the JUNGO STAKES *of the* EARTH

the JUNGO STAKES of the EARTH

ABDEL AZIZ BARAKA SAKIN

translated by Adil Babikir

AFRICA WORLD PRESS
TRENTON | LONDON | CAPE TOWN | NAIROBI | ADDIS ABABA | ASMARA | IBADAN | NEW DELHI

AFRICA WORLD PRESS
541 West Ingham Avenue | Suite B
Trenton, New Jersey 08638

Cover art: Courtsey of Ibrahim El-Salahi
Cover design: Joshua R. Porter
Book design: SpiralUp Solutions (P) Ltd.

Cataloging-in-Publication data may be obtained from the Library of Congress.

ISBN 978-1-56902-424-9 (pb)

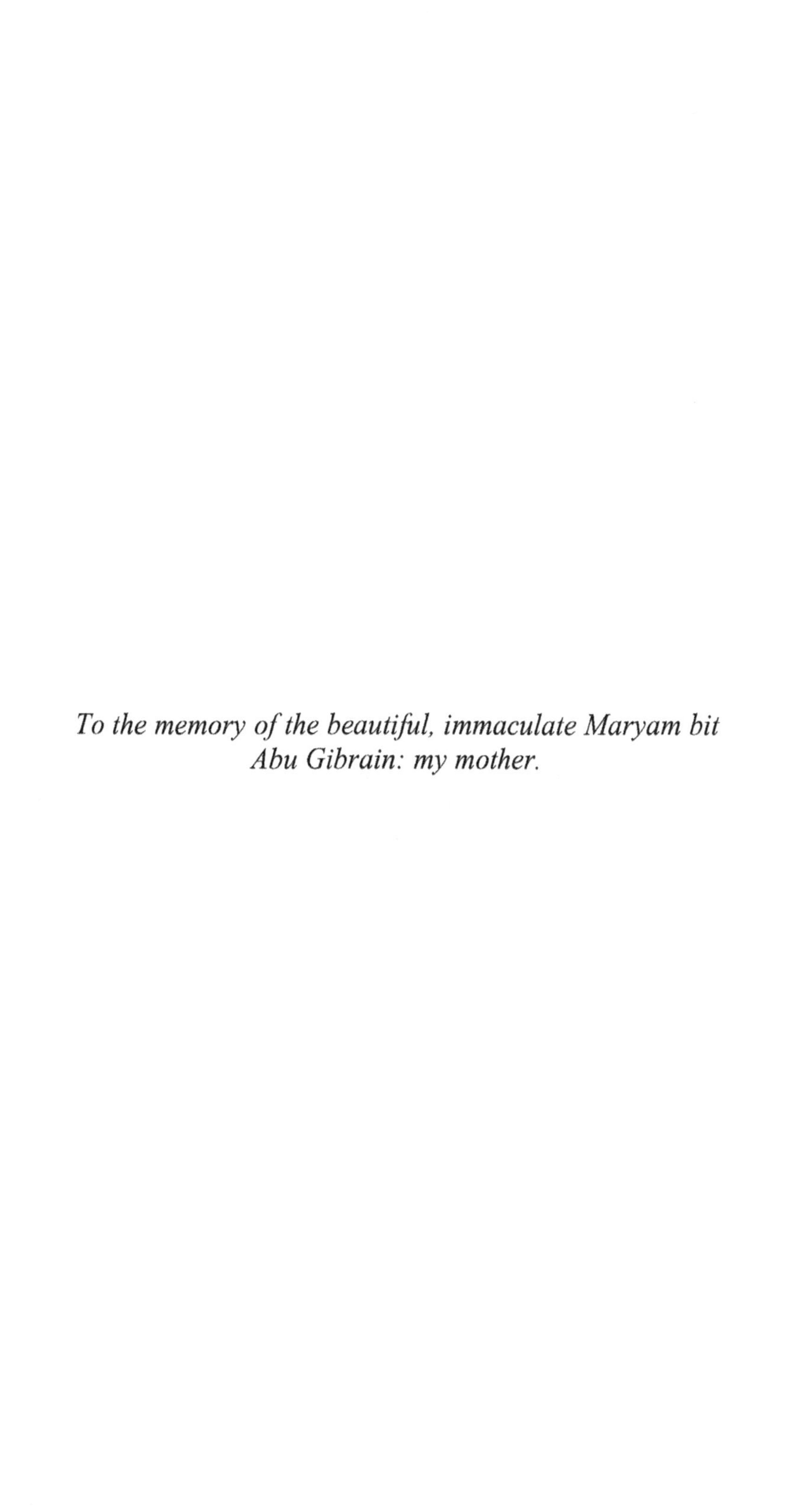

To the memory of the beautiful, immaculate Maryam bit Abu Gibrain: my mother.

"The Jungo are the stakes of the earth."
—Source unknown

"First they ignore you, then they laugh at you,
then they fight you, then you win."
—Mahatma Gandhi

CONTENTS

FOREWORD

Abdel Aziz Baraka Sakin

The Postmodernist Storyteller at His Best

*Kamal Elgizouli**

Abdel Aziz Baraka Sakin is one of the best and most prominent novelists and short story writers in Sudan, perhaps the most prolific, with eight novels and four anthologies of short stories in just a decade. Of these, *The Jungo: Stakes of the Earth* is widely celebrated by critics and readers as his most seminal work. The unique setting, brilliant narrative and the superb and nuanced intellectual discourse are but some of the attributes that set this work apart as a true masterpiece of contemporary African or Arab literature.

In the context of Sudanese literature, one could say with certainty that Sakin's *The Jungo* stands as a masterpiece that is comparable to any of Tayeb Salih's *Season of Migration to North*, *Wedding of Zein*, or *Bander Shah*. The exception is that Sakin's novel is the masterpiece of our time in its ability to embody the complexities of Sudan of the last two decades, the subtleties and the tragedies brought about by the disastrous impact of the current Islamist regime in Sudan that reigned since June 1989. In *The Jungo*, Sakin selects an unusual setting: the extreme southeastern parts of the Sudan, the societies on the borders with Ethiopia and Eritrea. In Sakin's novel, readers are first introduced to the *Jungo*, a marginalized population of seasonal workers (mostly male) from Western Sudan, little known outside their immediate perimeter, let alone at the center. The novel follows their journey throughout the agricultural season, during which they

* Kamal Elgizouli is a well-known poet, writer, a respected lawyer, and human rights activist, who served as the secretary general of the Sudanese Writers Union.

are hard at work on the sesame fields, as well as their relaxation rituals following the harvesting season. It reflects their interaction with a diverse local population and their relationship with their employers and the harvest, with women and alcohol.

The eponymous character, the Jungo, is just one element of a larger world at the triangle of the Sudanese–Ethiopian–Eritrean border. It is a world of its own, inhabited by the marginalized such as prostitutes, women who brew local alcohol, an army of the underclass, and the unemployed from across the Sudan, in addition to Ethiopian and Eritrean refugees who have been in the area for more than four decades.

Right from the beginning, readers are taken on a voyage of discovery, both illuminating and engaging. The novel offers fascinating insights into the daily lives and the complex humanity of the marginalized population who are brought together by the political economy of the failed postcolonial nation state. It explores, almost in an ethnographic fashion, the complexities of a society that can only be described as postcolonial and postmodern as well – a pastiche of people, movements, affiliations, and linkages that exist at the margin of the national economy, but also connected to it.

Given that modernism and experimentation, in the novel as a genre, are intrinsically inseparable, *The Jungo* shares the same emphasis on questions of challenging and breaking away from the norms, as well as probing untrodden paths. In that sense, *The Jungo* can certainly be classified as an epic modernist novel. In the gripping narrative of *The Jungo*, Sakin seamlessly employs elements associated with socialist realism and magical realism to decry the agonies resulting from social injustices and related structural and social inequalities. However, this same work also shows Sakin as a postcolonial writer, who is also very well versed in postmodernist style and associated discourses. His ability to combine complex structure and nuanced narrative with a brilliant intellectualism is an evidence of such postmodernist outlook. The rich setting of the novel brings together, and in a surreal manner, characters such as the Jungo, prostitutes, a woman with an ambiguous gender orientation, an

Ethiopian woman who bears a child with a magical sign, internally displaced people, a fundamentalist corrupt official, a homosexual who grew up in prison with a strong-willed mother, a vaguely political activist character, and much more.

Here, Sakin presents an intellectually engaging narrative that addresses the relationship between "the private" and "the public," through the dialectics of the individual self and the collective. He does so by tracing their points of harmony and disharmony, coherence and incoherence, and their ups and downs and their struggle through life. Yet the boundaries between the private and the public are quite blurred. Although at times they appear to dissolve into one, the overlap is by no means perfect or absolute. Still, Sakin's engagement in this highly intellectualized discourse does not sacrifice any of his fictional tools, depth, or mastery of narration.

The Jungo is a postcolonial novel par excellence, which is evident from the fact that the consequences of colonization and the struggle for decolonization are prominently featured here. Examples are issues of arbitrary borders, identities carved out of having different nationalities and ethnicities brought together under one nation state, civil wars, conflicts, and the consequences of the failure of the postcolonial ruling elites in managing such rich diversity. The novel's postcolonialist orientation manifests itself in foregrounding subjectivities of the oppressed and the marginalized by the nation state. It is fascinating how Sakin has managed to bring to the open the inner beauty and complexities of his characters, and their setting despite its gloomy outlook. More to the point is the use of the vernacular and its importance in localizing the global and globalizing the local, which reflects Sakin's depth and brilliance in his use of language, specially the colloquial.

Apart from the above elements, this work owes its brilliance to the author's fertile imagination as well as his superb narration techniques, resourcefulness, and skillful employment of images and symbols. Together, these attributes translate into an outstanding work of fiction that should encourage serious critical studies and reflection of contemporary Sudanese literature in Arabic, which, with the exception of few, rarely exit in English translation.

ACKNOWLEDGMENT

The translator would like to thank Dr. Yahya El Hassan for his review of the translation, Dr. Dina Osman for her helpful notes, and Kareem Abuzeid for his insightful edits.

1 THE MOTHER'S HOUSE

The Jungo are similar in every way. They hop about like old crows dancing around a prey. They wear new shirts with filthy collars, which the sweat, the sun, the hot wind, and the dry black earth have turned into scenes of perpetual battle against the elements and life. They prefer jeans with large pockets and brand names printed in large letters: CONS, WANT, LEEMAN, WINSTON, and others. They have no idea what these names mean, but they like them nonetheless and pay big money for them. The fake leather belts around their waists make them seem like foreigners, but their figures bear resemblance to familiar objects, particularly the neatly wrapped sesame bales. Their shoes that were, until last December, shiny and elegant, are now filthy, riddled with holes, and discolored beyond recognition. They don't bother to comb their hair and, as we later came to learn from Wad Ammoona, they even have thick pubic hair. They allow their hair, reddened by the sun, to become thick and tangled, attracting colonies of pollen.

A Jungo assumes different titles during the year. He is a *katakaw* between December and March, when he works on the sugarcane farms in Kenana, and in the sugar manufacturing plants of Khashm El Girba, Asalayah, and Geneid. In the period between April and May, when he is hired to clear shrubs and trees and burn them into charcoal, he is called *fahhammi*, which is the name given to a charcoal maker.

He assumes the title of *Jungo* or *Jungojora* between June and December, i.e., between the beginning of the rainy season up until the end of the sesame-harvesting season. Throughout the year, though, women call him a *faddādi.* Men, in turn, refer to the women who make sorghum wine (known as *mareesa*) and arrack as *faddadiyat.* We also learned from some Jungo who had come from al-Fashir and Nyala in Western Sudan that they used *Jungojora* to refer to what we, in the East, called *Jungo.* Accordingly, they would use *Jungojoray* for the *singular*, not *Jangawi* as we do.

It wasn't the first time—and it wouldn't be the last—that the two of us were going somewhere we'd never been before. Since being fired from our jobs five years ago under the so-called "layoffs for the public good" policy, we had traveled extensively all across Sudan. Born to a wealthy family, my friend had enough money to spend his whole life traveling around at his leisure. As for me, I was poor but single and was responsible for no one but myself. My parents had passed away, and my brothers and sisters were all married: some lived abroad, others lived in Sudan, and everyone led independent lives. My friend helped me out with travel expenses, and, in return, I was a good companion. As we say in these parts, choose your companions before hitting the road.

The smell of sweat steaming under the scorching September sun was unbearable.

"There are nothing but men here, it seems," my friend remarked.

"I saw a woman a while back," I replied.

Unlike everyone else, the good-looking young man who was sitting near us drinking coffee was not interested in the heated discussion about the harvest, profits and losses, and the threat to the crops from insects like *antat*, *gabour*, and *ka'ouk*,[1] and from birds like *om owaidat* and *wad abrag.* Even the coffee he was clearly enjoying couldn't deter him from eavesdropping on our whispered conversation.

---

[1] Three types of insects that ruin the sesame harvest. *Ka'ouk* is believed to have the ability to suck out the juice of the plants from a distance by simply flying over the field.

"Don't tell me you haven't been to the Mother's House?" he blurted out in an overly excited tone. "You've got to go there!"

"The Mother's House? Whose mother?" I asked.

"Yes, the Mother's House. She's everyone's mother."

Then he added in Tigrinya, presuming we knew all languages of the world: "Gatha Addai."

With the last sip of his coffee, he rose to his feet. We followed him. He was in his twenties, markedly handsome, neither tall nor short, with a radiant tan complexion. He was obviously well looked after: clean-shaven except for a thick mustache, his hair neatly combed, and wearing a branded perfume. He was well-groomed and stylish, unlike most people in al-Hillah, and there was a striking suppleness in the way he walked and spoke, and in his immaculate face.

Looking at me, he said, "My name is Wad[2] Ammoona," then added with a smile, "Actually my name is Kemal Eldin, but no one here knows me by that name. My mother's name is Ammoona. She calls me Wad Ammoona, and people seem to find that easier. So let it be Wad Ammoona. After all, on the Day of Judgment people will be called out by their mothers' names."

My friend said, "No problem. I wish people would call me by my mother's name. I'd be the happiest person on earth."

"What's your mother's name?" Wad Ammoona asked.

"Mariam."

"And you?" he asked, turning to me.

"Zeinab. Zeinab Abbakar."

He said, "My mother's real name is Amna. Ammoona is her nickname."

I asked, "So the Mother's House is your mother Ammoona's, right?"

"No! The Mother's House is the Mother's House—we're almost there."

"Where are you from?"

---

[2] Wad means "son of."

"From Qedaref," we said in one voice.

"Oh, Qedaref!" he said, letting out a deep sigh. "So you must have seen the Qedaref Jail. It's in the al-Nour district."

"Of course. Everyone in Qedaref has seen it," my friend responded.

"I was raised there," he said as he led us with large strides deep into the place.

Wad Ammoona would later come to learn that my father and my friend's father had both worked in the same jail. He led us past straw huts through endless lanes, meandering like snakes, up and down on rough terrain grooved by wagons, trucks, Land Rovers, and *barbaras*.[3] The place smelled of incense, and a languid southerly wind, warm and pleasant, carried the smell of *mareesa* and some local liquor. Without knocking on the metal gate in the center of the straw-and-wood fence, we entered the Mother's House, or Gatha Addai as they called it.

[3] Barbara is a pickup truck with a tractor engine.

2

THE PRISON, THE PRISONER, AND THE JAILER

This is the sum of the accounts I collected from several narrators, including my darling Alam Gishi, the Mother, Mukhtar Ali, al-Safyah, and Wad Ammoona himself (direct accounts as well as quotes from his memoirs), with some editing, interpretation, rectification—and sometimes distortion—of Wad Ammoona's anecdotes from prison.

He decided that, from that day on, he would no longer clean dishes, even if they carried out their threat to throw him out onto the streets. It wouldn't matter; he could survive outside the jail, sleep by the wall opposite his mother's room, and eat whatever she threw over the fence to him. He knew how to catch birds and mice, and how to make delicious grilled meals of them. And thanks to the fighting skills he had learned from his mother, he knew how to fend off the bad guys. He didn't know them personally, but he'd recognize them once they attacked him. His mother used to say, "No matter how many attack you—twenty or even a hundred—be sure to grab hold of just one of them. Bite him! Scratch his skin with your nails! Jab your fingers into his eyes! But never surrender. Never cry or run away. There's no room for the weak in this cruel world!"

Al-Shama's fingers, running through his hair, interrupted his train of thought.

"Please, Wad Ammoona: pick the lice out of my hair."

He was not particularly fond of al-Shama. Her breath smelled worse than piss, and her hair was filthy and infested with lice. People say she killed her husband.

"Today your mother was sent to serve at the commissioner's house. I don't know what that man wants from her. He won't leave her alone," she told him.

"I'm not washing the dishes anymore," he told himself, picturing himself yelling at the prison's cook.

The prison's cook, a skinny man with long fingers and hands that always held a ladle, strongly believed that Wad Ammoona had a bright future as a cook. "Wad Ammoona and I have many things in common," he said. "As a child, I was like him: handsome, chubby, lazy, and at my happiest when in the company of women."

But what Wad Ammoona hated most about the prison's cook, apart from his dirty, oily plates that always needed someone to wash them, was the fact that he was a sodomite. That was what everyone in the ward used to say about him. And Azza always warned Wad Ammoona never to be alone with him or allow him to touch his private parts, and she always urged him to tell her or his mother if the cook ever used obscene language with him. But Wad Ammoona couldn't see any danger, and always ignored Azza's advice and shrugged off his mother's daily flow of boring, useless warnings.

Yesterday, after Wad Ammoona had finished washing the dishes and stacking them on the steel cabinet, the cook invited him to a coin flipping game.

"If you win, you kiss me; if I win, I kiss you," he said.

Spitting out a ball of snuff near a big cooking pot, he quickly took a coin out of his pocket, flipped it, and snapped it down into his palm. "Heads or tails?" he asked Wad Ammoona, revealing crooked yellow teeth behind his broad smile.

He sprayed saliva into the air as he said this, and some of it caught Wad Ammoona in the face. He wiped it away, looking disgusted. The things he hated most about the cook were his moist lips and the smell of snuff.

Al-Shama interrupted his train of thought once again. "Your mother should be here any minute now," she said, braiding an extension into her hair. "The Commissioner's making her life miserable. He's forcing her to do his laundry and that of his sons, daughters, and even neighbors. He might as well be offering her laundry service to other people for a fee. Your mother is bound to collapse—it doesn't matter if she's as strong as a heavy-duty machine. The good news, though, is that it's almost over. It's just this year for all of us. Your mother's only got six months to go. It's almost over, son."

"I'm not playing games with you," Wad Ammoona said firmly.

"No problem," the cook whispered, trying to sound soft and kind. "Just come and let me give you a kiss."

Wad Ammoona moved away, trying to escape. Having safely reached the door, he said, "No! No kisses."

"No?" The cook's voice was now serious and threatening. "If you don't, I'll tell the staff sergeant about the glass you broke! You'll see!"

"And I'll tell my mother."

"*Your mother?* What on earth would she do?" the cook sneered. "She's got enough on her plate!"

"So," he continued, speaking softly now, "how are you going to fill your belly? Come on, Wad Ammoona! Let me kiss you, or you can kiss me—whichever way you like!"

The cracking of the prison's metal ceiling under the midday heat sounded like an explosion of small bullets. The whole place reeked of the sweat of exhausted women, dripping from fungus-infested armpits and pubes, and of tiled floors and rancid oily hair. The sound of buzzing flies mixed with the loud laughter of the guards and the sound of the sergeant calling out "Water, girls. *Water!*"

Al-Shama took a small amount of money from her purse and handed it to Wad Ammoona as a token of appreciation for picking her lice, and also as advance payment for future services.

The long ward was inhabited by twenty women: two old women convicted ten years ago for possession of two sacks of hashish; a pretty young girl who was a habitual jewelry thief; Wad Ammoona's mother, an arrack seller who was serving a sentence multiplied sevenfold by a religious judge as punishment for her failure to quit the illicit business, despite frequent lashes, fines, and imprisonment; al-Shama, who had been convicted of killing her husband, although she claimed he had been driven by jealousy to put an end to his own life by drinking a dye powder dissolved in orange juice; and many others.

Of all those women, Wad Ammoona cared for only one. He didn't know how old she was or what crime she had committed. Generally quiet and reticent, she would frequently sing for him in a melodious voice and tell him long stories that helped him overcome his boredom. And despite the frequent bouts of illness that would confine her to the ward's floor for long periods, she was by far the most cheerful, serene, kind-hearted, lenient, and patient inmate. But his mother did not want him to get any closer to Azza.

"You'd better keep away from that whore," she would shout, even in the presence of Azza and whoever else happened to be around. In response, Azza would simply laugh and sit on the floor, inviting Wad Ammoona to ride on her shoulders. "I'd get on at once and she'd rise to her feet and run back and forth past the space between the two wards, my long legs dangling in the air!" he recalled.

The staff sergeant suddenly entered the kitchen. The perplexed cook ordered Wad Ammoona to fetch the empty plates from the male ward.

"Hurry up boy!" Wad Ammoona rushed to the male ward.

He quickly shoved al-Shama's gift into his pocket, running his right palm over it carefully to ensure it was secure.

"Go wash your hands. Do you want to eat with filthy hands?" she said, kissing him on the cheek.

He put al-Shama's gift into his savings box, to join the rest of the money he had received from guards, prisoners, and from the cook himself. He couldn't tell exactly how much he had saved so far. What he knew for certain, though, was that it had been increasing, slowly but surely. Even when they sent him to the nearby shop or to the souk to buy snuff, cigarettes, or the like, and allowed him to keep the change, he would not treat himself to one of those mouthwatering candies on the shelves that were so popular with children his age.

He knew all the male prisoners. There might be new faces from day to day, but the new arrivals were quickly identified, right from the very first day, by their name, tribe, crime, hometown, village, and nickname.

He quickly picked up plates tossed out of cells and wards, and carried as much as his tiny body could tolerate back to the kitchen. The staff sergeant was still there. Seeing Wad Ammoona tottering back with his load, he yelled at the cook:

"Do you want to kill this woman's child, or what?"

The cook rushed toward Wad Ammoona and took the plates from him, murmuring an apology.

"Now run back to the ward. Your mother is waiting for you. She must be back by now," he told Wad Ammoona in a disingenuously soft voice.

"I am going to see Azza," Wad Ammoona told al-Shama.

"Don't you know she was sent to solitary confinement?" she asked, gloating.

"I know. I took her water a while ago—poor Azza!"

"She's not poor," al-Shama replied wrathfully. "She's a criminal!"

"What did she do? She told me she'd done nothing wrong."

"She was caught red-handed with contraband."

Only at this point was Wad Ammoona able to establish a link between yesterday's events, those of the day before, and what he had just heard from al-Shama.

THE DAY BEFORE YESTERDAY

Azza was standing by the eastern wall, not far from the guard tower, exchanging brief word, and cigarette, with Biraima, the guard. She told Wad Ammoona about some belongings she had entrusted to a woman from al-Homra in Ethiopia who was now in Qedaref but could not come down to the prison for fear of police.

"She's a repeat offender," Azza noted. "Disreputable," she added sarcastically.

Wad Ammoona was confused by the last word ("disreputable"), which he did not fully understand. He smiled, imagining it meant something similar to rotten food.

"What does that mean?" he asked.

"Well," she said, craning her long neck in a way that added further ambiguity, "she was detained several times."

"Like my mother?"

"No," she retorted. "Your poor mother has nothing serious against her, just the matter of the arrack—her problem is that the judge took an interest in her."

Biraima tossed down a packet of cigarettes (Bringi brand), which landed right on Azza's lap. When she looked up, the guard winked at her. She laughed, and he smiled back.

"Would you help me out, Wad Ammoona?" she whispered, pressing him against her bosom so strongly that he could smell her armpits.

"How?"

"Bring me my stuff from Alam Gishi."

"Alam Gishi? I thought you said it was a woman from al-Homra."

"That's right. Didn't you know that Alam Gishi's from al-Homra?"

"Where should I meet her?" he asked submissively.

"At the Showak bus station," she replied, scrubbing her nails against the bars.

"But how can I get there?"

"That's easy," she said, smiling. "When the cook sends you out to buy him cigarettes, just swing by the station. You'll find her there waiting for you. That will be after the noon prayers, as usual."

"But what if he doesn't send me on errands today?"

"I'm sure he will," she said. "Hide the package here."

"Where?"

"Right here. Here!"

He was not sure whether or not it was intentional, but her hand remained in his pants for a while, and before giving any further instructions, she pinched his penis softly.

YESTERDAY

Wad Ammoona had made it a habit to sleep beside his mother in the same bed. In fact, she was the one who insisted on him sharing the bed with her. Her fear was by no means unjustified.

To her, everyone was a threat: women and men alike, inmates, guards, prison workers—there were no exceptions. He was not the only child in the company of his mother at the jail. There were three baby girls, but they were all infants and therefore in no immediate danger. Her child, however, was nine years old and was surely in danger, for a number of reasons. First of all, his body was big for his age. Despite the poor food and meager portions, he had developed a puffy body and long legs that made him look far older than his age. Plus he was markedly handsome. His mother was aware that the cook was a pervert and that he was always hovering around her son.

"If he touches my son for one second, I'll give him a death that people will talk about till Judgment Day," she thought to herself.

The women too were a possible threat to her son. He hadn't reached puberty yet, but they still knew how to use him.

"Listen, whores. If I ever find my son with any of you, I'll send you to hell," she once warned them. They laughed off her threat, saying they wouldn't want him to miss the "training opportunity." But deep down, they had no doubt she meant what she said.

First the mother, then Wad Ammoona, and then everyone else in the ward woke up to a noisy fight, the cause of which, it turned out, was nothing but hashish.

It didn't usually take the jailers long to figure things out. They took the shortest course of investigation: a severe beating, followed by pinching with pliers. Almost immediately, a sergeant named

Ghalaba came to the female ward, pulled Azza to her feet, and smashed the massive palm of his hand against her face.

"Follow me."

"It's hashish, then, isn't it?" Wad Ammoona, who now seemed to have pieced things together, asked al-Shama.

"Yes, it is."

"Where'd she get it from?"

"She wouldn't say."

"What if they beat her?"

"They've already done. But she's stubborn: she won't confess, even if they beat her to death."

He sat outside the door to her cell. Her hand—strong, confident, and warm—held on tightly to his through the bars. Signs of a beating were evident on her face. Wad Ammoona had become used to such scenes and was no longer terrified seeing them. He had frequently seen his mother with a swollen face and festering wounds on her back. He once saw sergeant Ghalaba molesting her, and when she tried to fend him off, he punched her in the face several times.

"They're going to arrest me," he said in a feeble, trembling voice.

Laughing, Azza assured him that the thing he had brought her from Alam Gishi was not hashish or contraband. She opened a bag that was lying by her side and pulled out a bundle, the same one he had brought.

"Open it," she said, holding out the bundle to him.

"No!" he said, pulling back his hands.

"Open it up and see for yourself."

When he tried to run away, she opened the bundle herself. It contained medical cotton pads, nothing else.

"They're just cotton pads. Women need them. But they're banned here because prisoners can use them to make Molotov cocktails."

Although not fully convinced, Wad Ammoona still felt a deep sense of relief.

"I didn't sell hash to the jailers. So don't worry about me, or about yourself."

Just before sunset, his mother returned. He had already taken a bath and washed his other galabia and plastic sandals, and was lying on the bed waiting for her. He'd nearly fallen asleep when she threw him a small bag containing an apple, a piece of candy, a loaf of bread, and *tahniyah* (sesame pie).

"We spent the whole day doing laundry at the Commissioner's house. We must have done the whole village's laundry," she said.

"How was your day?" she asked in a soft voice, running her fingers through his hair. "Did they send you out to the grocery store and the market?"

"I washed dishes for the cook and chatted with Azza. Haven't you heard, mother? She was severely beaten today!"

"She deserved it," Ammoona snapped as she threw herself on the bed beside him.

"Why?"

"That girl's no good. Why does she go around selling hash?"

"She didn't have hash, mother. It was cotton!"

"Cotton? She was selling cotton?"

"Yes, I swear to God. I saw it!"

"Don't you want to keep away from that woman? Haven't I warned you?"

Wad Ammoona kept silent for a while, before starting to gnaw on his apple.

"Bring me an apple every day, will you?"

"I will."

Once his mother fell asleep, he picked up what was left in the bag and headed toward the cell. Darkness had already started to spread over the place, but he always managed to find his way with the help of the faint light of the corridor. The guards were hospitable: they always welcomed him, chatting with him and sending him on errands. Azza at first refused to take the *tahniyah* he held out to her, but when he started to cry, she accepted it. She was extremely hungry, and looked gaunt and pale. In the faint light, she looked like a ghost, but her warm palm was always there to reassure him that she really existed and to convey her affection. This was the first time she had asked him about his father.

"My mother said he was a Yemeni who used to run a grocery store in al-Hillah. He married my mother, but they got divorced later, and he went back to Yemen."

"Don't you have any brothers?"

"No. It's just my mother and me. My mother's relatives are back in our village."

"Where's your village?"

"I really don't know. My mother always says 'our village,' but I've got no idea where it is. I was born in al-Hillah and never left it except to come to Qedaref. I came to this prison with my mother several times—they told me that started when I was an infant."

"I'll be let out before your mother. If she agrees, I'll be happy to take you with me. I have family here in Qedaref. You can stay with us until they let your mother out. Ok?"

"My mother won't agree," he said sadly. "If it were up to me, I'd go with you without a second thought."

"I'll do my best to persuade her. You should have gone to school by now. How old are you?"

"Nine years old. They won't let me into school. I'll become a driver or a mechanic."

"No. You're going to school and you're going to become a doctor," she said emphatically.

"My mother said I can't go to school without a birth certificate," he said, presenting her with a large piece of candy.

Her eyes glistened in the faint light of the corridor.

"I'm going to get you an age assessment certificate. I'll get you into school. I know the principal. He visits us at home in Qedaref. I also know the person in charge of issuing the age assessment certificates. You'll have no problems. The only trouble will be getting your mother's blessings."

A tall skinny figure approached them. It was Ali, the guard better known as Jack Taweela—a cheerful man who always led the other guards in prayers.

"So you found someone to chat with," he said to Azza.

"Allah is generous."

"I came across your father this morning," he said, grabbing hold of the cell door.

"I imagine he didn't bother to ask about me."

"He said, 'If you let her out, her brothers will kill her, so she'd better stay with you.'"

"No one can kill me," she said defiantly. "I'll be out in a month, and we'll see."

"Leave this town," he said, staring at her face, which was glued to the bars. "Go somewhere else and make a living there. You're an educated woman, and you have a career."

"You call singing a career?"

"Sure! Singers can earn a fortune."

"I'm going to sell tea here in Qedaref, and none of them—neither Ahmed nor al-Sadek nor any other fool—will dare touch me."

Hoping to change the subject, the guard said, "The Commissioner said he'd transfer you to the ward tomorrow but that he's first going to make you sign a pledge not to commit any more crimes here in the prison."

"I take refuge with our Lord!"

"You'd be out of harm's way if only you stayed away from the girls of the eastern district," he said, laughing.

"I did nothing wrong, *mawlana*,"[1] she said in frustration. "What's wrong with being found in a house full of bachelors? Why didn't they jail the bachelors too?"

"They ran away."

"Their names are known, and they all live here in Qedaref. Come with me now, if you like, and I'll bring you all of them, one by one," she said bitterly. "And who said they were bachelors?"

"That's a matter for the investigators and the judge to decide," he answered in a low voice. "I'm just a prison guard. My job is to guard. If they bring inmates, I keep them in custody. If they don't, it's not my place to question anything."

---

[1] A title for a devout person or someone knowledgeable about religion.

Wad Ammoona failed to grasp why a woman should be arrested for entering a bachelors' house. He again interpreted it as tantamount to selling rotten food.

Jack Taweela went on his way. Azza sat with her back to the steel door. On the other side of the bars, Wad Ammoona went about combing her hair with his bone comb, while Azza started singing in a melodious voice:

My darling sent me some strange mail,

Full of blame,

Claiming I was neglecting him.

He didn't like that song, preferring the one that goes

This is truly our beautiful world,

Look at it,

Its flowers, its trees, its palms.

She sang him the second one. When the bell for lights out sounded—or rather, when they hammered on the steel bar that hung at the center of the prison to announce that it was already nine o'clock—Wad Ammoona groped his way back to the women's ward. His mind, for the first time, was filled with thoughts about his father, and about school.

He had never seen his father in person, not even a photo of him. His mother had never made it a point to talk to her son about his father. What he had said to Azza was part of what he'd overheard from one of his mother's conversations with a neighbor several years ago. He had embellished it a bit when talking to Azza.

School, on the contrary, was something he had never thought about before, as if it had absolutely nothing to do with him. It was a dream beyond his wildest imagination. It was two years now since he came to the prison with his mother to serve her current term. He was seven years old back then, the age when everyone was supposed to go to school. He wasn't there to watch his friends go and hasn't heard anything from them since he left. He kept seeing them in his mind, playing by the creek or the water depot; catching birds, butterflies, locusts, or rats; playing "doctors and nurses" with girls their age; pushing flat tires around; getting on the backs of stray donkeys; heading to the market during the gum harvesting season to steal some gum from the old women selling it; and playing "war games" in the afternoon against boys from the neighboring district. But going to school had never crossed his mind.

His mother was still asleep and would wake up only when it was time for the dawn prayers, when all the prisoners were forced to join the mass prayers in the central courtyard—men at the front, followed by women, and behind them Wad Ammoona by himself. He decided to ask his mother about his father after the dawn prayers, and to ask her to send him to school. When he finally fell asleep, he dreamt that he was in school and carrying an empty bag. The principal, who was none other than the prison cook, shoved some books and notebooks into his bag, and handed him a big pot full of lentils and *tahniyah*.

"Take this to Azza," he ordered him. "Tell her this is her father's corpse."

He dragged the "corpse" through the corridors, down to where Azza was. Together, the two of them got on a horse and rode away. Evil gangs were chasing them through stars and forests, but they managed to ride into the sky and jump on board a big white cloud.

As if addressing each of them individually, Jack Taweela lectured them extensively on what was waiting for the sinful on Judgment Day. He talked about thieves; murderers; homosexuals; prostitutes; alcohol brewers, drinkers, servers, and dealers; dissidents, politicians; fugitives; liars; debtors; mutineers; adulterers; forgers; those who don't pray; and those who don't fast during Ramadan. He then talked about the punishments for the infidels, a category that included communists, Shiites, Christians, Jews, pagans, Americans, those who commit adultery with both a woman and her daughter/mother, men who have sex with men, conjurers, people who eat pork, murderers, and those who unjustly seize the property of orphans.

And so as not to deny his audience the right to repent, he asserted that a repentant would be fully pardoned and regarded as free of sin. He concluded with the statement: "Exalted is your Lord, the Lord of might, above what they describe. Peace be upon the messengers. All praise be to Allah, the Lord of the worlds."

"Now you may go back to your wards, may Allah bestow His mercy on you all."

Tugging on the edge of his mother's dress to slow her down as the crowd returned from prayers to go back to sleep, Wad Ammoona asked his mother, "Where's my father?"

"My God!" She stopped and stared at his face as if looking at him for the very first time. "What on earth reminded you of your father today?"

"I just need to know."

"He's in Yemen. He divorced me and went to Yemen before you were born."

"Isn't he coming back?"

With a yawn, she replied, "I swear to God I have no idea. When you grow up, go and look out for him in Yemen. Okay? But I'm really tired now and need to sleep."

After a brief pause, he continued, "I want to go to school."

"Are you out of your mind, boy? What's wrong with you today? Just calm down, will you? Do you think it's that easy? Who would you live with? Who would pay for your food, the school fees, and the books?"

"You don't even have a birth certificate," she continued, as if he were responsible for that.

But she added softly, "Let me just get out of this jail and get a job, even as a maid, and I'll get you enrolled in school."

"Azza will be out in a month's time. I'll go with her. She'll enroll me in school," he said, rubbing his face.

"Did she tell you that?"

"No, it's my idea," he said hesitantly.

"We'll get out together. No devil will ever take you away from me. You're *my* son, Wad Ammoona, understand?"

3

A WOMAN NAMED ALAM GISHI

"This is the place where we learned the value of work," the skinny, moderately tall woman said in Tigrinya, while nonchalantly stirring a pot on a small stove. Then she added in Arabic, the language of the borders, "My man is skinny—like you."

She raised her eyes toward me, as if trying to place me inside the hut.

"Your man? Do you have one?"

Her swift, involuntary motion intimated how poignant my remark was.

We heard a beautiful song outside. She called out, "Wad Ammoona, please come in." He entered, elegant and handsome as ever, wearing a clean blue galabia.

"Hey, how are you doing?" he greeted me in a soft voice.

"I'm fine."

Then he turned to the woman, who said, "By God, please prepare a *sheesha*[1] for your friend."

"Regular flavor or apple?" he asked, with a big smile on his face.

"Regular."

"Shall I add some *green stuff*?"[2]

"No thanks."

---

[1] A hookah, or water pipe.

[2] Hashish.

"We also have some Ethiopian stuff, and Eritrean—even *Abu Humar*,"[3] he added, still smiling.

"I know *Abu Humar*. But what do you mean by the Ethiopian and Eritrean stuff?"

"Gin and cognac," he replied, astonished at my ignorance.

"No thanks, Wad Ammoona. Maybe later."

He went out, followed by strong smell of Fahrenheit-brand cologne.

"What an excellent boy," she said proudly. "He was brought up with us right here in the Mother's House."

"But he said he grew up in Qedaref Jail," I said.

"That's right. He entered the jail with his mother, as an infant and later as a child. He was a teenager when he came out, and he's stayed at the Mother's House ever since."

As gently as a breeze, Wad Ammoona came in, put the *sheesha* in front of me, and went out without uttering a word. The boiling of the water in the pot subsided after she added more water. She stepped outside the hut to grab what she needed to make coffee. I felt awkward with the white bed sheet wrapped around my waist and looked like a pilgrim exhausted by the hajj rituals.

I knew my friend could do in a single hour what took a man like me a full day. I knew that no mystery could stand in his way; he had a passion for decoding all secrets: those of a woman, a room, anything. So I wasn't too worried about him. I enjoyed a delicious meal of chicken *zigni*, one of my favorite Ethiopian dishes, flavored with their famous *dilleikh* chili. The smell of roasted Ethiopian coffee evoked endless memories, and I later came to associate that smell with my affair with Alam Gishi.

I was as exhausted as an old donkey. Taking public transportation—particularly the *barbara*—to al-Hillah was considered by many to be tantamount to suicide, or at least extremely reckless.

"Wise people take the bus. It's safer and faster. The *barbara* is a shortcut to death," she said.

---

[3] A nickname for arrack.

She was massaging my back with a mixture of colocynth, *Abu Fas* cream, olive oil, and dough, and talking incessantly about a host of things: Addai, Wad Ammoona, the bank opening a branch in al-Hillah, and the telecommunications company that would connect al-Hillah to the capital Khartoum and also link it with Asmara, Addis Ababa, and even America. She described Wad Ammoona as "the only man in the house, and the women's right-hand man." In a brief report, she divulged a whole bunch of al-Hillah's secrets.

Although barely thirty, she looked like an old timer, an expert in everything, and there was an aura of splendor about her—at least that's how she appeared to me. She was beautiful and enigmatic, her face concealing joy and sorrow, or revealing both at the same time. Like a true professional, she drew my left leg counterclockwise, pulled it upward and at the same time took my right hand and pulled it strongly. My body creaked and groaned like a dry leaf in a strong gust of wind. Had it taken longer than a few seconds, I would definitely have screamed. But when she finally let go of me, an unspeakable sensation of comfort and numbness had already come over me.

"I'm going home," she said abruptly.

"Home?"

"Yes," she replied. "I do my work here with Addai, but I don't spend the night here. I go back home to my husband and kids."

Then she asked in a professional tone, "Do you want a girl to sleep with?"

I wasn't sure, to tell the truth. I wasn't really disposed toward sex, having tried it only a couple of times. I can only describe those attempts as imperfect, and the memories of them were painful. I had been shy around women. But I was surprised to hear myself say, "I do."

"Alam Gishi," she instantly replied, as if she had expected my reply. "She'll spend the night with you. She's working today. A sweet girl. You'll like her."

She was about to say something else when Addai's voice pierced through the silence. The way she ended her short sentences added charm to her soft voice. She excused herself to enter. "Your friend's the strangest man on earth!" she said to me as she stepped in.

This wasn't news to me. She hadn't discovered a new continent, as her tone seemed to suggest.

"Yeah, he sure is," I said in an indifferent tone that she didn't like. "Do you want me to come with you? Or would you rather bring him down here? He must have caused some trouble, I'm sure of it."

"We kicked him out," she said theatrically.

"Kicked him out? Why? Where is he now?"

While I was gathering up my belongings and getting rid of the white sheet, the Mother started telling a story I had trouble following. From what I could gather, my friend had been dismissed two hours earlier, and if I wanted to find him I would have to follow her right away.

"Two hours? Why didn't you tell me sooner?"

Taking a long drag from her sheesha, she said, "We tried to deal with the problem ourselves."

Having freed myself entirely from the bed sheet, I asked anxiously, "Where is he now?"

"Come along. Follow me," she said, releasing smoke in small circles that gradually dissolved in the open air of the hut.

I put on my shoes and was ready to go. Although she alluded that they might kill him and throw his body in the Basalam River, I wasn't really worried because I knew that no one could kill him, at least not in this locality. He was one of those rare people who you couldn't imagine dying anytime soon, one of those men who always gave you the impression that they would be at your funeral digging a grave for you and praying for your mercy and who would then maintain a sad face through all the days of mourning.

We first passed by a small *rakuba*[4]—an open hall—where a small electric lamp was casting a faint glow that barely reached beyond its immediate perimeter but was still strong enough for us to see Wad

[4] A thatch and wood structure, which usually serves as the living area of homes.

Ammoona sitting on a short stool. He was brushing his feet against a pumice stone that women used to soften their soles. Behind him stood a woman in her forties (about Addai's age), fairly tall. Her brown skin looked darker in the light, though her facial features suggested she had a lighter complexion. They were whispering as she bent down to remove some hair from his back with some wax. Their whisper died down as Addai and I passed close by.

"Are you selling this boy at the auction?" Addai asked.

"Cleanliness is next to godliness, Addai," replied Wad Ammoona cheerfully.

Deep in my heart, I considered Wad Ammoona a pervert: using wax to remove body hair, and a pumice stone to scrub his feet. And God knows what else!

A few steps away, as if she had heard my thoughts, Addai said, "Wad Ammoona is a real man, the best one in this village. I raised him myself. Addai's upbringing was flawless."

"But he told me he grew up in the prison."

"What kind of upbringing can one have in a prison? He wasn't good for anything when I took him in."

I nodded in agreement. We proceeded down a narrow alley behind the large enigmatic huts that loomed like massive ghosts squatting on a dark ocean. The Mother, petite and plump, was walking ahead of me, surrounded by the scent of sandal extract (Crown brand), the darkness lending an enigmatic charm to the shuffling of her sandals.

Greetings kept coming to us from everywhere, through hut fences, from *rakubas*, and from thatched huts.

"Good evening, Addai."

"Good evening, ma'am."

"Mother Addai."

"Addai."

The greetings mingled with the sighs of lovers, drunkards mumbling, and erotic bodies crying out fervently to angels of pleasure—or to demons of pleasure, it made no difference.

She said joyfully, "Life's a game that ends in a grave."

I nodded in assent, or rather to say, "Oh, I see." We overheard a woman crying loudly for someone to come save her from death. She was begging her partner to let go of her, to take it out, to allow her to catch her breath, to lift his heavy body off her, to finish up quickly before she died.

My instinctive chivalry almost drove me to rescue her, but Addai grabbed my hand with unexpected firmness for a woman her age.

"Never believe women! Those who believe women deny the prophets," she told me.

Turning toward the woman's voice, she called out, "Show some courage, girl! Shame on you!"

The voice died down, lending an air of death to the place. We crossed into an even darker alley outside Addai's housing complex. Drunkards and passersby greeted us with one word, "Addai."

She replied mechanically, but softly,

"Hello, son."

"Hello daughter."

"Hello brother."

"Hello ma'am."

"Hello friend."

She could identify every one of them by their dark faces, their drunk husky voices, their figures, their gait, their breath.

"Your friend's the first person to ever be kicked out of my house," she said abruptly.

"Actually, he's the second," she added. "There was just one before him, over thirty years ago now—Mengistu."

"Mengistu?"

"Yes. Mengistu Haile Mariam. Before becoming President of Ethiopia, he was a bandit in the Zahanah forest and around al-Homra creek. A really tough man. May God forgive him."

"Where is he now?"

"May God forgive him. He died a long time ago."

I nodded, didn't tell her I meant my friend, not Mengistu Haile Mariam.

It occurred to me that the shuffling of her slippers was loud enough to be heard in all the nearby houses. We passed by al-Safyah, a skinny woman who was to be the focus of many stories in al-Hillah in the days to come. She was black, like everyone here, where night covered everything with its dark veil. She was carrying something in her hand, and two men were following behind her. The two women exchanged greetings, while the two men and I remained silent. I caught the smell of locally distilled liquor, mixed with the odor of armpits and the sweat of hard labor.

When they moved away, Addai said, "The Jungo descended on al-Hillah today. Look at them, carrying the *googo*."

The *googo* was a small bag the Jungo always carried on their shoulders, mainly to keep their belongings in it, although they credited it with supernatural powers too. I asked her if the woman was also a Jungojoraya, and Addai replied that she was the most famous Jungojoraya in the entire East, from al-Homra to the southernmost parts of Qedaref, from Hawwatta to Fashaga—everyone knew her. She even went on to claim that it was that woman's grandfathers and the djinn who had first inhabited these lands. She spoke confidently, every now and then swearing by God that these localities were inhabited by djinn.

"The book mentions this," she said.

"Which book?" I asked.

"The book of faith," she quickly replied. "Is there any other book?"

I nodded as if to say, "Of course not."

Every now and then I found myself thinking about the fate of my friend. But Addai hardly left me a chance to do this. She was either talking or dragging me quickly behind her through the darkness. Familiar with the topography and the meandering alleys, she took steady strides while I stumbled about like a drunkard—I came close to falling down on more than one occasion. We crossed another two rows of cane-and-straw houses and huts. We must have walked about a mile, making a large arc across the town. When we reached what I thought was the end of the arc, I overheard his loud voice—shouting was another one of my friend's bad habits, though it was by no means a sign of distress but rather an indication that things were going very much in his favor.

"I'm not going to pay a single penny," I overheard him say. "It's a matter of principle."

They were in a big enclosure fenced in with canes and thorns. At the center, a large hut and a *rakuba* were giving out a faint light beneath which the figures of five men came into view. I asked them to let him go.

"Who are you?" retorted one.

"Leave him. This is his friend. He'll resolve the situation," Addai interrupted, her large eyes gleaming anxiously in the darkness, like a cat lurking in wait for a mouse.

"I need to show these guys," my friend started, his tongue heavy, his voice numbed by alcohol, "the difference between vice and virtue. The difference is the money they want me to pay. Money can only reduce the intimate, blessed, and wonderfully human encounter I just had with the beautiful creature sitting there (he pointed at the dark hut) into an act of prostitution."

Suddenly, a voice emerged from the darkness: "I want my money! This is business. That damned communist talk doesn't work with me. I want the money I'm entitled to. I just want my due. Two long and painful rounds of sex and you call it prostitution? Massaging, sucking, biting . . . You think it's all free of charge? Why should you get it all free of charge? You're not my boyfriend. You're not even my girlfriend's brother."

The argument must have started over two hours ago. We could see people in small groups scattered around the pale shape of the *rakuba*, under what was once afternoon shade but was now utter darkness. We could smell sesame seeds being grilled and could hear the gurgling of a *sheesha* nearby, and the modest laughter of two ladies.

"Who brought you here?" he asked me. "This woman?"

"My name's Addai. Not *this woman*. Understand?" she said nervously.

"Treat Addai with respect," a man yelled at him.

"I want to go back," I told Addai.

"Back where?" she asked, astonished.

"To the hut."

"You want your money back?"

She had seen me pay a huge sum to "the woman" at the Mother's House.

"Did you pay money for sex?" my friend blurted out in protest. "You're certainly immoral."

Ignoring him, I said to Addai, "I want to go back to the hut. I want to sleep. Can I?"

She had apparently understood what I was up to. "You're different, not like your friend," she said.

He said sarcastically, "See you in the morning, genius."

I nodded in assent, as if to say, "As you like."

A man commissioned by Addai led me through two short dark alleys back to the Mother's House, where I met a woman who had been waiting for me for a long time in the hut. Her name was Alam Gishi.

4 AL-SAFYAH'S INVITATION

We met her at the al-Ganzai souk, a bazaar for cheap second-hand clothes held on the sidelines of the grand souk, near the livestock yard, in an isolated spot specially selected to protect the privacy of buyers and sellers alike. The Jungo frequented it from time to time—mainly during the austere months before the harvest season or when they were paid for their work in the harvest—to sell or trade clothes, shoes, and whatever remained of their personal belongings, or to buy more items. They also tended to visit it to fetch special items unlikely to be found elsewhere, such as the so-called "Mecca garbage" or "gifts from the dead": heaps of used clothes donated by charitable people and the relatives of the deceased from Saudi Arabia and other Gulf States. Although these clothes were meant to be given to the poor in different parts of Sudan, they somehow found their way to bazaars in villages and remote suburbs, where they were in high demand because they were usually in good condition and still showed glimpses of their brand names.

We saw her from a distance, bargaining with a seller over a dress.

"Al-Safyah . . . What a great woman!" he whispered to me. "I want to talk to her, friend."

He would bestow that title on me only when he was about to speak about an issue he considered to be of the utmost importance.

"The simple, neglected creatures living on the margins are troves of amazing secrets. Allah always stores His divine wisdom in such people. I want that wisdom."

"So you see her as a life project?" I asked sarcastically, echoing his jargon.

"*Exactly*! She'll be a true addition to my life experiences. Imagine if I got to know about every experience she's ever had—and also her dreams, expectations, frustrations, how she thinks! Everyone I meet here tells me stories about her. Mukhtar Ali told me some too. But I want to hear the truth myself, first hand."

"Who's Mukhtar Ali?"

"A kind old man I met last night. I spent the night with him at his house."

In his usual straightforward way, he offered to pay for her dress. She showed a shy reluctance, but eventually accepted and thanked both of us. We followed her to the dried fish market, and he volunteered to pay for her purchase: two pounds of dried fish, a bunch of *kawal*,[1] 250 grams of white beans, slices of dried meat, two coils of sheep bowels, and 250 grams of *kambo* (a traditional Sudanese dishes). "You've bought me a whole week's worth of *mareesa* and food for five poor workers," she said gratefully. "We're heading back to the fields in two days."

"Why shouldn't we go with them to the fields?" He whispered to me. "I want to see the Jungo in action, in their natural habitat. I'm even prepared to join them at work. I'm eager to learn how they live—first-hand, not on hearsay."

I burst into laughter: I was sure he simply wouldn't be able to follow through. He was just a petit bourgeois embroiled in contradictions, vanity, and fancy dreams, trying to spend his idle time somewhere that would provide him with excitement, pleasures, and thrills. But working in the sesame fields? No way!

Our relationship had been built on candidness. We had worked in the same government department until we were both laid off for the so-called "public interest." We had grown up in the same place—the prison guards' housing complex in the city of Qedaref, although

[1] A popular dish made from a wild plant.

he had lived in the officers' quarters (his father was a senior officer and the prison's commissioner, while mine was just a guard). We remained close friends at school, at al-Hillah, and even at home—we had spent over thirty years together. We were open books to each other due to our almost identical backgrounds. We had both gone to the al-Noor Ankara primary school and used the area behind the veterinary quarantine and the space adjacent to the cemetery as our playgrounds. We joined forces in fights against children from the Dalasa and Salamt al-Baih quarters. We swam in the Majadeef creek together and in the Mekki al-Shabik puddles, and played war games at the foot of Mekki al-Shabik mountain.

We read the same books and were both enchanted when we discovered the worlds of Kahlil Gibran, Mikhail Naimy, Ilya Abu Madi, and Ibrahim Ishaq's *Old School Festival* and *The Story of the Girl Miyakaya.* As we got older, we came to know the writings of Nietzsche and Van Gogh's fine paintings, and memorized the poetry of Amal Dunqul, Nazim Hikmet, and Mohammed Mohiyaddin, and read the poems "The Blind Prostitute" and "Maria and Amboy."

In our early adolescence, I fell in love with his sister, and he fell in love with mine—those were our first love affairs. I didn't know exactly what he and my sister were doing, as they were careful to keep it secret. His sister was two or three years older than me, and we were intent on exploring every part of our bodies. My sister was two years younger than me, so I presumed it was a different thing for them since older girls, being less self-conscious of their bodies, always took the initiative in love affairs. I presumed that my sister, given her young age, couldn't be as skillful as his sister. I always thought of her as naive, and hardly attractive. She was dull and boring at best, and I couldn't stand her company, since the only thing she was good at was alerting my father to my mischievous acts.

We went to the same university, the same college, picked the same major. Our first ever sexual experience was with the same woman, a nymphomaniac lecturer in our department.

As I said, I knew him inside out.

"I'm not going with you to the fields. I'll wait here," I told him.

"With Alam Gishi, right?" he said, laughing.

"Of course."

Al-Safyah suddenly said, "You're my guests tonight at Addai's house."

"Addai's house again?" he asked. "I've just been stripped of my original Jovial watch and all the money I have. They nearly killed me."

"You'll be al-Safyah's guest," she said confidently as she rushed past us, leaving behind the smell of armpits and *mareesa*-flavored sweat.

"You're my guests of honor tonight," she added. "Do you drink?"

"We do," we answered in one voice.

"The imported stuff is on us," my friend added.

"*Abu Humar* is on me," she said.

We giggled as we went deeper into the narrow alleys, through huts, thorny thatched fences, and the smell of *mareesa*. We were met by drunk men and women, lovers, children—everyone greeted al-Safyah with a single word:

"Al-Safyah . . ."

She always replied with two soft words, "Hello father."

"Hello ma'am."

"They say you left your friend behind with the gang and headed to Alam Gishi," she blurted out. "What if they had killed him?"

"Who told you?" I asked in surprise.

"Everyone here knows it," she said calmly. "There are no secrets here."

"I know no one can kill him," I said defensively.

"Not for another twenty years at least," he said. "I have a project that will take twenty years to complete. After that, I'll be ready to die."

"A project in Fashaga?" al-Safyah asked innocently.

He tried in vain to explain his 20-year project to her. But I managed to explain things more clearly.

"But only Allah knows when one is destined to die," she said.

"True," he said, "but life is in man's hands."

"Both life and death are entirely in Allah's hands," she asserted.

"So humans are helpless? Is that what you're saying?" he asked in frustration.

"I don't know. I only know that both life and death are in Allah's hands," she said calmly.

I could feel how uncomfortable failing to win the argument had made him. He didn't usually give up that easily, that was for sure. He must have been trying to save his energy for another battle, in a different arena. He whispered a harbinger of that battle in my ears:

"You know, boy? This woman al-Safyah is wildly sexy, like a hot bitch."

"And you're a dog on the loose . . . "

"Exactly, exactly! A randy dog!"

Three of us sat in one corner of the Mother's House: Wad Ammoona, Alam Gishi, and I. Wad Ammoona made all the arrangements and sat near the door. I could tell he was split between an overwhelming desire to chat with me and the feeling that he should let Alam Gishi and I have some privacy. I tried to gauge Alam Gishi's desire to sleep with me against her willingness to keep Wad Ammoona's company.

I said to Wad Ammoona, "You said you were raised in the prison? My late father, may Allah grant his soul peace, was a guard in Qedaref."

Both Alam Gishi and Wad Ammoona seemed deeply relieved. Taking a deep drag on his sheesha, he said,

"The prison . . . Yeah. I was brought up in the prison."

5 THE FIERY WAD AMMOONA

The air of the hut was full of Abyssinian incense. Voices passed through reed fences into the darkness inside. We were able to recognize a soft, charming song calling out to us.

"That's Boushai," explained Wad Ammoona, then continued with his detailed account of his life in the prison, speaking in relaxed, soft tones. Alam Gishi and I shared the white pillow on the bed: her legs were crossed over mine, and she occasionally clawed the sole of my foot with her toenail, kindling a wild lust in me that was only kept at bay by Wad Ammoona's endless stream of captivating stories. The night was pleasantly warm, as was usual that time of year. Alam Gishi suddenly got off my lap.

"I'll make coffee for you."

Making coffee was one way people in those places expressed their love and affection for special guests.

Wad Ammoona continued telling his story about Azza. Azza couldn't persuade his mother to let her take him along when she was released. All mediators—jailors, prisoners, and even the prison superintendent himself—failed to convince her. His mother only caved in after what happened to Wad Ammoona that night.

Wad Ammoona was on his way back to the women's ward after running errands for the staff sergeant. When he reached the hallway to the cells, which was the quickest route to the western wing of the ward where his mother lived, a soft hand grabbed his arm firmly while another muffled his mouth. The smell of onions and garlic revealed the aggressor to be none other than the cook.

"Don't panic. It's me," he whispered, then slowly removed his hand from Wad Ammoona's mouth.

"What do you want?" asked Wad Ammoona.

"Azza's going to be discharged tomorrow, and I understand you're going with her. So I came to say goodbye. Shame on you for not saying goodbye, Wad Ammoona!"

"Okay, goodbye! Now let go of my arm!"

"No, not this way," the cook said, trying to sound gentle and polite. "There's a better way to say goodbye. I'm hosting a small party in your honor, in the pantry, just the two of us. I brought some candles, and I have some presents for you: new clothes, a pair of shoes, a ball, candy, and other stuff I'm sure you'll like."

Wad Ammoona struggled to free his arm. "If you don't let go of my arm, I'll scream and my mother will come and kill you."

The cook pulled a bunch of coins from his pocket.

"You'd better let me go," Wad Ammoona said.

The cook put back the coins into the pocket and quickly unzipped his pants. Out came something that Wad Ammoona could not immediately identify in the darkness, but when the cook pushed it against Wad Ammoona's belly, he felt a long hard object.

"It's so simple, and won't take more than a minute. I'll give you whatever you want," the cook said.

As the cook's mouth, which reeked of snuff, poor-quality cigarettes, and liquor, advanced toward Wad Ammoona, the latter quickly grabbed the cook's thing. It was big, dark, and smooth. He put a good part of it into his mouth, between his sharp teeth, and executed his mother's advice to the letter.

Everyone inside the prison, everyone in the surrounding area, and everyone who happened to be passing by at the time sprang to the air in terror as the cook let out a fierce, desperate scream, the like of which none of them had ever heard before. The small birds that were asleep on the *neem* trees in the central courtyard of the prison took to the air in fright. The old *sinber* birds that had taken refuge in the *sunut* tree by the pond at the southern end of the prison flapped their wings in horror. There were subsequent screams, but they were significantly lower in volume—only Wad Ammoona heard them. Then the cook fell over.

"I spit the whole head of his penis out my mouth. It was disgusting," Wad Ammoona remarked.

After the dawn prayers, his mother said, "Now you can go with Azza. I'm not worried about you anymore. Just take care of your teeth. I'll give you money to buy *masaweek*."[1]

The smell of Abyssinian coffee filled my lungs, and the warm air carried Boushai's voice, fresh and lovely, from the al-Omda quarter into Addai's hut.

"Despite what he did, the cook didn't lose his job," Alam Gishi remarked. "He's still there—as fat as a mule."

I happened to know that cook and had heard his story, though not with all those gruesome details. We had lived in the same housing complex, the one for the prison staff. My father worked in the same prison. The cook was a dubious character, but he had never been known to have molested any of the neighborhood children.

But I didn't tell them I knew the cook. I didn't tell Alam Gishi that what she had said about his still working there and being as fat as a mule wasn't true. The truth was that he died one year after that incident from a snakebite in the prison's storeroom, where they kept the grain. I didn't tell them we were relatives.

Alam Gishi moved around briskly with the pan, bringing it close to our nostrils so we could smell the coffee roasting.

"I was only ten years old when I left the prison," Wad Ammoona said, "but I was as experienced as an adult, aware of everything."

"Praise be to God! It's as if Wad Ammoona was never a child," boasted Alam Gishi as she poured more coffee into the grinding pot. She started pounding the beans into powder, the rhythmic beat in tune with the song she began to sing in the Hamaseen dialect.

---

[1] Sticks of the *araak* tree that are widely used for brushing one's teeth.

"Sorry to bother you with prison stories and all this trivial stuff," Wad Ammoona said. "I should leave you now with Alam Gishi. I'll stay in a nearby hut, though, in case you need me."

I insisted that he should have coffee with us before he left. Alam Gishi hinted that she would like that too. He accepted on one condition: that he would only share the *bikriyah*—the first round served—with us and would take the subsequent ones with the Mother.

There was only one bed in the room, yet it was as big as two beds combined. It was made of *sunut* wood, had huge, heavy legs, and was covered with a white sheet embroidered with the image of two peacocks facing each other, their mouths close together. The Abyssinian style of embroidery was evident in the intense use of yellow, red, and green colors. With her smooth tan skin and her long slender legs that revealed traces of henna, Alam Gishi looked stunning. On one foot, she had a henna tattoo that looked like a cross or maybe a rose. Whatever it was, it was clearly fresh, and it was beautiful.

I'm not an expert in sex. In my early adolescence, I, like most of my friends in al-Hillah, had sex with goats, young donkeys, and even calves. It wasn't particularly fun, but it was still important—it allowed you to boast of your virility and stopped the others from calling you impotent, or a girl.

One experience I had before puberty was particularly thrilling and might still have been influencing my approach to sex. My aunt, al-Tayah, used to send me, every morning before I went to school, to deliver a bucket full of sorghum to the mill for grinding, which I would then pick up on my way back home. She would use the flour to bake *kisra*[2] and sell it at the grand souk. The mill owner was a young woman who had no children. Her husband, who worked at the vegetable market, didn't come home until sunset. She was particularly popular among the teenage boys and seemed to have had an affair with every single one of them, including myself. Yet my experience with her was a unique one. When I came back to pick up the flour one day, she led me into the house through the mill's back

[2] A type of bread baked in thin sheets from sorghum dough.

door. There she undressed and helped me take off my clothes. She explained what was expected of me and showed me her sex. I became quite frightened when I saw it, as it was totally different from the image that I and my friends had had of it. We had thought of it as something beautiful like a rose, but the thing that lay in front of me looked like a large rat covered in black hair. It had a big mouth—and perhaps teeth as well—and it smelled awful. How come we had been so wrong all those years? But she was experienced enough to alleviate all of my concerns. Then I came to understand everything, or what I thought was everything. The weird thing, though, was that she always urged me—ordered me, to be precise—to urinate.

"Piss, come on, piss inside me!"

I didn't know how to urinate in there. Besides, my bladder was empty. But when I told her that, she beat me:

"Piss in me like a man! Aren't you a man?"

I only came to experience "men's urine" several years later, when that same woman came to me in a dream, stark naked. Her wild rat stared at me, and then she herself became wild and started to beat me:

"Piss in me!"

I wet my pants—a warm fluid that smelled of the *laloub* fruit that I used to eat a lot of. The "urine" came out, giving me an amazing feeling—a mixture of pleasure and pain. That was my only experience with a woman. I never "urinated" in a lady again—I never had the chance, or maybe I was too shy with women, and never met another woman as bold as she was. I don't know exactly. The only other experience I had were the innocent touches of my friend's sister.

So here I was, thirty-five years later, all grown up now but with barely any experience with women, finally face to face with a woman—an experienced woman, a woman in flesh and blood.

I didn't know how Alam Gishi understood all this, for she did everything alone, from putting on the condom all the way through to the "urination," which she wildly sucked from deep within me with indescribable lust.

6 MUKHTAR ALI

Mukhtar Ali continued his version of the story. He was now able to walk on his own to the lavatory and even farther to the corner grocer to buy batteries for his radio.

"Then we went into the sesame fields. Samaeen, the *jallabi*,[1] chanted *Allahu Akbar* ('God is the greatest') three times. The whole place fell into a deep silence."

Samaeen brought two big, horned sheep for the men to slaughter in celebration, and as a way of invoking Allah's blessing for a bountiful harvest.

When the sesame harvest is good, the spikes are elegantly stud like jewels on top of the lofty red stems, forcing the Jungojorai to bow. The act of harvesting turns into a festival of dancing. The Jungo move to the rhythm of the scythes and the crackling sound of the sesame bales (called *kulaigas*) as they are bundled and thrown backward, one after the other:

Kulaiga, kulaiga, kulaiga, kulaiga . . . Four *kulaigas* make one *hilla*. This year they managed to raise the price to eight pounds per *hilla*, three times more than last year. So each *hilla* is part of a fortune, each *kulaiga* part of a dream coming true. Each *hilla* earns eight pounds—another eight, then another . . . The money is safely entrusted to an old woman in the village.

[1] A merchant or investor who is not a native of the locality.

Eight plus eight plus eight plus eight plus eight plus ei . . . Mukhtar's head was getting heavy, his arms were numb, his legs—where were his legs? He felt as if he were being dragged away from the sesame fields, or perhaps from life itself.

"It wasn't until I fell down that Abbakar Adam saw me and came to my rescue."

Mukhtar Ali spent a whole week bed-ridden inside the workers' camp (*taya*), all alone. The others all went to work early in the morning, leaving him in the company of rats, birds, and the guard's watchdog.

"I felt like I was going crazy. I didn't want to die away from my home, so I asked Samaeen the *jallabi* to take me down to my sister's house in al-Hillah. He dumped me there. Shortly after this, my sister went to Hamdayeit to join her husband, who was a smuggler."

Samaeen never came back to check on him, even though he had promised to bring the medical assistant to him, or take him to the local hospital, or seek the help of Fekki[2] Ali Wad al-Zaghrad, a famous local healer. He didn't do any of those things and instead ran away—a cowardly act, as some Jungo described it.

Thank God, many sisters and brothers were there to help—particularly al-Safyah, a slender black gazelle, as agile as a bee. She had a distinct smell—the smell of stinky armpits and an endless supply of sweat caused by extensive exposure to the sun. That slender figure, that peaceful and convivial lady who was always seen in the company of scores of Jungo, would transform into a wild animal as soon as she entered the sesame fields, cranking out scores of *hillas* one after the other as if she were using a machine—praise be to God! Indeed, the fortunate *jallabi* who manages to win her to his team will definitely have a great harvest.

Mukhtar Ali continued, "Al-Safyah said to me, 'I'm going to teach Samaeen a lesson—that son of a bitch! I'll bring him to his knees.'

[2] A *fekki* is a devout or religiously knowledgeable person who people call on for treatment of all ailments, particularly serious diseases and psychological disorders.

She called in the nurse. She called in no less than Fekki Ali Wad al-Zaghrad himself. And she made me *madeeda*,[3] as well as red sorghum and millet porridge."

"They say al-Safyah is an incredible sex machine," interrupted al-Shaygi, who was actually from the Jaliyeen tribe but was called al-Shaygi on account of his facial scars, which looked like those that distinguished the people from the Shaygiyya tribe. "If only she'd been marriageable—I would have married her," he said, biting the back of his hand.

Everyone present burst into laughter, although some of them held the exact opposite view. Some fidgeted awkwardly, but none of them could resist the temptation to listen. Talking about women has a taste similar to *mouleeta*:[4] sour but savory, and no two bites are ever the same. Perhaps that's because it evokes such deeply buried memories: of a wonderful mother left behind somewhere; of a kind, half-forgotten sister; of a daughter they can't give birth to; of a wife or girlfriend back home whose features can no longer be made out.

Al-Safyah was particularly enigmatic; portions of her life were unclear, especially with regard to sex, and all the tales being told were mere fantasies that navigated through warm valleys and creeks, under aging *sunut* and *neem* trees, and on the feet of foxes, rabbits, and pigs—dreamy, peaceful myths . . .

"How do you know she's a sex machine?" Mukhtar Ali asked defiantly.

Abbakar Adam volunteered an answer: "I don't have any personal experience with her, but I heard about her affair with Wad Fur. You don't have to die to walk through a graveyard!"

Let's not go into their affair now. It's well and widely known, and we don't want to give the impression that our version of the story

---

[3] Millet or date pie.

[4] A plant juice used to flavor chili.

is the true one. Everyone in that area—men, women, and children—seemed to tell their own version of the story. No two were the same. But a different story was being told at Adalia Daniyal's house, on her *mareesa* day.[5]

The part that the Mother had allocated to us in her spacious property was at the farthest row of huts—a quiet spot apparently reserved for special guests. A row of small *rakubas*, about 20 meters long, ran in front of the huts.

The *sheesha* added to the convivial atmosphere, courtesy of Wad Ammoona, who was at his best. He couldn't reconcile himself to the idea of an all-male gathering and was desperate to bring in girls to add to the fun, but also to earn some extra cash. He clearly wasn't satisfied with just al-Safyah—or "the monster," as he called her. He kept whispering the name of Alam Gishi into my ear whenever he had the chance. When she noticed that Wad Ammoona was hounding me, al-Safyah spoke to him so harshly that he left in silence, depriving us of his hilarious jokes and amusing comments about al-Hillah and its people and prison, and of the fragrance of his classy perfume.

Taking a strong drag on her *sheesha*, as if she wanted to suck up the whole world in a single puff, al-Safyah said, "It was my grandmother al-Safyah who established this place. I was named after her. When she first came to this land, it was a huge forest of thorny plants, *laloub* and *nabak* trees. The place was full of hyenas and monkeys, wild boar, and djinn."

She related captivating stories about what the place had been like dozens of years ago, about prisoners who escaped from al-Homra jail in Ethiopia with the *ferro*[6] still tightly fixed on their heads; about djinn who lived and married humans; about humans who turned into

[5] The day when a *mareesa* producer invites her friends to her house and serves them freshly produced *mareesa*. They used to make *mareesa* in turns, with each woman having a specific day so that each one should have an equal share of the market.

[6] The *ferro* is a torture device made of iron that is fixed tightly on the head.

animals and crows; about dead people who came back to life; about people who, after seven rounds of death and rebirth, eventually transformed into *abu lamba*; [7]about cannibals; et cetera, et cetera.

"Tell us about your affair with Wad Fur," my friend interrupted her. To tell the truth, I was a bit on edge because I didn't know what her reaction would be. She rose to her feet, handed the *sheesha* hose over to me and, without looking at us, walked into a hut a few yards away—the larger hut that Wad Ammoona had lit up at sunset along with all the other unoccupied huts so as to ward off the djinn.

As she silently disappeared inside the hut, I felt an urge to rebuke my friend for his inept remark and tell him, once again, how rude I thought he was. "When will you learn to be polite?" I wanted to say, but I didn't utter a word. Instead, I set the hose aside and stood up. "Wad Ammoona!" I called out loudly.

In the blink of an eye, as if he had been behind the door waiting for me to call him, he sprang into the room and stood before me.

"Yes, sir," he said quietly and politely.

"Let's go."

Without asking where, he led the way and I followed closely behind, taking quick steps. We went into a narrow alley that led us to another alley past a row of *rakubas* and huts. We passed two *neem* trees near what we thought must be a pen (*zareba*), as the smell of manure and *mushuk*[8] seemed to suggest.

Another alley took us down a twisting route before spitting us outside the Mother's house into a wide path frequented by a host of people—drunkards, lovers, Jungo, *jallabis*, soldiers. Wad Ammoona went ahead, and I followed behind silently. It was only once he was inside Mukhtar Ali's house that he asked, "You wanted Mukhtar Ali's house, didn't you?"

---

[7] Abu lamba—literally "the one with the lamp"—refers to a creature that gives off light as if it were carrying a lamp, and that is believed to deliberately mislead desert travelers.

[8] *Mareesa* residue used to feed livestock.

"Yes."

I didn't ask him how he knew. Mukhtar Ali woke up once we entered the courtyard.

"Who is it?" he called out.

"Hello, Mukhtar. It's us," Wad Ammoona replied.

"Welcome, welcome. Come on in."

Wad Ammoona excused himself. "I'd love to stay with you, but I've got work to do at the Mother's House. We've got a big group of guests tonight. See you in the morning."

Without waiting for my response, he vanished into the same alley that would lead him, eventually, to the Mother's House.

I figured Wad Ammoona was hurrying back to the Mother's House because he was anxious to see what was happening between my friend and al-Safyah.

In a drowsy voice, Mukhtar Ali asked me where I had left my friend.

"At Addai's house, with al-Safyah," I answered.

"Why?" he asked objectionably, his voice now vigilant.

"That's what he wanted," I answered matter-of-factly.

"But with al-Safyah?"

"Yes. With al-Safyah."

"Haven't you heard what happened between her and Wad Fur?"

"Was it any different from what happened between her and you?" I asked.

"It was completely different," he assured me.

"Are you sure her story about Wad Fur is true?" I asked.

"No one really knows exactly what happened to Wad Fur. But we all know that *something* happened to him. Good? Bad? Only God knows. All we can do is seek refuge in God from all evils."

As he lay back down on the bed, I said, "I'm sure she won't be able to kill my friend. He's not someone who dies easily. And anything short of death would be a positive experience for him."

In an attempt to change the subject, he asked if I would like to sleep inside the hut, like my friend. I said yes, as that had been my habit since I was a young boy.

I didn't feel tired yet, so I decided to try to draw the old man into a conversation.

"How long have you been here?" I started.

He turned onto his left side to face me. "I really can't remember exactly what year I first came here. But it was a time when al-Hillah was still one big property fenced with *kitir* and *sayyal*.[9] Hyenas and foxes wandered about in broad daylight. There were only a handful of *jallabi* investors, and agricultural land was limited. I was the resident manager of the biggest farm here and had full control over it—the tractors, the workers, everything. The *jallabi* would only come when it was time to harvest. I was able to earn ten or even twenty piasters a day—a single piaster was a fortune back then."

"But I was hopeless with money. I would take all my money and camp in the mareesa houses in the Fariek Girish district in al-Homra: this drink's too sweet. This one's bitter. This one's sour. This one's underdone. This one's stale. This woman'sa virgin. This one's unmarried. This one's a whore. This one's decent . . . And so on until I'd spent my last piaster. I'd do it all over again the next day. That's been going on for over 40 years now. And it will continue until Judgment Day, or sooner, if we end up under the death tree."

"The death tree?" I asked in surprise.

"It's a big tree in Fariek Girish in al-Homra. When a Jungojorai gets too old, or becomes seriously ill, he goes on his own to that tree—or the *mareesa* maker drops him off there, and he sits under it until he dies. Of course he receives donations from friends: food, money, clothes, drinks, snuff, etc."

"Why don't they take him back home?" I asked in protest.

"No one would want to go back home after all these years, not when they're on the verge of death. It's shameful."

According to Mukhtar, a Jungojorai comes with the intention of serving just one season before returning home loaded with lavish gifts for his mother and sisters and getting married. But once the

[9] Two types of thorny plants.

season is over, he's seduced by wicked people and goes about wasting his money on *mareesa*, liquor, and women, promising himself that he will go home next year right after the harvest—an endless cycle, until he gets old and dies.

"In all my life," he said, "I haven't seen a single Jungojorai who returned home of his own free will! They only go back if their family comes and picks them up!"

"Strange," I remarked. And then, remembering the tree, I added, "I'd really like to see the death tree you mentioned."

"It's in Fariek Girish in al-Homra, near the house of Omda[10] Dawada. It's where people like us are destined to end up."

"Where's your family, Mukhtar?" I asked affectionately.

"I have no family. I'm over sixty now. Where would one get a mother, a father or even brothers at this age? And I was the youngest in the family."

"Don't you have any nephews?"

"I don't know them. And they don't know me. Our village in Darfur was wiped out by government shelling. There's only one place for fate to lead me: under the death tree. I don't feel any remorse, though. I've enjoyed my life. I'm still able to work and earn a living. And I'm convinced that whoever has lived in this village and tasted its women and *mareesa* can't live anywhere else. I've never deprived myself of those delights—from Khashm El Girba to Fariek Girish in al-Homra, and from al-Hawatta to al-Fazara. But let me give you one piece of advice, son: don't chase after extremes in your life."

It's too late for that now, I told myself. But I said to him, "May Allah protect us."

We woke early, as was the habit of the people here, who went to bed early and got up as early as the chickens—except for the drunkards and philanderers, who stayed awake past midnight but still got up early. I handed him the snuff I had left and went straight to the Mother's House.

---

[10] Local mayor.

The roads were bustling with passersby from the surrounding villages on their way to the Friday market; the *barbaras* were packed full of sesame and villagers. A truck passed in front of me, and then a water cart. The cart driver called out my name, and when I turned toward him he said, "Al-Safyah gave your friend a hard time yesterday."

"What?"

He repeated in obvious relish: "She showed your friend the stars in broad daylight!"

"When?"

"Yesterday," he said, drumming on the water tank to attract buyers, "after you and Wad Ammoona left him with al-Safyah at Addai's house."

7

THE AL-GANZAI SOUK

I missed Wad Ammoona the moment I entered the courtyard of the Mother's House; his absence could not go unnoticed.

"Wad Ammoona's training the bride," Alam Gishi told me.

"Training the bride? Training her to do what?"

"To dance. Don't you know that Wad Ammoona's a singer—and a seasoned dancer, henna painter, and hairdresser too?"

I nodded my head, though I meant to say, "No I didn't."

"The bride is Abrahait's daughter," she added in a seductive voice. "She's marrying Mohammed Awad Kajok, the *barbara* driver. You may have heard about him. Hammado is his nickname."

I nodded my head, as if to say, "Sort of."

Alam Gishi continued, "Had it not been for Allah's protection, Wad Ammoona would have been a girl."

I laughed. "He's already doing women's work. He doesn't seem to be a proper man," I said.

"No woman has tried him out so far," she said, laughing. "But no man has tried him out either, to the best of our knowledge—except for the matter with the prison cook when he was a boy. Nothing else. He's a grown man now, twenty years old. But no one knows who his father is."

"He said his father was a Yemeni."

"On account of his fair skin or what?"

"That's what he said. His mother told him."

"Everyone here knows the story of his mother," she replied.

Massaging my legs with *dilka*,[1] she continued, "Ammoona ran away from her home in a remote village in Western Sudan, about 28 years ago. The truck driver who picked her up on the road slept with her, as did his helper and the owner of the truck. When she got to Qedaref, she slept with the owner of the cart, who had given her a lift to the girls' quarter, and with the Yemeni grocer, and with al-Nazeer, the sheikh of al-Hillah, and with Wad Jibreen, the inn owner, and with the husband of her hostess, and with Ustaz Zakaria, the primary school teacher. Then she got pregnant and gave birth to Wad Ammoona. I heard all this from the mouth of Kaltouma bit Fadul, Ammoona's closest friend."

"And which of those men does Wad Ammoona look like?"

"Honestly, I haven't seen any of them. But his complexion's the same as his mother's. Haven't you seen her? She's got light skin, and a face as bright and beautiful as a full moon. She's old now, of course, but she's still pretty."

"Where is she now?"

"She's married to a prison guard in Qedaref. She had a daughter too. If you saw Ammoona today, you'd think she was only thirty years old: she's still attractive, and her skin glistens with *dilka*, *khomra*, and *henna*."

"Maybe it was his mother who spoiled him," she added.

"How?"

"He was a spoiled kid."

"Even though he spent most of his life in prison?"

"Even at the prison, he was pampered by the inmates—both the men and the women, and by the guards too. It's rumored the guards used to have their way with him."

The weather was nice, the sky clear and blue. We were sitting under the big *rakuba* in front of the hut, the perfect place for a chat and some coffee. I believe whoever invented the *rakuba* did so for the sole purpose of hanging out and talking.

---

[1] An aromatic dough used in massaging.

"Where's your friend?" she asked.

"With Mukhtar Ali."

"What a strange man!"

I nodded in agreement.

"One day he'll get killed."

"I don't think so. No one can kill him. He's simply not the type who gets killed."

"I assure you, he won't survive ten minutes in Fariek Girish in al-Homra. Have you heard what al-Safyah did to him?"

I said people here tended to add fanciful touches to stories and were prone to present their own fantasies as true stories.

She started to tell me what she thought was the true story. I interrupted her several times to highlight what I thought were weaknesses or contradictions in her account. But she went on relating her account as confidently as an eyewitness, although I know that neither she nor anyone else had seen anything.

I decided to drop the subject, especially since Wad Ammoona had now joined us. Redolent of *khomra* and other homemade perfumes, he seemed more delicate and feminine than ever. He said he was in a hurry and complained that the bride's sense of rhythm was so poor he could only train her with Ethiopian songs. "And even with Ethiopian songs, she's barely any better. The *dalluka* rhythm is going, but she's dancing to a different one. What an awful job!" he whined. Turning to me, he said, "Al-Safyah gave your friend hard time yesterday." He burst into laughter, which was interrupted only by the arrival of my friend, who said, "You all seem in good spirits."

Wad Ammoona excused himself on the pretext of having to run some errands for the wedding. We ate breakfast in silence, then headed to the al-Ommal souk, leaving Alam Gishi at home. When we arrived at the souk, a revolt against the *jallabis* was brewing, which stirred our interest because such events were quite rare.

The al-Ommal souk, the gathering place for laborers, was held every Saturday on the main square near the health center built by the Christian Outreach Organization to serve as a maternity center.

The square came to be known as the Medical Insurance Square after it was occupied by a medical insurance organization, which was believed to have been behind sending mothers and children astray.

Five *neem* trees served as the venue of "the Alalla Souk," frequented by porters, Jungo, masons, carpenters, and brokers. Land Rovers, *barbaras*, pickups, and *jallabis*' trucks were parked on the southern end of the souk, near the Shoak bus terminal and the workshops of the mechanics and iron smiths, and near the oil and spare parts shops. The *jallabi* merchants, with their flowing robes and bright faces, were encircled by workers, completely absorbed in heated bargains and arguments. We asked a pretty Jungojoraya called *Bit al-Malayka*[2] what was going on. "This is the first time the Jungo have ever all stuck to the same rate, with no exceptions," she explained.

It was clear that some arrangement had been made, that some agreement had been reached among the workers. The black and brown faces on which the previous night had left evident marks—those faces that had always been cheerful, tolerant, and carefree—were now more serious and were uttering a single phrase in unison: "Nine pounds for a *hilla* of sesame." The *jallabis* said they would only pay eight pounds to the Jungojorai to cut a *hilla* of sesame, contending that even eight pounds was an unbearably high rate, to say nothing of nine.

Yet both the Jungo and the *jallabis* knew it was the sesame that had the final say and that those bargains were a waste of time for the *jallabis*. Indeed, when the sun rose further, a scorching northerly wind blew, carrying the sound of Wad Ammoona's voice as he desperately tried to get the awkward bride-to-be to move to the rhythm of his sesame-themed songs. When the scorching wind blew over the fields, it ripped open the fat sesame ears, those ears that the *jallabis* wanted to remain intact until the Jungojorai's sickle reached them. The sun was working against the *jallabis* and even the moon was

[2] "Daughter of angels."

rising inauspiciously at sunset. They both seemed bent on ripping open the sesame ears, and once the golden grains fell, they would be picked up by an army of relentless ants that would store it in fortified underground silos, guarded by the blessings of loving queens, for use in times of hardship.

The Jungo were certain they were going to win the bargain, and the *jallabis* knew they were going to lose, but they still thought that prolonging the discussions might prove useful, so different people intervened: middlemen, brokers, agents, famous prostitutes, pension owners, water pump operators, wordmongers. "Fetch workers from the neighboring Fashaga," some suggested. "They're skilled and cheap. Ignore these rebels. They'll regret it."

The Jungo laughed at hearing this. "Workers from Fashaga? And you expect them to abandon work in their own sesame fields?"

"Let's hire people from the refugee camp," the *jallabis* suggested loudly to each other. The Jungo laughed, "Refugees? Are you dreaming? The refugees have now become richer than the natives. No refugee is interested in cutting sesame."

The Jungo loudly suggested to one another, "We should abandon this useless sesame business as well, and go find work laying cable for the telecommunications company."

"I for one will never cut sesame for eight pounds, even if I have to work like Wad Ammoona," said a Jungojorai in a coarse loud voice.

The *jallabis* responded just as loudly, "We'll bring in workers from Khashm El Girba."

The Jungo replied, "You won't find anything but singers and teachers there."

Then al-Safyah called out, "Let's go folks. The *Googo* wants us to head to al-Hillah. Let's continue last night's fun! The girls are waiting for you, boys!"

The crowd moved toward al-Hillah. When they reached the premises of the bank under construction, the sesame whispered to the *jallabis* pockets. "Ok. We'll pay nine pounds. May it bring you all the evils in the world," they finally said.

Spitting out a big snuff ball onto the ground, al-Shaygi said, "We consider this money you pay us *haram*,[3] so we spend it on drinks throughout the day, and piss it out in the evening."

So the Jungo accepted the job but decided to start only the next day, because once the *Googo* headed to a particular destination, they were obliged to follow that direction. They were now heading toward al-Hillah to continue the previous night's drinking, and they couldn't change course as that brought ill fortune.

Early the next morning, they would leave for the fields. They decided to work on all the plots except for the *jallabi* Samaeen's. They wanted to teach him a lesson. Their decision was a big relief to Mukhtar Ali, who burst into tears.

On our way back to al-Hillah, I asked my friend, "What happened between you and al-Safyah last night?"

"I'll tell you later," he said, looking away. "You'll know everything."

"They're saying she's brought disgrace on you," I said.

"What do they say she did to me?" he asked in surprise.

"They're saying she's got 'a thing' like a man's, but even bigger—half the size of a donkey's, as big as that of a large ass."

"I'll tell you the whole story," he murmured tensely. "That's not it at all. People here are obsessed with fanciful tales. True, it's a strange story, but it's got nothing to do with a donkey or a dog or whatever."

We sat in a café in the sorghum market, near the pharmacy. The Jungo went past us in small groups, speaking in loud voices and different accents, stirring up dust as their feet kicked against the ground, mimicking the *jallabis* and laughing. The owners started to shut down their restaurants, and the women selling food and tea packed up their utensils, aware that there was no chance of selling anything anymore. The Jungo were focused on one thing now: drinks. The women would have to follow them to al-Hillah to sell them arrack or set up seats for them. It was the harvest season, and

---

[3] Gained from illicit sources, and hence damned.

the harvest was the essence of the Jungojorai: they were creditworthy now. The real challenge was luring the Jungojorai into their houses, for women were quickly snatching them from the streets.

The café owner apologized to us for not being able to offer any drinks. "The clients have arrived. I have some arrack I want to sell. I'd better hurry up and try to sell a few glasses. Am I not right, brothers? Thank God they are staying for another night. A good chance for us. Am I not right, brothers?"

We nodded in agreement and simultaneously rose from the two stools, demonstrating full content with her wise decision and making gestures to assure her that she was doing the right thing. In gratitude for our evident goodwill, she left her room unlocked and allowed us to use the two stools, as long as we took them into the room and locked it before we left.

"Ok, brothers?"

"Ok, sister. Ok," my friend replied in a soft voice.

I thanked her. As she left with a basket packed with stuff on her head, she said, "My house is next to the Mother's House," looking my friend straight in the eye, a look that could be interpreted in many different ways.

"What did she mean?" my friend asked as she moved away, chanting one of those songs the women love.

"She's probably alluding to your story with al-Safyah," I said indifferently.

"Wad Ammoona must have spread that rumor," he said.

"What happened exactly?" I asked him. I assured him that Wad Ammoona had been giving dancing lessons to the bride-to-be, and after taking me to Mukhtar Ali's house, I overheard him singing to the beats of the *dalluka*[4] drum: "*Louleyeh: surely you will draw the evil eye, o Louleyeh of Abyssiniya.*" His voice could be heard by almost everyone in al-Hillah. My friend fell silent, as he usually did when he was absorbed in thought. I couldn't understand why he

[4] A local drum played mainly by girls, particularly at weddings.

didn't simply tell me the truth. Our relationship was built on honesty, not on barriers and silence.

A handful of army officers went past us, swaggering like peacocks. Some employees of the telecommunications company asked us if "Bakhieta" was in. We said she was at home, so they headed off in that direction. My friend recognized some of them, including the manager.

A group of workers passed by wearing blue, black, and white overalls covered with oil stains. Al-Hillah was currently witnessing brisk development, and everyone was optimistic and enthusiastic. Girls composed lyrics in praise of teachers, local councilmen, policemen, telecommunication engineers, and even the workers at the gas station on Hamdayeit road.

"Where's Bakhieta?" a man asked us, half his body inside the *rakuba*. I said she was at home. Looking at my friend with piercing eyes, he said, "You're newcomers here, aren't you?" I said we were.

"Staying at the Mother's House?"

"Yes."

He flashed a broad smile that revealed scattered and decaying teeth that had been turned brown by chewing tobacco. My friend thought the smile was sarcastic. He then told me what he claimed was everything that had happened between him and al-Safyah, in order to close that chapter, at least as far as I was concerned.

8

AWADEYAH CRIES FOR SEVEN DAYS ON END

In the early days, al-Hillah was inhabited by wolves, wild boar, turtles, and foxes. The djinn were everywhere: in ditches and mounds, by the river, and even inside al-Hillah itself, sharing homes with people. The whole village was one big home, a thousand meters long and much wider than that, fenced with dry thorny plants and guarded by dogs. It was the home of Habouba al-Safyah, our great grandmother. Inside, it was subdivided into scores of smaller homes: straw and cane huts and big *rakubas* made of *kitir* and *dahaseer* wood. At the center were pits that served as underground storage spaces for sorghum and millet and a place to ferment *kawal*.[1]

All the newcomers who chose to settle there found ample space inside the big house to build their own huts. Transitory travelers bound for Ethiopia, Eritrea, or the South were hosted at Habouba al-Safyah's guesthouse, which had its own prayer space, a large vessel used to store drinking water, and a *mostorah*: a pit roofed with strong wood and straw, used as a lavatory. This guesthouse hosted waves of pilgrims who came from Nigeria, the Niger, and Cameroon en route to Mecca. Even Moroccans with fair skin and long brown beards broke their journey here en route to the Bab al-Mandab Watergate, Yemen, and on to Mecca. Some stayed for more than a year, took up plots of land, and planted sesame and millet. Some even got married and had children.

[1] Edible herbs.

But one house alone was the focal point of that place, and its proprietor was famous throughout the East, thanks to impressed pilgrims who carried tales of her to Mecca and back home. In fact, Habouba al-Safyah was not the founder of that mansion, but she was the most famous of the many al-Safyahs who had lived here. They were the descendants of a man who had fled from prison in al-Homra. That happened in a year dubbed "the year of the comet"—comets only appeared when extraordinary events were underway.

In that year, a big comet strutted its long tail for a full week. Habouba's grandfather had been accused of robbing a *Gishi*'s[2] house in Ethiopia and was going to be beaten to death or left to starve. Back in those days, groups of prisoners roamed residential quarters, souks, and restaurants, a whole group of them all tied to a single hemp rope, eating leftovers and begging for food, money, tobacco, and snuff. That was the only way for them to avoid starvation. The prison authorities were generous enough to provide them with shelter against the elements, and feeding them was not part of their job.

Grandfather Abdel Razek was sitting with some friends in a restaurant in al-Homra near the Hamdayeit souk, so named because the scores of Sudanese who frequented it took Hamdayeit road and crossed the Setit River to reach it. They were sitting and eating *zigni* with *injera* and *dilleikh*, the most popular dish in Ethiopia, when Abdel Razek saw his twin brother Abdel Razzak bound from his feet to a hemp rope along with twenty others. He was in a miserable state, emaciated, his face reduced to bones, his body reeking.

They gave each other a long and warm embrace, until they were separated by the guards and prisoners, who were too impatient to waste their precious time with such sentimental nonsense. The twins chatted in their own tribal dialect. Abdel Razek gave his twin some food and money, as well as a promise to free him from prison. Abdel Razek was aware that his twin was too shy and innocent to steal. He was also aware that Abdel Razzak could die in prison if he didn't

[2] An Ethiopian police chief.

come to his rescue. They were in a foreign land where he knew no officials or dignitaries who could help. The bar owner whom he regularly visited was no help either. When he explained his twin's ordeal to her, she said she could not help for fear of death at the hands of the *Gishi*. And he had no money to bribe the guards with. Only one option was available to him, and he went for it without hesitation—he had to rescue his twin at any cost.

In narrating this story to us, Mukhtar Ali gave us the impression that he had personally witnessed every single episode, and been one of the story's main characters, although he occasionally said something like "this happened over one hundred fifty years ago."

We were walking leisurely through the alleyways with no specific destination. That was Mukhtar Ali's idea: to stroll under the morning sun and gain some essential vitamins. "Even snakes get out of their holes to improve their sight." He looked healthier today. He was optimistic, quick to laugh at the slightest thing, and he was talking loudly, something he did not usually do.

We found ourselves in the alley leading to Adalia Daniyal's house. Spotting us, she called out over the straw fence: "Come in. Your friend's here. Come join us for a drink."

We accepted the invitation gratefully. It was early in the morning, and *mareesa* was the best way to start the day, just as the morning chat was the best net for catching the previous night's tales. We called it the morning journal. The *mareesa* unleashes the imagination, which in turn unlocks the tongue, so you have heart-to-heart conversations, and the angels of wonderful stories come down.

We found my friend sitting on a big stool like some mythical sheikh who survived the *Anaj* massacre. Beside him on another stool was al-Ajouz, an old man who was the most famous *om kiki*[3] player in al-Hillah and the neighboring villages; in fact, the residents had not seen or even heard of anyone else who played the *om kiki*. They seemed to have just concluded a rousing round of songs, as they were

[3] A local musical instrument, similar to a violin except that it has a single chord.

now talking about the birth of a new song whose opening verse was *Awadeyah cries for seven days on end.*

We overheard the last statement by al-Ajouz: "The al-Kalash brothers are the true composers. I heard them sing it in Ganees and Kurmuk, in Hai al-Zihoor and Yabous, and at parties in Rosairis. I brought it from Gaisan. But I was the first to sing it with the help of the *om kiki*."

My friend turned to me: "Where have you been *man*?" he asked cheerfully. I laughed. Adalia Daniyal laughed. Mukhtar Ali laughed. My friend burst into hysterical laughter. "You're the only one who knows why you're laughing," he said to me.

"We all know the story," Adalia said, swaying her breasts in a kind of dance. "That's life. One day it's in your favor, the next day it's against you."

Adalia Daniyal brought in *asaliyah* and *mareesa*, and the Mother brought in *Om fitfit*[4] soaked in chili pepper and peanut butter.

"I have *mouleeta*,"[5] she said. Al-Ajouz said he loved *mouleeta*. I asked the Mother if she had *abanghazi*.[6] She pointed at the chili mixture with a finger that bore a large gold ring, and said it had already been added.

Adalia served us cups of *mareesa*; the thin layer of henna on the nails of her soft black hands was charming and sexy. A few Jungo were present; the majority had left early in the morning to go cut sesame. Mukhtar Ali kept reminding us every now and then of his victory over Samaeen the *jallabi*.

"That son-of-a-bitch Samaeen. He couldn't find a single Jungojorai to work for him."

Taking advantage of a brief pause, al-Ajouz chanted in a melodious voice:

---

[4] Sheep intestines, served raw.

[5] A plant juice used to season chili.

[6] Sheep's bile—also used to season chili.

Far-off Gaisan
is the home of my darling.
Far-off Gaisan
is the home of my darling.

Because his songs couldn't be performed without a chorus, we volunteered to chant the opening verses after him. That wasn't difficult, since everyone knew all the songs. True, my friend and I were strangers, but chanting two stanzas in the five-tone scale—stanzas that contained two Arabic words, five words in Albarta dialect, and three in Angassana dialect—was not too difficult. True, we occasionally missed the tune and rhythm, but we nevertheless performed our role as chorus with great enthusiasm, thanks to Adalia Daniyal's *asaliyah* and *mareesa*.

In fact, no one could be called a stranger in al-Hillah. The moment you got off a *barbara*, a gloomy bus, a Land Rover, or a truck by the souk or anywhere else in al-Hillah, you became one of its founding members, and you quickly came to know everything about the place. You were immediately authorized to give a historical account, whether true or invented, to prove that your ancestors had lived in al-Hillah ever since it was a wilderness inhabited by monkeys, hyenas, and those djinn who had survived the Kingdom of Solomon and Balqees.

Adalia Daniyal danced beautifully, swaying her large swelling breasts in a way that imprinted itself in my memory forever. A young Jungojorai from the Wataweet tribe—his name was Agahzi, which means "bitter"—volunteered to play the *kalash* (a swift rhythm that requires a good deal of skill) with the help of a plastic vessel used for serving *mareesa*. When the song came to an end, we all clapped in self-praise, for the song had been performed by all of us together.

Adalia Daniyal's dance tempted us to order the remaining stock of *mareesa* that she couldn't sell to the Jungo. We even paid her, of our own free will, for two extra buckets of *mareesa* that we didn't drink.

My friend put a large bank note in the gap between her breasts, in the space called "the cat's valley." Mukhtar Ali whispered to me as we went out: "Who else could she have sold her sour *mareesa* and her dead stock of *asaliyah* to if you hadn't been there?"

At night, I put my bed near his. At my request, he told me the story of al-Safyah's family. According to him, al-Safyah's grandfather, Abdel Razek, had come to this place after a dramatic escape from al-Homra prison. He was the first person in the history of Abyssinia to escape with a *ferro* placed on his head. He might well be the first such man in Italy too, since it was the Italians who had introduced the *ferro*—an iron device used to torture rebels and thieves—to Abyssinia.

A neighbor passed some coffee to us over the straw fence, reminding us that it was Saint John's Day. We offered our best wishes and apologized for our belated congratulations. It slipped our memory, we said.

"Alam Gishi sends you her greetings," the neighbor told me.

"Where is she?" I called out.

"She's here with us," she said ceremoniously. "Do you want to see her?"

Having stayed in Mukhtar Ali's house, we missed the great party that Addai hosted in celebration of Saint John's Day. We missed a delicious feast of chicken and *om baba.*[7] There was no dancing or singing, though, as Wad Ammoona was busy training the clumsy bride-to-be. Despite this, it was a great celebration, as we later heard—"hilarious" was how Alam Gishi described it.

I should mention here that Alam Gishi's name had been haunting me the past few days. She and I were accused of being on the edge of taking an important step. We were expected to get married in the coming Eid al-Adha (Qurban Bairam). The least optimistic theory was that I adored her. She was quite sure that I loved her. Everyone was quite sure of that—except me. All I knew was that Alam Gishi

---

[7] Popcorn.

was the one who had put a happy end to my virginity, breaking, to some extent, the psychological barrier between myself and women. I had been terrified that any experience with women would end in utter failure. I had also been obsessed with the strange idea that if I failed with the first woman, I would become impotent for the rest of my life.

None of the old memories I occasionally called upon to defend my claims of virility did me any good: the memory of the woman at the mill who molested me when I was a child, the memory of my friend's sister, the memory of an ass and a goat that I and my friends had sex with when we were adolescents, the memory of a female dog that we raped after placing a palm leaf collar around her neck, the nymphomaniac university professor, and other perverted acts.

It was Alam Gishi who helped me regain my self-confidence, with high professionalism, great intelligence, and unspeakable lusciousness. I found myself dealing with a perfect, natural woman—a human being. In a single night, we had sex at least ten times: throughout the night, at dawn, and again before and after breakfast. I paid her lavishly. And that was it. We never had sex again, although we met, drank coffee together, and touched each other. But love is something that I never thought about. The truth is I had never fallen in love. My friends often called me frigid.

Alam Gishi was a tall woman with a soft, golden complexion—you could almost call it reddish. She had two wide Abyssinian eyes surrounded by dark circles that lent them the unique charm associated with the inhabitants of rainy mountains and highlands. Although she had a beautiful body, she was not ravishingly attractive, otherwise she would have had a successful career as a barmaid in al-Homra, Gondar, or even Addis Ababa. As she always said, the visible side of her charm was not strong enough for her to compete with professional barmaids and led her instead to the new farms inside the Sudanese territories. Sudanese men were known to have special affection for Ethiopian women, preferring them to their countrywomen. The reason, asserted Alam Gishi, was the fact that

Sudanese women were circumcised, and lacked affection. The lack of affection was due to circumcision, she said.

I asked the kind neighbor to wish Alam Gishi a happy Saint John's Day for me and to tell her that I would join them shortly. She sucked some air into her mouth and let out a clicking sound from her tongue: a gesture that in these areas means "okay."

I helped Mukhtar Ali take a bath, his first in more than two weeks. He had been warned against coming in contact with water. "Even for the purpose of washing up for prayers, use clean sand instead of water" was the advice he had heard from old victims of the "blood stroke," the local diagnosis of his mysterious illness.

When we were done with the bath, we found Alam Gishi waiting for us outside the hut, lying down in the *rakuba* on a bare *angaraib*,[8] deliberately exposing her legs in an alluring manner. "Since you weren't willing to visit me," she said, "I decided to take the initiative." "But keep in mind that there will never be a second visit: I have dignity too."

Mukhtar Ali started cleaning up and getting dressed. I want to make a confession here: while it was true that Alam Gishi loved me, *I* was apparently the one who felt jealous, as I asked her to quit her work as a night girl with Addai and work as a cook in the residential complex of the new telecommunications company. "A decent job," I said.

"My work with Addai is decent too," she said in a coquettish tone, concealing her legs with a still more seductive motion.

"It's not, at least not in my opinion."

"On the contrary, it's business. Anyone who's interested has to pay. Frankly, I don't enjoy sex with clients. But business is business." And as if to confirm the last statement, she translated it into Tigrinya: "*Sareh sareh bayo.*" "What's wrong with it?" she asked.

Years later, after reading Mahdi Amel's book *A Critique of Everyday Thinking*, I realized that the problem lay in the way I had been

[8] A wooden frame bed, with strings made of dried local plants forming a net to sleep on.

brought up and the values that I held as someone "different"—someone who belonged to a different sex and a different culture. I must admit that she had opened new dimensions for me in my relationships with women. I enjoyed having sex with her, but I tended to view sex in terms of right and wrong. I had clearly long suffered from a form of schizophrenia: split between being an opportunist and someone self-important; on one hand, I enjoyed the experience, but on the other, I couldn't stop myself from judging it.

My friend whispered to me, "Come, come. I'll tell you my story with al-Safyah."

"I thought you told me that yesterday," I said.

"That was all a lie. You had me cornered, and I had to find a way out." He called Mukhtar Ali to join us and be witness. "It's an interesting story, I promise."

Mukhtar Ali and I sat on an *angaraib* and a stool beside my friend.

9 A LUSTFUL HYENA

He woke up to the voice of al-Safyah calling him in. He had slept on the same chair he had been sitting on. The large hut was devoid of furniture except for two *sunut* beds. The lighting was fairly good. She asked him to sit on the opposite bed.

You wanted to know my story with Wad Fur, didn't you?"

"Only if it doesn't bother you," he said, trying to be diplomatic.

She took a long drag on her *sheesha*. "In the last rainy season, I was working on the al-Zubaidi Farm. Have you heard of it?" Before he had a chance to answer, she continued. She was the only woman among twenty Jungo men. She still remembered their names, as well as the day, month, and hour that everything happened. She and Wad Fur were on the same team. She noticed that Wad Fur was interested in her, that he was always eager to be in her work group, that he kept near her and flirted with her. Her faultless feminine instinct told her that he liked her—and that she liked him too. She wouldn't turn him down if he asked her hand in marriage. Why should she? He was young, energetic, and responsible. More importantly, he treated her with respect. She wanted to have children, a house, and a husband. Above all, she had desires that needed to be fulfilled.

So she neither pushed him away nor left the door wide open. Rather, she made him believe that he was in command, unaware that he was being lured to play a part in a carefully orchestrated plan. This was a proven trap that women set for foolish and rash men—the blind lovers. Fortunately for women, these attributes were indiscriminately shared by all men.

"Put your faith in God, girl," she said to herself. And the poor man took the bait. After a series of initiatives that were consciously ignored by al-Safyah, he ran out of tricks, and out of patience. One moonlit night, he said to her, "Let's go to the reservoir. I can't sleep. Look how beautiful the moon is."

My friend yawned, and drank some water from a cup on the table beside him. He skimmed over a lot of details, telling only what he considered important. He mentioned that she had insisted on giving every tiny detail of what had happened between her and Wad Fur. Perhaps my friend was the only person in the world who understood her. She hadn't disclosed those things to anyone else because no one had ever asked her; everyone simply contented themselves with rumors. "I'm exhausted," she told my friend. "This story's been weighing on me for a long time. Please be patient and let me tell you the whole thing once and for all." He cautioned us that her account was very lengthy and elaborate. Mukhtar Ali and I made it clear to him that he didn't need to skip anything. We had the whole night ahead of us and had nothing else to do.

They went to the *hafeer* (reservoir) and climbed to the top, which was the only place that wasn't covered with grass. She was scared to death of snakes. In fact, the *only* thing she was afraid of was snakes. He assured her that he had a charm with proven power to protect against all evils. He showed it to her, tightly tied to his left arm beside his knife. They spread a straw mat on the ground.

"He ran away," she said suddenly.

"Who?"

"Wad Fur. He ran away!"

"Why?"

"He ran away from me," she said, her tone becoming more bitter.

After pulling herself together, she continued, "I really wanted him. Everything was going great and I was getting close to my climax. But suddenly he pulled out and ran away like a madman."

He sensed she could not continue speaking. He didn't want to force her to continue. He took pity on her and decided to go to bed with her immediately, because his intuition told him she was in desperate need of a man in her life. With the exception of Wad Fur, no one had recognized her needs as a woman. No one was sensitive to her true needs. They treated her like a man dressed in women's clothes.

He was shocked to discover that she smelled horrible. "I'm sorry, but I hardly had any time for myself," she said as she used one of Mother Addai's old bed sheets to wipe down her body a bit. She wasn't wearing anything under her gown. That was a blessing, as he couldn't bear the sight of dirty or shabby lingerie. The mere sight of it was a turn-off to him.

"From her *googo* she took out a can of *khomra* perfume and started to massage her body. She had bought it from a peddler last year. It was very poor quality, and smelled awful. There really was no need for her to make all that effort. The plan I set for myself was very simple. I would approach her body until it responded and she reached her climax. Then it would be over. Something similar to a contractual relationship. That was, in my opinion, what al-Safyah needed. And that was what I needed to convince myself that I had done a great deed, noble and exceptional—to give her something that she had been deprived of all her life.

She made a different suggestion: I should wait until she had had a proper bath. I turned that suggestion down too. The matter was simple. She rose to her feet and shut the door. She might have been afraid that a client would barge in on us, or that Wad Ammoona might try to see what we were doing. Or it could well be that she was afraid that I'd escape just as Wad Fur had done."

He objected to the idea of closing the door, but apparently his objection was too late this time. She made another suggestion: to keep the light on. He agreed to that one. He was eager to finish the matter as fast as he possibly could.

There was one final surprise that could have been fatal had he not been strong-willed. He said that it wasn't easy for him to describe what he had seen. And from the way he talked, we sensed he was telling the truth.

"What happened could not possibly have crossed my imagination or the imagination of the most wicked devil, assuming devils possess the power of imagination. 'I haven't cut a single hair since I was born,' she said in a somber tone. 'They say shaving your sex brings ill fortune. But it's also because I never had time for such things. I spend all my time working. But I'll take better care of myself from now on.' Let's finish this up, I told myself. I was determined for her to have an unforgettable experience, for this to be a turning point in her life. 'I do clean and comb it every Friday,' she added."

He continued his detailed account. "Al-Safyah turned into a hyena!" he swore.

"A hyena?" we asked in one voice, like actors in a TV show.

"I put my hand on her naked body and started to caress her ears and big nose. Almost instantly, her body was covered in hair: black, thick, ugly hair that looked like a donkey's and that was growing at an amazing speed. Then her facial features started to change, her canine teeth protruded, and she started to utter a coarse sound.

Then she attacked me, like a hungry lion attacking a wounded, helpless prey. That happened in a few seconds. I don't know how I managed to escape: through the closed door? Through the small window? Through the wall? No idea. Somehow I found myself outside the hut, then outside Addai's compound, and then outside al-Hillah altogether. It all happened in the blink of an eye."

He took off his galabia and showed us some scratches on his back and buttocks, and we laughed.

10 THE *FERRO* SONG

Early one morning, Alam Gishi sent me a message through Wad Ammoona: she wanted to see me at Addai's house at once. Addai's house could either be very near to or very far from Mukhtar Ali's house, depending on the time—day or night—and how close your relationship was with your neighbors. Those who were fortunate enough to have good relations with their neighbors could use the so-called "neighbor access doors" to reduce a good deal of striding through alleyways into no more than twenty meters.

I generally maintained good relations with my neighbors, so I entered the house of my immediate neighbor, Soad, and exchanged greetings with her husband before crossing to the house of Bit al-Broon, a kind old midwife with broad tribal scars on her cheeks and a permanent smile on her face. She had no husband or children and lived in the company of her niece, who was asleep at the time. We exchanged greetings before I crossed the road to the house of Adalia Daniyal, the pretty Dinka lady. She wasn't home, so I continued on my way until I found myself in front of the door to Addai's compound. I was stunned to see that Wad Ammoona had arrived before me. In response to my obvious confusion, he said that the policeman al-Haj who happened to be driving his motorcycle past Mukhtar Ali's house had given him a lift.

"You never came to check in on me again. It's been a week since I last saw you," Alam Gishi reproached me in a friendly tone.

Wad Ammoona added in his unique soft voice, "I swear to God, Alam Gishi has never opened her thighs for anyone else since your night together."

"You didn't find me attractive, did you?" she suddenly asked, looking me in the eye.

Wad Ammoona interrupted again, "Who on earth wouldn't like Alam Gishi?"

"City people are difficult to please, Wad Ammoona," she said in a coquettish tone, swaying her breasts like a dancer in action. "Maybe they prefer girls like the ones on TV."

Wad Ammoona asked, "Didn't you prepare *dokhan*[1] for him?" Alam Gishi gave him a shy look. I felt tremendous embarrassment, although I was fully aware of the trap being set around me. "No. No. It's not that, of course," I said. "Alam Gishi is beautiful and clean, perfect just as she is."

"Tonight I'm going to give her a special treatment for you—*dokhan* and *dilka* massage. I'll turn her into a true bride for you. Anything else I can do for you?"

"Thanks, Wad Ammoona. You're impeccable, though I like her just the way she is," I said out of courtesy.

"OK," said Alam Gishi. "I have something else to discuss with you: working for the telecommunications company."

"Have you made up your mind?"

"I thought I should give it a try," she said, moving her breasts in that same fascinating way. "Perhaps God wants to direct me to a different source of livelihood."

Alam Gishi was aware that my friend had a personal relationship with the manager of the telecommunications company that had recently descended on the area. He was the one who had originally suggested that Alam Gishi should serve as a cook at the employees' residential compound. The employees were only going to be joined

---

[1] A steam bath that married women in Sudan take, usually before having sex, using a combination of aromatic wood and locally produced perfumes.

by their families after the tower and ground connections had been set up and the equipment installed.

"Ok, I'll tell him you've agreed."

They invited me to join them for morning coffee, but I apologized as Mukhtar Ali and my friend were waiting for me. We had recently made it a habit to take our morning coffee at the old lady's coffee shop. On my way out, Wad Ammoona asked if I was planning to come that evening. I told him I was. He winked at me. I smiled at his gesture and nodded a thank you in anticipation.

My day usually gets off to a lethargic start; quite fitting for the jobless like me, who have an income source that protects them from starvation; quite fitting for someone whose mission in life was to wander around leisurely. We always took our coffee in the same place: our host was an old lady who had turned her *rakuba* into a coffee shop to serve the Jungo and other workers who passed by her house at the eastern end of Hamadayeit Road, where scores of workers were building a gas station.

Today, however, I had to drink my coffee alone; my friend had decided to go into al-Hillah instead, and Mukhtar Ali had accepted the invitation of an Ethiopian neighbor to join her and her husband for morning coffee; only a fool would turn down such an invitation—people here strongly believed that no one makes better coffee than Ethiopian women.

The old lady served me a coffee with extra ginger, thinking I was from Kasala, when in fact I was from Qedaref.

Two policemen went past us, followed closely by the al-Hillah sheikh and some members of the local committee. They greeted us and hurried on toward the gas station.

"A worker was stabbed at the station yesterday," my host told me.

"Who stabbed him?"

"Boys from the nearby refugee camp," she said, moving a small piece of hot coal with a teaspoon. "They got into a fight gambling. They were both completely drunk."

"Is he badly hurt?"

"They put him on Osman Eisa's truck, but he died before reaching Khashm El Girba."

"You knew him, by the way," she added, though all her attempts to help me remember the poor guy were in vain. One of my bad habits was that when people I had known only casually died, I failed to remember what they looked like. I might even fail to remember if I had ever met them. Strangely enough, I could always remember casual acquaintances when they were still alive. I had no explanation for this.

"He was one of my customers. You saw him in this very *rakuba*."

"Was it the Barnawi boy?"

"He looks Barnawi, though he's actually a crossbreed."

She went on to explain to me that 99% of all al-Hillah residents could not be identified with a single ethnic group or tribe. All of them were crossbreeds: born to mothers who were either Ethiopian, Bazarian, Bani Amer, Hamaseen, Bilalawi, etc., and to fathers who were mainly from Western Sudan: Masaleet, Bilalah, Zaghawa, Fur, Fellata, Tama, though some were also from Humran, Nuba, Shukriyah, Shuluk, Nuer, and there were a few from the Shaygiyah and Jaalieen tribes as well.

"Anyone who claims they're descended from the pure blood of one tribe or house is surely a liar," she said.

"Even Adalia Daniyal?" I challenged her.

"Her mother is Dinka, her father Asholi, and her husband Lakoya."

"What about you?"

"My mother is Bazawi. My father had an Ethiopian mother and a Muslati father. My son is married to a lady from the Hobab, from the famous Kentibai family. You know the Hobab are very pretty. All the people around here have such mixed blood, yet each clings to his father's tribe! The blood's from the mother. The soul's from the mother. Nonsense. What does the father contribute, other than the seed?"

She then went about describing how each person in the village had mixed blood. She concluded with a statement that was a commonly known fact: "The men here are crazy about Ethiopian girls." To support her contention, she told me the story of someone who had been seduced by the devil into breaking off his hajj pilgrimage. Sitting in the shadow of a *laloub* tree in Massawa on his way to Mecca, he saw a vagina hanging on a branch above his head. He kept throwing stones at the organ. It shook but never fell down, and the pilgrim continued throwing stones until well past the hajj season. He returned empty-handed.

"What about al-Safyah?" I asked.

"Her grandfather is Muslati, and her mother is Amhara on her mother's side and Fur on her father's. In their house there are Bazawis, Hababwis, Qamrawis, Engriabis, Robatabis, even Halfawis, Mahasis, and Donglawis."

I asked how a human could turn into a hyena. "It's all in the milk," she said in a confident scholarly tone. She poured me another cup of coffee. "It's all in the breast milk. Feeding a child from different breasts is not a wise thing to do. Some women who move about from one house to another allow their children to be breastfed by other women. You don't know people. Not all people are people. Some of them are *baatis*,[2] some turn into crows, lions, hyenas, or *barta barta*.[3] Some are even cannibals. Al-Hillah is teeming with djinn disguised as women, men, donkeys, cats, and trees. May Allah protect us. Even an owl wouldn't hesitate to breastfeed a child if she found it alone. May Allah protect us all. O Lord, protect us and protect all Muslims. Amen, lord of all the worlds."

I asked if it was true that al-Safyah's family was the first family to live in this area. "Who told you that?" she replied, sounding a bit confused. "Whose family? That drunkard was brought up by our family. Her mother abandoned her immediately after birth and left God knows where. I was the one who named her al-Safyah, after my grandmother. My family was the first to live here."

---

[2] Humans who can come back to life after death.

[3] Mythical creatures that have eight legs.

She then told me what she insisted was the authentic story—all other versions were distortions or fabrications motivated by prejudice, ignorance, and envy. When her ancestors first came to this place, there was nothing here but foxes, hyenas, monkeys, wild boar, turtles, rabbits, falcons, bustards, and the occasional tiger. There were thick forests of *kitir*, *laloub*, *hashab*, and *seyal* trees. *Sunut* trees grew beside creeks and ponds while *aradaib* and *tabaldi* trees dominated the highlands and the riverbank. The whole place was known to be inhabited by djinn and *abu lamba*, which came out at sunset.

Her family was on their way back from the hajj. They had come through Yemen, Bab al-Mandab, Massawa, Ethiopia, and were en route to Qedaref when they were stranded in this very place by the onset of the rainy season. They built the first house here. Her grandfather and his sons cut down the trees, cleared the land, and planted sorghum, millet, and sesame. According to her, that was over 100 years ago now, maybe 150 years ago. She heard that story from her grandmother, who in turn heard it from her grandmother, who in turn heard it from her grandmother.

Her great-grandfather was named Abdel Razek and had a twin called Abdel Razzak. According to her grandmother, who was quoting her own grandmother, the twins traded firewood and agricultural products, which they sold to the Ethiopians in al-Homra, Bahar Dar, and in Gondar, farther away. They would travel for days on end, leaving behind their father and a young sister named al-Safyah. According to her grandmother, who was quoting her own grandmother, al-Safyah was barely ten years old at the time, but she could remember the moment when her brother Abdel Razek arrived with the iron device pressing hard against his head, his eyes red and protruding, his tongue dangling out of his mouth like a dog's. He was unable to utter a single word, but from his chest he let out a sound like the cry of an owl.

Her father, mother, and twin brother Abdel Razzak, who had escaped from jail only two days earlier, rushed to his rescue. She still remembered the single sentence he finally managed to utter:

"The *ferro* is killing me." He was sweating profusely. Her father started to recite verses from the Holy Quran. "The hacksaw. The hacksaw, father. The hacksaw," muttered Abdel Razek.

His twin brother Abdel Razzak brought the hacksaw and they managed to cut the *ferro*. It was a tense moment, and they were all relieved when it was finally over, as if he were being reborn at that very moment. No one paid attention when Abdel Razek broke wind, fouling the air with the smell of a long restrained fluid. He then vomited before falling into a deep sleep. His father woke him up at midnight. He ate something and fell asleep again. The whole family stayed by his bed, staring at him with perplexed eyes. Abdel Razzak kept repeating a single sentence every now and then: "I'm the one to blame." His mother tried to comfort him: "He's your brother, after all."

The old woman continued her story with great enthusiasm. Some flies had flown into the coffee I'd forgotten to drink.

"Until recently, prisoners in Ethiopia weren't fed at the prison. Instead, groups of them were bound together on a single strong rope and sent to beg for food at the market and *endayas*.[4] While Abdel Razek was having a meal with fellow merchants at the al-Homra souk, he saw his twin brother Abdel Razzak tied to a rope along with other prisoners, begging for food. His heart almost stopped beating. He fed him and gave him some money and told him in the Masaleet dialect that he would come to the prison the next Friday. He'd be dressed exactly like his twin was then—the same shoes, the same head cap. 'I know those people very well,' he told his twin. 'I've lived with the *shifta* and *falloul* bandits for a whole year.'"

"So they traded places on the appointed date. The other prisoners reported the matter to the authorities three days later, though they knew about the trick from day one. True, Abdel Razek and Abdel Razzak were identical twins. But Abdel Razek's personality was significantly different from his twin's. He led a life of great extravagance and was the type of man who would leave for several months

[4] Local bars serving locally produced drinks.

in pursuit of adventure and pleasure, alcohol and women, and team up with vagabonds in the Ethiopian forests. He was a moody, hot-tempered, violent man who never hesitated to break religious taboos, and who had only ever prayed or fasted in his youth. In contrast, Abdel Razzak was genial and peaceful, and although he was not particularly devout, he had never drunk alcohol, smoked, or tried snuff."

"Abdel Razek tried his best to imitate his brother Abdel Razzak, but failed miserably. What's bred in the bone comes out in the flesh, as the adage goes. The prisoners informed the management, hoping to earn some privileged treatment, or at least avert punishment in case the trick was discovered by the jailors themselves. After beating him severely, the prison authorities asked him to choose between the stake and the *ferro*. Both meant a gradual, painful death. He chose the *ferro*. The iron device was fixed tightly around his head. 'If you fail to bring your brother back in half an hour, you'll die,' they told him. 'And remember, we have the only key to the *ferro* here. Now *qaltif*!'—a word which meant 'move!'"

"He at once went off in search of his brother, hoping to hand him over and rid himself of the *ferro*'s torment. He looked for him haphazardly, with no clear plan and no hope. He went running in every direction calling his brother's name. He was terrified, but at least he was moving away from the prison. They were certain he was going to come back. He had only options: to come back or be killed. And they were certain he wouldn't die far from the prison. They cared more about the *ferro*, which was the property of the prison. As for his body, they would simply throw into the deserted well at the foot of the mountain."

"Moments later, he came to his senses and remembered how the *falloul* bandits handled the *ferro*. A *falloul* would convince himself that what was around his neck was not a lethal iron device but rather a snake that could kill him with a single bite. There was a chance it might not hurt him if he treated it kindly. He had to be patient in order not to die from a snakebite; he had to placate the 'snake' until he had crossed the border. To calm himself, he started to sing a song in Tigrinya. It was a long song composed of very few words:

I won't die;

I won't die; I won't die;

I won't die;

I shall live; I shall live; I shall live.

He repeated the last line over and over again, hoping that the 'snake' would finally release him. He chanted his way toward the Sudanese border to the west. He avoided paths, roads, donkeys routes—all the trodden access routes to Hamdayeit—and instead headed south, following a rugged course across the small *taleh* forest that was crossed by two creeks. He knew this land well. Two years ago, he traded 100 quintal of gum arabic for ten sacks of red sesame. The deal was made with Burhani Kidani, the 'cunning Ethiopian,' as he loved to call him, one of the most famous *falloul* in al-Homra creek and the dreadful Zahanah forest. He was aware that the man who sold him the gum didn't have a single pound to his name, and knew little about gum harvesting—they said he could barely distinguish a *taleh* tree from a *kitir* tree. Yet the poor farmers could not sell their gum harvest to anyone else, and they had no choice but to accept the price he set. In most cases, he was not unfair to them, and even offered them protection against other bandits and thieves. If Abdel Razek was fortunate enough to come across Burhani, he would certainly help him get rid of the *ferro*."

"Ahead of him, the sun was blood red and menacingly high in the sky. They had deliberately sent him off at that time of day to further reduce his chances of survival. As the day wore on, he came across many *fallouls* and devils, all of whom ran away as soon as they saw him. Shortly before sunset, his legs finally led him home."

The two policemen came back. They stopped briefly at the coffee shop and asked the old lady about a boy, mentioning his name, surname, and the name of his mother, followed by the words "the whore."

"He went to Zahanah with his friends," she told them. "They were invited to a Saint John's Day celebration."

11

AN OBJECTIVE DIALOGUE AND CARAMEL

My friend assured me that his affair with al-Safyah—which he called the "al-Safyah scheme"—was far from finished. To him, it was a battle he was determined to fight to the last breath. That came as no surprise to me. We had been friends for over thirty years now, partners in readings and travels, in frustrations and achievements, in times of work and times of idleness. It would have been out of character for him to declare that he had backed off from his so-called al-Safyah scheme or become scared.

"My analysis of al-Safyah is this," he said in a confident tone. "When she becomes sexually aroused, hair starts to cover her entire body, her nails and ears grow longer, and her facial features change to something that resembles a large wolf, a lion, or a monkey. She then unconsciously attacks her partner, who has no choice but to take to his heels."

He wondered what would happen if her partner held fast till the end. "Let's seriously consider the matter. We shouldn't leave her all alone with such a big dilemma. We're all humans, after all, bound by a common destiny. We all come to life through one and the same route. If any of us stumbles on the way, the others can't get through either." He continued to ramble on about an issue he believed in, and he seemed unlikely to back off.

Alarmed by the specter of an inevitably dreadful scenario, I said, "I sincerely hope you won't put yourself in jeopardy."

"You mean I shouldn't meddle in this?" he asked nervously.

"Exactly!"

"But isn't our mere presence in al-Hillah a sort of meddling? What have we got here? We're former employees of the Ministry of Health who, having been sacked under the public interest policy, have now turned into squatters—every day we intrude on a new land and a new people."

He meant to say that intruding on a place meant, by definition, meddling in the affairs of its people. He often maintained that he was keen to make a lasting impact—which he called a *wow* effect—on every place he visited. The key to this was to do things no one else would do, or to "take the rough course," as he put it. That was his guiding philosophy. Wherever we went, he took the roughest of courses, searching for alienated individuals, communities, and places, constantly putting himself at risk.

I told him Alam Gishi had agreed to take the job. He and Mukhtar Ali then cooked a meal that we thoroughly enjoyed: white beans, *frendo*, and dried meat. We bought *injera*[1] from the Mother's house, and Mukhtar Ali brought us some *dilleikh* from his hut, where he always kept a good stock. Alam Gishi came in and made us some coffee with ginger and cardamom before the three of us headed to the company's office near the crop market.

The place was teeming with construction workers, but we somehow managed to gain access to the manager, a short, skinny man, elegantly dressed, with an inviting smile. He thanked us warmly for bringing Alam Gishi to help them at the residential compound at a time when her services were sorely needed. He considered it a great humanitarian gesture, a blessing from Allah, and an invaluable contribution to the company. "We need a woman we can trust," he said. "I wonder what we would have done without you."

Yet his warm words couldn't conceal a trace of disappointment that flashed across his face as he welcomed Alam Gishi. I later came to understand from Alam Gishi that they were hoping to

[1] Sorghum bread.

get a younger girl—"someone livelier and prettier than me," she said. "But they'll soon realize that I'm the prettiest woman in the world."

I said to my friend, "It seems your friend was expecting to find a beauty queen in this place at the end of the earth, surrounded by bushes and small seasonal streams, a place whose native inhabitants included monkeys; a remote spot that few people care for, a land whose original settlers were a bunch of castaways."

We headed back to the market, leaving Alam Gishi behind to get ready for her new job. It was noon, and the bank workers were hard at work. The bank would surely be up and running before the next agricultural season. Rumors were circulating that the bank was destined to change the map of wealth and power, and restructure production relations in favor of those in lower income brackets, small-scale farmers, and the poor. It was meant to extend interest-free Islamic loans to every producer and farmer. Some analysts interpreted the word "producer" to be an all-inclusive term that embraced literally everyone, without exception. Based on that analysis, it included, without limitation, the big *endaya* owners, peddlers, ladies selling date arrack, and charcoal sellers. Wad Ammoona thought about opening a small bar by the riverbank, similar to the existing one on the eastern bank of the Setit River overlooking Hamdayeit village, which was frequented by clients who would have to swim their way to the other shore, into the Ethiopian territories, carrying no passport, ID, or even a paper with their name on it. Wad Ammoona's bar would be a blessing for those pleasure seekers and would spare them the risk of drowning in transit.

Apparently the talk of loans was more than an unfounded rumor. Addressing the worshippers one unforgettable Friday, a speaker commissioned by the bank spoke at length about Sharia-compliant methods of investment, such as *salam*, *murabaha*, and *musharaka*. He quoted verses from the Holy Quran and sayings of the Prophet and cited opinions of renowned religious scholars. One of those quoted was an obscure name that no one in the village had heard of.

His name was al-Karadawi—perhaps in reference to *karad*,[2] who knows? All that the audience could make of the lengthy speech was that loans were going to be made available to everyone without discrimination: interest-free loans, compliant with the commands of Allah and the *Sunnah* of His apostle. The speaker made that very clear, leaving little room for speculation.

The first gesture of support came from the local council, which allotted a plot of land free of charge to serve as the bank premises. Not only that, it offered its truck to deliver stones, sand, and red bricks to the site at a nominal charge that covered only the cost of labor. The bank supervisors were supplied with fuel, electricity, and water free of charge, for the sake of God and the country's development and prosperity.

To gain a stake in these free offerings, the construction contractor sought to procure army personnel to serve as construction workers—free of charge, that is. And why not? They were sitting in their barracks, doing nothing but playing cards and waiting for wars that were unlikely to break out in the foreseeable future. It was his bad luck that the military commander at the time was a hardheaded man who had little appreciation of the bank's role in development. Not only was the contractor's request turned down, he also received a verbal admonition: "Beware. Beware. Beware. Who do you think you're talking to? This is the army, not a charity, for God's sake!"

Apart from that one outright rejection, the bank encountered no difficulties in acquiring all the facilities and blessings it needed. Most people felt duty-bound to do anything in their capacity to help. To them, the bank was a savior, a messiah.

We stopped by Aziza al-Zaghawiyah's coffee shop for a cup of *karkadeh* (hibiscus tea). Two brokers who were sitting near us were clearly disappointed that the price of sesame was so low this season, despite the scarce supply. In their experience, low production always meant high prices. But not this time. "The harvesting season will be

---

[2] A dry fruit of the acacia tree, used for tanning skin and treating many diseases.

over in a week's time. After that, there won't be any more left," said one. The other was more optimistic. "The sesame company hasn't entered the market yet to buy its annual quota for export. So the prices will definitely go up, even higher than last year's."

My friend interrupted: "It's the peanut and sunflower crops that are to blame." Without asking for permission to join in their conversation, he cranked out impressive figures about the production of peanuts and sunflower this season. He noted that the price per pound of oil from both varieties was declining and was destined to fall further. He factored in the use of sesame in the production of cooking oil and in confectionary. Although cheap, the peanut was losing ground to the sunflower, which was preferred by exporters because it was both cheap *and* healthy. Then he elaborated on what he called "the future of sesame production in Sudan" and whether it would be the same as the gloomy future of cotton and gum arabic.

They gaped at him. "Are you from the security agency?" one of them asked. We laughed. "No," my friend replied sarcastically, "I'm from Qedaref."

The man, still staring at him, said, "Oh yeah. I know. You must be al-Safyah's man. But what do you do?"

My friend was enraged. "This village is good for nothing but gossip. What a miserable place!"

"Let's go back to the sesame," the other man said in an attempt to turn the discussion away from a delicate subject. Suddenly, the conversation was drowned out in a roar of voices: horns blown from vehicles and *barbaras*, mixed with the ululations of women and girls, songs and noise. The place was soon enveloped in a thick cloud of dust from the tires of all the vehicles.

"Is this the right time for a marriage?" Aziza al-Zaghawiyah exclaimed. "The harvest season's not over yet!"

"Guess who the groom is?" a broker said. "It's Mohammed Awad, the driver of al-Barnawi's *barbara*. Those people can get married anytime after the end of the rainy season, once the roads are accessible again. This is his third marriage."

The wedding procession was comprised of twenty *barbaras*, five Land Rovers, the Hamdayeit bus, the al-Showak bus, the al-Hafeera truck, and a tractor-trailer belonging to a merchant from Zahanah. Wad Ammoona was a star as usual. Assisted by an enthusiastic chorus of women, he sang beautifully in his feminine voice—the few rough edges to his voice were due only to long hours of rehearsals and drinking large amounts of coffee at the bride's house, where the coffee fire had been burning for over a week.

"Damn him," one of the brokers exclaimed. "You can't tell if he's a man or a woman."

"He's Wad Ammoona, that's what he is," Aziza commented with a laugh.

"He's a hopeless effeminate. By God, if he were my son, I'd have killed him."

Aziza responded, "Why are you so concerned with him? This is how his Creator wants him to be." Then she added, "Did you know who Mohammed Awad married?"

"Of course not," I said.

"Zeinab, daughter of Abrahait al-Felashawi."

"Al-Felashawi? You mean from Felasha?" I asked.

"Yes," confirmed one of the brokers. "They say the Felasha are Jews." Turning to my friend, he added, "They're the ones Gaafar Nimeiry sold to Israel, correct?"

"But are there any Felasha here?" I asked.

"Only one family—the family of Abrahait, son of Is'haq," the broker replied.

"But Abrahait is a Muslim," Aziza noted. "He attends the Friday prayers. Everyone's seen him there."

"Those Jews include Muslims and infidels," one of the brokers said in a confident scholarly tone. "They're just like the djinn—they have Muslims and infidels in their ranks."

"And by the way, some Muslims are truly Jews. They're the ones who don't pray or fast, and who practice usury and steal from orphans. What do you call those people? Aren't they Jews?" He took his case one step further and solemnly swore that if he were to find an interested buyer—be it an Israeli or someone from any state in the world—he would sell them Abrahait and his family and make a fortune. "Isn't selling them *halal*?" he asked. "Our Lord never prohibited the selling of slaves, let alone the Felasha. Isn't that right?"

I nodded in assent, though in my mind I meant to say, "No comment."

My friend, who was listening attentively, whispered in my ear, "We have to visit the Abrahaits. I'd really like to talk to a Jew, be he Felasha, Ashkenazi, Sephardim, or from any other Jewish group—even Bani Gorayzeh or Bani al-Nadheer."[3]

"I won't go with you," I said, "after what you did at the church last week with Mother Mariam Kudi, the pastor."

"Who was to blame for that—me or her?" he responded nervously, in a louder voice. "I wanted to engage her in a dialogue about religion. That was truly my intention, but unfortunately Mother Mariam misunderstood me. She wanted to debate with an Arab Muslim, but I was trying to present myself as a man who embraces the entire spiritual heritage of humanity, including Christianity itself, Nietzsche's *Thus Spoke Zarathustra*, Wad Daifallah's *Book of Tabaqat*, and the holy texts and other important books."

I told him the problem lay in how he expressed himself, not in his intentions. And I wound up accompanying him, after all, because I didn't want to be accused of abandoning my friend when he got himself into yet another bind.

Finding Abrahait's house wasn't difficult; it was next to the souk, and Abrahait was well known. Besides, it was easy to find a house that was hosting a wedding party. We knocked on the door, and some women and young girls invited us in, suggesting there was no need to knock. We stood by the door, unwilling to enter except with the host's permission. A moment later, Abrahait came toward us, smiling—a tall man elegantly dressed in a clean pair of white pants and a white shirt. He welcomed us in, speaking with an Amharic

[3] Two Jewish groups that inhabited Medina before the advent of Islam.

accent, and gently rebuked us for knocking on the door like strangers. He softly called in his daughter Judith, who approached carrying water, sweets, and popcorn, a charming smile hovering on her tiny beautiful mouth. She bent in front of each of us, poured water from a blue jug into glasses marked with images of Ethiopia's famous flag and lion.

"The Lion of Zion!" my friend whispered in my ear, his voice beaming with excitement. I ignored him so as not to attract attention. We congratulated our host for the marriage of his daughter Zeinab to Mohammed Awad Kajouk, the *barbara* driver, wishing the bride and groom happiness, prosperity, and many children.

He said coffee was ready, as was breakfast. We said we had already had coffee with Aziza al-Zaghawiyah and had had our breakfast at home. Suddenly my friend, in his typical rashness, broached the subject he was interested in.

I was very impressed by Abrahait's eloquent and intelligent response. He was so cool and composed that it seemed as if he had been born with the answer to my friend's question, some 55 years ago now. It seemed as if he had tested it out on all types of people, and perhaps on animals and djinn as well, before adopting it as the standard answer, an effective and conclusive response to all the nosy meddlers, to all the lazy loiterers, to the curious and inquisitive, the suspicious and distrustful, to those with poor faith, and to the extremists among men, djinn, and all other creatures too.

The vehicles of the wedding procession circled around the house, with Wad Ammoona chanting some of those women's songs. Abrahait's teenage daughter added more *om baba* to the sweet tray, glancing at us from corner of her wide eyes before running outside to welcome the approaching procession.

"I'm a Muslim," Abrahait said in a clear voice. He looked piercingly into our eyes as he flashed us a smile.

"I'm a Muslim." He wiped his face with his palms before adding sharply, "I bear witness that there is no god but Allah and that Muhammad is the messenger of Allah. I pray, pay the *zakat*, fast during Ramadan, and I'll go on hajj as soon as I can afford it."

Then he added in an icy tone, trying to maintain a smile, "Now you can leave in peace. Give my regards to the chief of security. Tell him Abrahait, son of Is'haq, sends his regards."

That, my friend later told me, was enough proof that Abrahait was a Jew, and an extremist. We denied any connection with the security authorities as we dragged our feet apologetically toward the door. Judith, his beautiful teenage girl, was glued to the door, stealthily listening to the conversation between my friend and her father—a very short conversation. My friend had asked him, "Is it true that you're a Felasha Jew?"

She looked pretty in her white dress. To tease us, she stuck her tongue out at us: it was covered with small black spots and smelled of caramel.

12

RAHAT CUTTING AND *DOKHLA*

Wad Ammoona sat on a big stool in front of me, his enigmatic eyes gleaming with joy. He apparently had something important to tell me but needed a prod, which I gave him by asking, "What's up?"

Stretching out his immaculate legs, which glistened against the lantern's light, he said, "Do you know how much you owe me?"

"How much?"

He counted on his fingers as he shifted his eyes from side to side and said, "Three and a half pounds for the *dokhan* wood and *taleh*. Ok? Seven and a half pounds for the *dilka* that I bought from Addai. Ok? Then there's fifteen pounds for the bath soap and cologne. And five pounds for the *dilka* massage I gave her—that's just for the work I did with my hands, that is," he said, stretching out his hands in a feminine way.

"Another five pounds for hair removal. By God, I removed every single hair on her body. She's glistening like the full moon now. You'll see for yourself. And then there are two pounds for *sobaa amir*."[1]

"*Sobaa amir*?" I asked in surprise.

"You'll know what I mean later. You're going to love it, believe me," he said, laughing.

"So how much in total?"

"Fifty pounds—but let's round it up to seventy, ok?" he said smiling.

---

[1] A highly effective adhesive.

I gave him a hundred pounds. In the blink of an eye, he prepared a *sheesha* for me and offered to massage my body with *dilka* free of charge, or to remove my armpit and pubic hair. I politely told him that there was no need. He replaced the bed sheets; brought in a fresh supply of milk, soup, and hibiscus tea; arranged the coffee utensils; and set up a big cassette recorder with two speakers. He did all this with incredible speed and professionalism, and then announced, "Your bath's ready. The water's just right. You'd better hurry up before it gets cold."

He handed me a fresh towel, a toothbrush, and a bar of Lux soap, then led me to the bathroom, swaying his large butt. The bathroom was a small and roofless structure made of straw, cane, and *sunut* branches. There was a large cement washbasin on the floor, as well as a plastic stool and a bucket full of warm water. It had a tin door fitted with a short rope to tie it to a pole made of *sunut* wood. A kerosene lantern occupied a remote corner of the room, beyond the reach of the water. Using a small plastic vessel floating in the bucket, I started to bathe. I usually spend a long time in the bathroom, washing my body over and over again and playing with the remaining water. I love water, especially when it's warm. It was the perfect temperature that day and was scented as well. I felt tremendous affection for Wad Ammoona, Alam Gishi, the Mother's House, and the entire place.

After a thorough wash, I dried my body with the help of the big white towel that smelled of sandalwood and went out. The hut was filled with aromatic smoke. Alam Gishi was standing at the center. I didn't recognize her at first, since she was completely wrapped up in a *garmasais* robe, which was usually worn as part of a wedding ceremony. If I hadn't seen Wad Ammoona standing right in front of her, I would have thought he was the one wrapped up in that sexy silken dress.

The moment I stepped in, Wad Ammoona pressed a button on the big cassette recorder and a song by a male singer in a high-pitched voice started playing:

Al-Loul, al-Loul, Loul Liyyah

Surely you will draw an evil eye,

Loula of Abyssinia,

You're not a tame one,

Loul Liyyah,

I feel like an exile in Khartoum,

I love Kasala, and Addis Ababa is my home.

Alam Gishi's body started to sway to the rhythm of the song, her hands covering her face. "Come in," Wad Ammoona said, grabbing my hand, leading me to her. "Cut the *rahat*, so you can see your bride's face."

I walked over to her as if I'd been hypnotized, and without uttering a single word inserted my hand under her gown and felt about her waist for the *rahat*. I found a thin straw strap. I tore it and threw it onto the ground. Wad Ammoona picked it up and waved it in the air, ululating joyfully, trying hard to keep his voice as low as possible.

Ayooooy Ayooooyyy . . .

Alam Gishi went into a feverish fit of dancing, swaying her hips, chest, arms, head, feet, legs—every inch of her body. The slippery *garmasais* slid to her feet, exposing a very short skirt held together by two straps that stretched over her shoulders and down her back. The black skirt was embroidered with a piece of gold thread. That charmingly revealing dress coupled with the fragrance she was wearing made her seem like a bride from the 1950s.

I stood there motionless, mesmerized, while Wad Ammoona clapped his hands rhythmically, letting out restrained ululations every now and then.

When Alam Gishi finished her dance, Wad Ammoona said to me, "Congratulations, bridegroom. Tonight is your great night—your *dokhla*."[2] He pushed the stop button. He didn't seem very impressed by my performance, though. I could sense that from the way he twisted his lips and from the look in his eyes. He went out. It all seemed like a dream.

Noticing that I was not at my best, Alam Gishi hounded me with anxious questions. She sat me down on the big bed that Wad Ammoona had neatly set up and asked if I felt like a cup of coffee. Before I could answer, she embraced me. A fresh wave of strong local perfume brought me back to my senses.

I had very limited experience with women, which I owed almost entirely to my first encounter with Alam Gishi. Now, however, I felt like I was beginning from square one again, and my old fear of failure returned. To tell the truth, I was so scared of Alam Gishi that I wanted Wad Ammoona to stay. He was a cheerful person, albeit more pragmatic than humane. Nevertheless, I always felt safe in his presence, if for no other reason than because I didn't expect him to put my sexual capacities to the test. True, he was eccentric and hard to fathom at times, but he was also entertaining and reassuring.

I asked Alam Gishi to make some coffee. She rose to her feet, but instead of doing as she was told she held my hand and asked me to stand up. Looking me right in the eyes, she said, "You're afraid, aren't you?"

"Afraid of what?"

"Of your bride," she said, putting her arm around my waist.

"But . . . "

"Is it because of the ceremony we prepared for you?" she interrupted. "We wanted to make you happy, but you . . . "

"I *am* happy," I interrupted.

Putting her head on my chest, she said, "Let's go to sleep. We'll have the coffee later. You look drowsy. Come, let me put you to bed."

She took the towel off my shoulder and threw it onto a *stool* in the far corner of the room, then put out the light.

---

[2] *Dokhla* refers to the first night a groom sleeps with his bride.

"Where's your friend?" she suddenly asked, running her fingers over my body.

"With Mukhtar Ali."

"Is he still set on going after al-Safyah?"

"He's hardheaded," I replied.

"And how's *your* head?" she asked, running her fingers through my hair. We laughed.

"I like men who are overly sensitive—you're that kind of a man, don't you know?"

"What do you mean?" I asked, burying my nose in her braids.

"Men in this village treat women like they treat sesame: grab, cut, and throw. But you're a sensitive man. You scream." We laughed. I kissed her. She dissolved in my mouth like butter.

We woke up early the next morning to the voice of Wad Ammoona calling out to Alam Gishi. When we opened our eyes, he was standing right in front of our bed. Only then did we realize that we had forgotten to close the door last night. He had shaved and was wearing a clean white galabia, and his thick mustache was perfectly trimmed. As usual, he was cheerful, brisk, and talkative. He congratulated us on the *dokhla*, though actually it was more his achievement, a work of art that he had created with great enthusiasm. I later understood that his greatest passion was to bring men and women together to enjoy themselves.

"Don't you want a bath?" he asked. "You'd better hurry before the water gets cold. I won't make you tea and breakfast until you're as clean and beautiful as I am." He said, theatrically showing off his clothes and face.

"*Okaay*," Alam Gishi moaned in a sleepy voice, ridding her body of the cover with successive kicks. "Out of the way. Let me put my clothes on."

While Wad Ammoona pretended to be busy arranging some items in the hut, we got dressed. Alam Gishi followed me to the bathroom, carrying a big towel. The bathroom was behind the *rakuba*, nearly ten meters away from the hut. To my surprise, she followed me into the bathroom, helped me take off my clothes, and then undressed herself. She invited me to sit on the stool. She asked if any woman had ever washed me before, and I replied that only my mother had. She said that was what she had expected. She sponged my back, legs, and arms. My thick hair made it difficult for her to sponge my chest, so she used her soft palms instead. As she did this, she hummed a lovely tune in Amharic. Pointing at my pubic hair, she said, "I'll ask Wad Ammoona to shave that off for you." The idea scared me, but she assured me that Wad Ammoona was an expert at it, and that his clients included the regional military commander, the chief of police, and others whom she named. I told her I wouldn't allow anyone to come close to those territories. She laughed.

It was a lovely morning, serene and quiet, thanks to the absence of the Jungo, who were not yet back from the fields. The voice of the Mother talking to Wad Ammoona reached us clearly as we stood outside, watching flocks of birds heading east. Alam Gishi had an extremely attractive body—an ideal body, I would say, despite my limited experience with women. The ladies who attracted me most were those with large thighs and wide hips. And Alam Gishi was surely one of those women.

"Did you enjoy last night?" she asked, interrupting my thoughts.

"It was the most beautiful night of my life! You're incredible!" She smiled and said nothing. In fact, from that day on, I considered myself almost a professional with regard to women. I still had some concerns, though. Was every woman smart enough to know how to treat a man who knows so little about her? A man who has an overwhelming fear of sex? In other words, could I be with a woman other than Alam Gishi? Or would the fear of failure keep me hostage to this one fantastic woman forever?

"You're hopeless," she said, again interrupting my train of thought.

13 THE POST-PARTY BENEFITS

Alam Gishi adapted herself to her new life remarkably quickly. She showed great passion for her new work even though the amount she was paid for cooking and housekeeping was less than half what she used to make as a night girl at Addai's house. She quickly proved very adept at finding new sources of income. For instance, she made an offer to the staff: there was no need for them to have their clothes washed at the laundry shop; she could take care of it. And what's more, she wouldn't mix people's clothes together. No. She'd do each person's laundry separately to prevent the spread of infection. And they'd see the difference themselves.

Then she came up with the idea of selling Ethiopian garments and other costumes in small installments to the staff and their friends so they could take their purchases home to their families at the end of the month. She then expanded her offerings to include Ethiopian and Zairian cassettes, original leather belts, and Italian shoes smuggled in from Ethiopia. Then the list swelled to include gin, brandy, *anisha*,[1] and cognac, and then condoms, Viagra pills, and appetite-stimulating drugs. Her income increased further still when she hosted a party at Addai's house one colorful Thursday for all the employees of the telecommunications company and their friends who were building the bank premises, as well as local government officers, some senior army and police officers, and local

[1] Ethiopian liquor.

dignitaries. They were treated to a variety of grilled meats served with ghee and honey, and *sheesha* whose tobacco was soaked in the Stim soft drink.

The star of the night was the old singer Adam Belala, or al-Ajouz, as he was better known, accompanied by his *om kiki* and the prettiest five girls in the Eastern quarter: Safiyyah Idris, nicknamed Safiyah Nasat; Sonayet, who had the most beautiful legs, especially when she danced; Ameera al-Dabbaba ("the tank"), a multiethnic woman with large eyes and even larger hips; Manahel Saeed, better known as Manahel al-Nubawiyah, a girl with a long, smooth neck, born to a Yemeni mother and a father from the Mahas; and Ammoona bit Khadoum, who had only recently arrived from Qedaref, accompanied by her Jungojoraya mother, but who did not take long to ascend to the top echelon of al-Hillah's women, thanks to her beauty, eloquence, and knowledge. For such a historic event, Alam Gishi could not possibly neglect to also invite an iconic figure like Astair Kedani Bashir, who was also a newcomer to al-Hillah, having moved from her place at Fariek Girish near the death tree. She had worked as a barmaid at the outdoor bar on the Setit River opposite Hamdayeit and had to flee to al-Hillah after being accused of murdering one of her fellow employees. She was pretty and straightforward but struggled with her Arabic. Boushai Shoul, daughter of a Shuluk father and a Homrani mother, was a singer whose presence was crucial for the success of any party in al-Hillah. Her beauty was praised in a song composed by one of her many admirers in al-Hillah:

The sweet fruit of papaya,

You are as sweet as mango, my Boushai,

I love you—wai!,

Wai . . . Waaai!

Needless to say, no party would be perfect without Wad Ammoona. Here he was, well groomed and attractive, briskly moving about—no one was immune to his prompt, impeccable services, his strong perfume, or the charm of his low-pitched voice. He danced, sang, performed *doubait*[2] and *madeeh*,[3] and made secret deals with whomever he set his sights on—deals for almost everything, from imported alcohol down to women. Everything had its price: a single woman, a divorcee, a married woman, a widow, a conservative woman, a prostitute, gin, whiskey, amulets, *mehayah*,[4] *anisha*, beer, cognac, and even date arrack, *mareesa*, and *asaliyah*. And he added another distinguished service to all this: home delivery, highly regarded by clients who were too proud or too shy to procure these services directly from the source. Praise be to God, Wad Ammoona had a solution for every problem.

Only one request irritated him, which was communicated to him in the form of a whisper into his ear, confirmed by a sudden pinch on his ass, a wink, and a gesture with the tongue. "I want *you*, Wad Ammoona. It's *you*, not anyone else, that I want, Wad Ammoona." That request, he later confessed to me, left a weird feeling in him, even though it was not the first request of its kind; neither the first pinch nor the first wink nor the first lewd gesture with the tongue.

"I told him to meet me the next day at Addai's house, but he didn't show up."

I asked him what would have happened if the man *had* shown up. "Frankly? Frankly? I liked him. But thank God he didn't show up," he said, laughing in that dubious way of his that always put him under suspicion.

It was a lovely party that we all enjoyed. Everyone was there, even those who hadn't received a formal invitation. People here didn't need a formal invitation to attend. Alam Gishi had spent a fortune to ensure its success. But the subsequent benefits were much greater than the party's costs.

---

[2] A type of chanting popular in rural areas.

[3] Religious lyrics, in praise of the Prophet.

[4] A drink made of a piece of paper containing writings by a sorcerer or a religious man dissolved in water—used as medicine.

I said to her at the Mother's House, our usual meeting place, "Your business is booming. You've become rich."

"City people love Ethiopian clothes," she said, avoiding my insinuation.

"And what else?" I asked shrewdly.

"Ethiopian and Zairian cassettes," she said.

"And what else?"

"What do you mean?" she asked defiantly.

"Women. Don't they love women?"

"I'm just a facilitator. That's a service that I'm prepared to extend to whoever wants it, including *you*," she boasted. "If you want a woman, I can arrange one for you."

For the first time in my life, I was so infuriated that I slapped her in the face. She rose to her feet, picked up an empty gin bottle, and hurled it at me. I ducked and the bottle dashed against the door with a bang. Addai and Wad Ammoona rushed in and, luckily, so did at least half the quarter's residents, or rather all the residents who happened to be awake at that late hour. I say "luckily" because Wad Ammoona and Addai alone failed to get Alam Gishi off my chest or release my throat from her strong grip. "You were on the verge of death," Wad Ammoona later told me. Alam Gishi later claimed she hadn't intended to kill me; she had just wanted to play. Anyway, I learned my lesson, and considered it one of the subsequent benefits of the party. So the quarrel was settled. No one blamed me, and no one blamed her. The one to blame was the devil. Cast your curses on the devil. People here go out of their way to avoid severing ties with one another. People need each other, just as they all need God, the Creator of all worlds.

"Now you can be sure that Alam Gishi truly loves you—because she realized that you hit her out of jealousy," Wad Ammoona said. "But do you really love her, boy?" he suddenly asked.

I fell asleep instantly, too exhausted to follow their chat about the Hamdayeit bus that had been robbed by the *falloul* bandits this afternoon at the Zahanah forest. It was impressive that the news of the robbery could reach us in no more than half an hour, when the bus itself, being the fastest ride in those parts, would need a full hour to reach al-Hillah from that spot. Isn't it true that the djinn alone are responsible for carrying news around in these lands?

14

THE JUNGOJORAI

(Pathetic in the Dry Season, Drives You Mad in the Rainy Season)

Thursday is a festive day here, a day that a Jungojorai believes falls under one single slogan: "Never fail to enjoy your Thursday . . . even if you have to sell your one and only shirt." They descend from fields and farm camps, from near and far, crossing sorghum and sesame fields, and *kitir* and *taleh* bushes; their feet beat heavily on the black clay soil, spreading panic among the wild rabbits, rats, and lizards; the wilderness echoes their ancient harvest songs. The *googos* on their backs are loaded with plant roots, prescriptions for local diseases as well as for snakebites, scorpion stings, and even the bites of the malicious scorpion ants. Their *googos* are also loaded with all the outfit items they've been able to acquire so far. When they become tired, they rest under a *laloub* or *taleh* tree and chat about employers, women, and Fariek Girish. In most cases, they avoid talking about money—that strange slippery creature that never stays in their pockets, hands, or *googos*. It can bring them *mareesa* and arrack. It can bring them grilled meat, *miris*, *kajaik*, and all kinds of foods beyond their wildest dreams. It can bring them women in the blink of an eye. But it also knows how to humiliate men and end their life's journey under the death tree in Fariek Girish in al-Homra.

This month, however, as long as a Jungojorai is perfectly healthy, fit, and able to make love, money is crucial for completing his outfit: a pair of shoes (Adidas or suede); a new pair of pants, preferably baggy jeans with big pockets and broad belts; one or more new shirts with big collars and bright colors; perfume that smells like incense; a new flashlight, made by the original English brand (Tigerhead); a sweater; a large cotton handkerchief; a can of Vaseline to be used as a snuff container; a big cassette recorder with two speakers, preferably a SANYO or International, with silver letters embossed above the "play" button; a large pack, also known as the *googo*; sunglasses, black or reflective, big enough to cover half the upper part of the face (the women are mad about them); a wrist watch (a Casio will do in the absence of an original Seiko, Citizen, or Jovial). A privileged few also carry a Bic ballpoint pen and a small notepad, two items that reveal not only the holder's education but also his standing in the work hierarchy, as he is most likely a project administrator, the highest post a Jungojorai can dream of, and the fruit of education and schooling.

Every Jungojorai can complete his outfit during the dry season, this December. On Thursdays, he does his best to procure a few items and also enjoy a wonderful day that he can boast of when he's back with his fellows at the farms, with the porridge pot on the fire, and his exhausted friends lying on canvas sacks spread on the ground, submitting their muscles and imaginations to the hands of magicians of relaxation. A true Jungojorai is not too attached to women. They dismiss as "mean" anyone who prefers keeping women's company to alcohol. *Mareesa* is their favorite drink during the day. At night, when it cools down and the effect of the *mareesa* wears off, they drink arrack, the best treat for relaxing exhausted muscles. They're now in the months of laziness, which start around mid-December—the post-harvesting months, when they enjoy a warrior's compulsory rest.

All this popped into our minds when our ears caught a conversation that sneaked in through the cane fence from the house of Khamiesa al-Nubawiyah, who was talking to a Jungo named Abdaraman.

"I am at fault, mother. Please forgive me."

"You have a sweet tongue, Abdaraman, but your deeds smell like shit."

At some point their voices died down, and I missed part of the conversation, but when Abdaraman explained what he wanted, his voice was audible again:

"Okay. Keep this new shirt as a mortgage and give me half a bottle. And if I don't pay you tomorrow, don't give me the shirt back."

Khamiesa laughed loudly. "So it's the same story as the cassette recorder. For five long months you drank arrack, *mareesa*, *asaliyah*, *kani moro*, *baganiyah* . . . And when you had had enough of it, you took back the recorder without paying a single penny. You even cheated the girl you promised to marry. Once the weed clearing work began, you vanished, and no one's seen you since, until today, now that it's the dry season and you're jobless again."

"The girl? I'll marry her right now. Call Fekki Ali al-Zaghrad. Let him recite the *fateha*[1] for us."

"What a hypocritical son of a bitch!"

"I swear by my grandfather Barambageel. By God, mother, I'm not a liar. I swear by my father's head, I'm dead serious."

A soft voice came from a remote corner deep inside Khamiesa's house: "I don't want him, mother. I don't want him. A Jungojorai is pathetic in the dry season and drives you mad in the rainy season."

Abdaraman laughed. "Hey Kaltouma, hold your tongue for now. When I marry you, I'll show you stars in broad daylight!"

Another voice joined the conversation. He talked about the sanctity of matrimony and swore that he would divorce his wife unless a *mazoun*[2] was summoned to consummate the wedding, and Abdaraman got private access to Kaltouma right away.

The voice of Kaltouma came from a remote corner deep inside Khamiesa's house: "I don't want him. I don't want him. He only comes to me when he's broke. Where were you at high season when your hands were full of money? Where were you after

---

[1] The *fateha*, meaning "prelude," is the opening chapter in the Holy Quran. It is recited as part of marriage ceremonies.

[2] A *mazoun* is a registrar of weddings.

sesame and sorghum cutting? I don't want him, mother. I just don't want him."

"I swear to God this is a doomed year. I had to sell my recorder and my glasses, which I bought from Qedaref. It's still January. I wonder what will have happened to us by June."

Khamiesa al-Nubawiyah said, "The girl said she didn't want to marry you."

"You listen to a girl? Would *any* woman refuse to get married? Is this sweet thing resistible?" asked Abdaraman. "Mother Khamiesa, please give us half a bottle of arrack. We'll drink it while waiting for Musa Wad Mahgoub to get Fekki al-Zaghrad to consummate the marriage. Then I'll go in to see your daughter, and we'll become husband and wife."

"I don't want you. I hope half your body is thrown to the dogs."

Other voices supported the proposal that Khamiesa should offer half a bottle of arrack in honor of her daughter's prospective husband, in early celebration of the happy event and as a prelude to the special night. Alcohol, as they say, is a prelude to the bedroom in the same way that ululations are preludes to weddings. So cheer up Kaltouma. But Khamiesa adamantly refused. If he was serious about marrying her daughter, he would have to come tomorrow with some witnesses, and of course the dowry.

"Witnesses are easy to find, mother Bakhieta. But money in such a hot dry season? I doubt you'll find much of that," Abdaraman said. As if talking to himself, he added in a low tone, "If I had money, I would have paid for the half bottle. I would have drunk it and slept in peace, unbothered by marriage and all this nonsense. Why do you think I want to get married just now? Isn't it because I can't afford a half bottle? How would I have any money before the sesame and shrub cutting, or the work making charcoal? Impossible—unless I had a djinn for a servant. Right, folks?"

"I don't want him, mother. I'm saying it once and for all: I just don't want him. Why would I want to marry a penniless Jungojorai? Look at him: he wants to marry me just to get a half bottle of arrack! I don't want him!"

The distant conversation reached us in whispers and murmurs, interspersed with Kaltouma's cries and curses. Her bitter words pierced through the reed fence to pervade the whole space and mix with the mumblings of the drunkards, the cries of bats, the noisy battles of dogs, the meowing of cats, and the sounds of bodies on beds. Suddenly, ululations erupted from the courtyard of Khamiesa al-Nubawiyah and cut through the darkness of the eastern quarter. From the very first moments, the entire village knew that Abdaraman, son of Ab Bakar al-Bilalawi, had married Kaltouma, daughter of Khamiesa al-Nubawiyah. People instantly began commenting that this was Abdaraman's fourth marriage in four years in al-Hillah and that it would not be his last if circumstances permitted. They also noted that although it was also the fourth marriage for Kaltouma, daughter of Khamiesa al-Nubawiyah, she was presented to the marriage official as a "virgin" so that the official would not ask for her divorce certificates, even though he was the same person who had officiated all her previous marriages.

However, everyone said that Abdaraman, son of Ab Bakar al-Bilalawi, would not emerge unscathed from this marriage; he was destined to meet the same fate as Kaltouma's ex-husbands, or worse. The first was still in jail, the second was killed in this very house of Khamiesa al-Nubawiyah, and the third disappeared, and no one but God knew if he was dead or alive. The reason behind all this was that Khamiesa al-Nubawiyah was not a woman who took insults lightly. She had a witch called Altera who would take revenge for her sooner or later. And while Abdaraman admits that the Jungo often insult others, he tells himself that it's the cruel law of life that has made them so.

What people here say is more than mere prediction. They *know*. They read the future without ambiguity. They actually see it.

15 MUTUAL ADVICE

Al-Safyah became his "immediate" life project. And I'm using the word "immediate" deliberately here; it's a very clear-cut word, and I'm sure my friend would be upset if he knew that I was using it in this context. He's moody and rash and would not hesitate to implement any ideas that sprang to his mind, no matter how contradictory they might be. That's how I've known him to be since our early childhood. Now that he had come up with his so-called al-Safyah scheme, I had no doubt that he would get to the cold dark bottom of that idea and taste its salty sediment. What I called meddling, he called "challenging tasks." That was the difference between our two personalities. It wasn't a difference of degree, as many of our mutual friends believe, but rather one of concept, which boiled down to our approaches to life.

I love people but always keep some distance, while the first thing he does is eliminate any distance between himself and others. I couldn't see how al-Safyah could attract a city boy like him who had so fully absorbed Arab-influenced concepts of beauty through schooling, the TV, the radio, newspapers, the street, religious education, and family. That model was conveniently at his disposal, and he could avail himself of a wide range of attractive options that perfectly suited his taste. He's by no means psychotic. Nor is he randy, although he's more experienced with women than me. His desire for al-Safyah was driven by the hot blood of adventure boiling in his veins. He's a man who will never give up on mysteries, on puzzles to be solved.

That was why I wasn't surprised when I heard him say, "I want to get to the bottom of this al-Safyah affair."

"You're going to die," I replied.

"I won't die. A gypsy fortune-teller I met in Port Sudan told me I was going to drown. And she said that would happen at an old age, perhaps in my eighties or even nineties."

"Did she tell you whether your entire body and limbs—your eyes, for instance— would be drowned?"

He laughed as he closed the outer door behind him—a laugh that seemed laden with fear this time. My instinct told me he was going to call off the adventure. That was for certain. I knew him well.

In recent days, Alam Gishi had fallen victim to an oppressive feeling of loneliness, particularly after midnight. Addai had devoted her to me, or she had devoted herself to me. She would come to me at Mukhtar Ali's house, and we would go to Addai's house together. For the first time, she said she wanted to have a child with me. "That's what I want, a baby girl, a pretty girl that looks like you."

I liked the idea. It filled me with erotic thoughts and took hold of my tongue and the decision-making chambers of my brain, as if it were originally my idea, as if I had simply been waiting for her to take the lead. And so that my daughter would not be disgraced as a bastard in this backward community, I said, "I'll marry you."

"Of course you will," she said calmly.

"Yesterday a Jungojorai named Abdaraman got married to Kaltouma, daughter of Khamiesa," I told her.

She laughed. "She's conceived three times from Abdaraman. He'd been living with them, eating, drinking, and copulating—all on credit. The wall of the room is full of scratches to document his debt."

"Was he her boyfriend?"

"Of course! He was her *man*. She adores him and can't live without him. Was the wedding yesterday? Those Jungo only get married when they're broke. They only marry rich women. And this Kaltouma is rich. She has money and gold. Her mother has djinn and witches who can get her anything she needs."

Wad Ammoona came in, engulfed in perfume. He was accompanied by Fekki al-Zaghrad and Addai, who looked elegant in her traditional white Hamaseen dress, a beautiful fly whisk in her hand. My friend was also present, as was Mukhtar Ali, who acted as my attorney. In the presence of all of them as well as some neighbors and drunk passersby, the marriage was officiated. Fekki Ali prayed to Allah to give us virtuous offspring that would be a valuable addition to the followers of Prophet Mohammed, may the blessings and goodwill of Allah be upon him. Addai offered to put us up for as long as Allah would permit or until we built a house of our own, whichever came first. Wad Ammoona volunteered to groom Alam Gishi for me whenever I liked, but he didn't tell me if that service would be free of charge or not. The company staff and others who had come from other cities threw a big party in my honor. They invited a singer from Qedaref who was the first to introduce a song that came to be known as "Mutual Advice":

We exchanged advice,

Be bold, she said,

Face reality,

For whether you like it or not,

We are destined to part.

From that moment on, people here began to sing that song at their parties. Wad Ammoona memorized the lyrics, and al-Ajouz performed it with the help of his *om kiki* after making some minor modifications to the melody to suit the instrument's solitary string and its strange musical scales. In fact, he was the one who popularized the song and made it available to all, and for all purposes: as a wedding procession song, as a *dalluka* song, as a *kalash* and *dobok* song, as a *kayta* and *nouba* song, and as a *tum tum* song[1] for the purpose of the bridal dance and *rahat*-cutting ceremony. He also

[1] Different types of rhythms popular in different parts of Sudan

performed it in the *mardum* rhythm at the request of some homesick Kordofanians[2] who yearned for the golden sands of their homeland, and in the *dalaib* rhythm for some bachelors from the Northern Province who were working here in the gas station. Thanks to him, "Mutual Advice" soon became everyone's favorite bathing song. The song name was soon given to a new ladies dress, a new shirt, a new style for wearing women's robes, and even a new style of riding donkeys. The only thing the villagers failed to do was make a special dance with the name of "Mutual Advice."

The date of our wedding was linked with the time when that song became popular in the East. We took that as a good omen, despite the sad story that was said to have prompted the song's composition and the tragic end of its poor poet, who was believed to have gone mad right after writing the lyrics. Not only that, he rambled aimlessly about until he finally fell into a deserted well on the outskirts of Khartoum. As if that was not in itself enough for a full-fledged tragedy, his beautiful girlfriend, a Christian from the South, became blind after she resigned herself to endless weeping because her father had refused to give her hand in marriage to the poet. Rumor had it that "Mutual Advice" was the first and last poem that man ever wrote. Despite all that, Alam Gishi and I took it as a good omen that our marriage was associated with that song because the lyrics contained words like "mosques" and "churches," "bells" and "temples," and most importantly because it mentioned the sickle, which here in the East is widely regarded as a good omen in dreams.

---

[2] From Kordofan province, in midwest Sudan.

16

A TRIBUTE TO ETHIOPIAN WOMEN

These days the women were complaining of slow sales. They had an immovable stock of *mareesa* that had gone bad due to the heat. The date arrack was no better either. *Asaliyah* was both costly and highly perishable, so they made it only when they had a solid order. Cash was in short supply in al-Hillah, while bartering flourished. Summer was a time when it was every housewife's responsibility to protect the stability of her family. It was a matter of life and death, and relying too much on the man in that season would only precipitate divorce and family discord, and might even put both the wife and the children at the risk of being beaten up.

I was listening attentively to Alam Gishi. We had become very close and were now working hard to achieve our goal of giving birth to a baby girl. During a break in our lovemaking, which we called "warrior's rest," we were drinking coffee with ginger. She was talking to me in a soft voice as refreshing as the smell of the Ethiopian coffee, as a morning breeze by the riverbank, as the sigh of an Ethiopian girl in love. Wait a minute. Let me say a few words in praise of Ethiopian girls. Let me describe the fascinating black rings around their eyes, the distinctive marks of highland dwellers. Let me describe their peerless shoulders.

I could be classified among the impotent, a category of men who need a special type of woman to decipher their ordeals. But my impotency did not take long to dissolve at the magic touches of that woman's lustful fingers patiently probing my body, at her experienced, knowledgeable, frenzied yet serene Ethiopian self. While I'm in this ecstatic state, let me say the following: women in this world fall into one of two categories: Ethiopians and non-Ethiopians. The Ethiopians are Ethiopians. As for the non-Ethiopians, they're diverse: employed, unemployed, refugees, expatriates, Jungojorayas, skinny, those with large hips, scholars, teachers, prophets, students, lovers, tall, drunkards, lawyers, judges, journalists, high-heeled, lustful, those wearing thick spectacles, merry, dancers, naked, clothed, adulterers, chaste, virtuous, devout, poor, hungry, mothers, friends, sisters, girls, poets.

My wife and darling Alam Gishi was asking me why men were scared to death of being impotent. Wad Ammoona once confided to me that he had seen himself in a dream as a woman. "I was very happy. But I want to be a man, a man who can have sex with women ably and effectively, who can ejaculate inside them and cause them to conceive and give birth." I, for one, could not comprehend why Wad Ammoona would want to be a woman when being a woman simply meant that one had to bear the man, which was the worst fate that could befall anyone. I wonder how such a boastful selfish creature could be tolerated.

Alam Gishi said she had previously married a man from Hamdayeit; his name was Mousa Harba Harba. He was the only Jungojorai in a family employed in the smuggling business. She lived with him in al-Jairah, in a house on the riverbank. The houses of the poor looked just like those of the wealthy there, and the couple lived like everyone else, in a big hut with a *rakuba* built of straw and *adar* grass, fenced by thorny *kitir* bushes and sorghum cane. Like most women, she made local drinks. Each Tuesday she made a big barrel full of *mareesa*. He did nothing but play cards with soldiers under the shady trees. Sometimes he went hunting for rabbits, wild boar, monkeys, and pythons in the Zahanah forest. Other times he visited the al-Kitra souk to buy or sell something. She confessed to me that they had two daughters: two beautiful girls who were now living with Mousa's family in Hamdayeit. The elder was in the 7th grade, and the younger in the 5th.

One hot, dry, and dusty summer three years ago, he divorced her for no obvious reason except that she had told him, "Be a man. Stop being lazy and join the army or the smuggling business." He placed his daughters in the custody of his rich father in Hamdayeit, and when he returned, he stayed with a divorced woman in the souk district. Yet he kept visiting her regularly, at midnight, at least twice a week. He claimed that since she had not remarried, he still had rights to her, including the right to call off the divorce at any time and to sleep with her whenever he wanted. So long as he had not issued her with a divorce certificate, she was still his legally wedded wife. "If I ever find a man with you, I'll kill both of you," he warned her.

No one stood by her side. And she had to accept his terms because they were pretty much in line with the norms.

"You're different," Alam Gishi said as she handed me a cup of coffee, its smell wafting into the air. "You're not like the men here. That's why I fell in love with you and told myself you were the one who deserved to be the father of my daughter. I want her to be a copy of you. Understand?"

I had nothing to do. The days stretched out their limbs like a sleepy dog under a damp water container. There was no more work for the men to do; it was now time for leisure, for keeping women company, and men wouldn't hesitate to mortgage their personal belongings to have that company. Some men worked clearing land and making charcoal. It occurred to me that I should acquire some land on the bank of *Maghareif* creek and prepare it for the new season before I died of boredom. I wasn't the type of man who would allow a woman to take care of his living expenses in return for sex. The amount of money I had left from my social insurance pay was enough to buy a large plot of land at a cheap price. So why shouldn't I embark on this adventure and renounce my idleness? I consulted my friend, but he said he planned to spend the summer in the city, and might go to Addis Ababa or maybe to Cairo. The international book fair was happening in February, and he wanted to attend. He suggested that I take Alam Gishi to the city. Life, he said, would be unbearable here in the summer.

"You didn't ask me about al-Safyah," he said suddenly.

"Everyone knows all the details," I said, laughing.

He was aware that he had become one of the legends of that place, one of its most thrilling myths. The mere mention of his name would unleash different versions of his story with al-Safyah, narrated by different tongues, everyone telling it to everyone else any way they wanted and whenever they wanted. Yet the version closest to reality was the one that I told because I was the person closest to him. Besides, as you will notice, I consulted many sources and compared the various versions and weighed them all against each other.

I even held a so-called mini-seminar at Adalia Daniyal's house on her *mareesa* day. It was attended by Fekki Ali, who was believed to have the ability to read people's hidden intentions, both good and evil, and to foretell the dates of people's death and birth, using his collection of references such as *The Jaljalotiayh, The Principles of Jurisprudence, The Sun of Greatest Knowledge, Abu Maashar al-Falaki, The Right Approach to Using the Djinn*, and the famous *al-Taseen Book.* No one hated superstition more than he did, so he depended on "knowledge . . . knowledge of the book."

My friend was present too, but no one bought his version—not even me—because it was the farthest from reality. And although he asserted and swore several times that his version was the most accurate, everyone dismissed it as a fabrication. The audience of the mini-seminar at Adalia Daniyal's house on her *mareesa* day, in the presence of Fekki Ali, unanimously dismissed his version as the ramblings of a drunkard. Though he protested that verdict, he stayed on and listened patiently to the authentic version of his story with al-Safyah, which was recounted by others quoting *him* and narrating incidents that presumably occurred between him and al-Safyah, even going into minute details with unshakable confidence. He did not try to object because no one would have listened to him. What he considered factual they regarded as fables, lies, and conscious distortions of incidents that people considered their own. He had certainly been part of the incident, but he wasn't the only person involved.

The gathering ended. The three of us went to Mukhtar Ali's house. We performed the evening prayers together and then had dinner. The others went to bed, while I headed to my hut at Addai's house, where Alam Gishi was waiting for me with Wad Ammoona.

17

GIFTS AND ADVICE FOR WAD AMMOONA

The bank was inaugurated just in time, before the beginning of the new farming season. The employees were temporarily put up in the telecom company's residential compound while the final touches were being put on their own accommodations, built of a combination of permanent and semi-permanent materials to suit the local environment. The huts had a base of red brick and stone while the upper parts were made of straw, as was the custom in al-Hillah. And like all other houses here, the compound was surrounded by a fence made of canes and thorny dry plants.

The first person that the bank employees got to know was Alam Gishi, who was working in the company's residential compound. And when they asked for someone to work as an office boy, she recommended Wad Ammoona without a second thought. To her, he was the only suitable candidate: obedient and easygoing, he wouldn't complain or grumble, and he'd be very willing to do all kinds of tasks, from small ones such as lighting a cigarette to important ones such as asking for a woman's hand on behalf of one of the employees. Besides, he was always neat, cheerful, and sober—he never drank during the day, regardless of the temptations. Even at night, he only drank when he was certain that no one needed his services. He was a rare person in a place where men were universally known to be rude, rash, and filthy. "Wad Ammoona's the one for the job—no one else," she told them. "He's attractive, smart, good-mannered, and obedient." She didn't fail to mention that he was paid peanuts at his current job at Addai's house. Nor did she fail to mention other attributes that some of them considered great advantages. He accepted the offer, and didn't forget to thank her.

Before taking up his new job, he bought a brand new pair of pants and a shirt, both of the "Mutual Advice" brand. It was the Mother who had given him the money to clean himself up enough for the new job. He had long been in her service, and as a caring mother, she wished him success and advised him to get rid of the one bad habit that had stayed with him since childhood: "Avoid chitchat and idle gossip," she warned him, referring to his habit of spreading stories around.

From Qedaref, where she had settled with her husband, his mother Ammoona sent him a new pair of shoes—authentic leather ones—along with her best wishes. She too warned him against a bad habit, the one bad habit she felt he had acquired since starting work at the Mother's House: "Never reveal people's secrets," by which she meant the love affairs and habits that people would rather keep in the dark.

Adalia Daniyal gave him a beautiful SEIKO watch with a golden background, which she had bought from a Jungo the previous season. She warned him against the one bad habit she had noticed in him, "Refrain from pimping," she told him, and by that she was referring to his inability to resist arranging for a beautiful woman to sleep with a man and his desire to receive full credit for those encounters. Whenever that happened, Wad Ammoona felt fully satisfied with life—it gave him unspeakable pleasure.

Fekki Ali summoned him to give his blessings for the new job. He presented him with an amulet that protected against envy, jealousy, and evil people, both men and women. He warned him against the one bad habit *he* had noticed in him for over two years now: "Avoid gossip and idle talk," by which he was alluding to an incident that had involved Fekki Ali and the police, when Fekki Ali had been taught a lesson that he would not soon forget.

Boushai called Wad Ammoona and gave him a cassette of Ethiopian songs and a bottle of perfume. She assured him that he would win all hearts if he could rid himself of his one bad habit: lying. She was alluding to his testimony at a gathering held at Addai's house last autumn. The topic of discussion was her virginity.

From her prison in Qedaref, Azza sent him a woolen shawl of her own making and told him that he had one good habit that he should never lose: keeping his word. She was clearly referring to his commitment to pay blood money on her behalf so she could be set free.

Many others sought to see him to present him with token gifts or personal advice. He apologized politely: time was running short, and he had to report to work.

So off he went, with one piece of advice fixed in his mind, one that his inner self had whispered in his ears: "Don't let this opportunity pass you by, Wad Ammoona. Rise up, up, up."

Even at that moment, it had certainly never occurred to Wad Ammoona or anyone else that he would rise so high as to become a federal minister in just ten years. But that's an amazing story for another time, and one that I'll leave for my friend to tell in his book *The Revolt of the Jungojoraya.*

Early in the morning, six Jungo men accompanied by three Jungojoraya (Jungo women) and al-Safyah visited us at the Mother's House. I met them in the sitting room. They said they intended to ask the bank for a loan. The bank had been created primarily to serve the poor farmers, as had been preached at a Friday sermon last year, although none of those present now had been present then—not even Fekki Ali al-Zaghrad, who had had to entertain some djinn guests who had paid him a surprise visit, as he later explained.

They wanted a loan so they could buy a plot of land to cultivate. They wanted the bank to buy them a good branded tractor fitted with a plough—they specified the make, model, and even the color. If they were fortunate enough to have a good rainy season, they would be able to repay the principal loan the very same year. "And we would still have some money left to divide among us," Abrahait said with a wide smile that made his mustache look even longer and thicker than usual. "And the next year, we'd be able to repay the interest to the bank. After that, the tractor, the plow, and the project as a whole would be all ours. Am I right, brothers?"

"You're right, Abrahait," I said. "But, as you know, we'll need a feasibility study."

"What's this feasibility study?" asked a tiny well-dressed Jungojorai who had a pen and a notepad in the pocket of his Tetron-brand shirt.

"Can we buy the study from the Qedaref souk? And how much does it cost?" al-Safyah asked.

I asked them to give me some time—three days at the most—to prepare the study. I could see their dreams of success and wealth hovering above us, filling the air with a sense of jubilation. Before they left, Abrahait took me to a corner and apologized for his rashness the other day, saying he had mistaken my friend for a security agent. He complained of non-stop harassment by security agents and fanatical religious groups over his alleged involvement in the transport of the Ethiopian Felasha to Israel in 1985. On behalf of the group, Abrahait presented me with a present: a bottle of cognac—very useful, they said, particularly for a man newly married to a beautiful Ethiopian who used to work at Addai's house.

Alam Gishi and I held a small celebration one morning to do honor to the gift. We discussed the Jungo's crazy idea. "Do you think the bank will lend them the money?" she asked suddenly.

"I don't know. Maybe. Let's write up the feasibility study," I said, though deep inside I already knew what the result would be. I could see the Jungo being forced off the bank premises in humiliation.

"Those people are supported by Fekki Ali al-Zaghrad himself," Alam Gishi announced.

Fekki Ali, as was well known, did not draw his power from the Holy Quran alone, nor merely from witches, trees, or black magic. He used the Quran and other books, as well as magic, soothsaying, and the science of letters. He had invisible djinn at his service, and he could do whatever he wanted.

"Fekki Ali has a far-reaching hand. He can turn water into curdled milk," she said.

I was a friend of Fekki Ali's, and I admired his simple way of life, as well as his high level of self-esteem. I liked the smell of his clothes and his body, a mixture of gum and tanned leather that lent him an enigmatic air. His religious opinions were neither progressive nor backward, but rather strange, particularly with regard to drinking alcohol and accountability. He believed that Allah classified people not as Muslims versus non-Muslims, but as women, men, and children. Women and children had no responsibility to worship God because they were not eligible to enter Paradise, which was exclusively the domain of men; and it was therefore men who had to pay in advance here in this worldly life the cost of the reward they were going to receive in the hereafter. As for alcohol, it was forbidden for the foolish and abusive only, because they would use it only for amusement, whereas the elite and the decent—which included rulers, scholars, and judges—were allowed to drink, and alcohol would be their best companion.

"I have taken all my ideas from no lesser being than Iblees[1] himself. Iblees used to be an angel, one of the best informed and the closest to Allah. People should not think so little of him," he told me.

The Ethiopian cognac had a pleasant taste and left you with none of the unpleasant aftereffects of alcohol: migraines, heartburn, and nausea. It only caused you to urinate more frequently than usual and to increase your level of sexual desire, whether you were a man or a woman. The Ethiopians had both imported and locally manufactured cognac, and the Eritreans had a locally manufactured equivalent. I prefer the Ethiopian. We had a great time that day, and at night we dreamt of the Jungo who came to us on zebras, followed by sesame plants and sorghum stalks, and some *sinber* and *ashoshai* birds laid eggs on the Jungo's heads. They took the feasibility study, leaving their zebras behind in the custody of the rainy season and the scorching sun.

---

[1] Satan.

18

THE JUNGO ENTER THE BANK

Please note that I deliberately glossed over all the detailed accounts that my friend had confided to me about what had happened between him and al-Safyah, retaining only those details that matched the other accounts about him and Wad Fur. I depended primarily on the details that came out at Adalia Daniyal's house on her *mareesa* day, one Saturday when she organized something like a seminar to discuss what had come to be known in these localities as the "al-Safyah affair."

You will also notice that my account is influenced by what Fekki Ali considered indisputable facts. First and foremost, that al-Safyah had two sets of genital organs: one for each sex. The male organ was large and mature, concealed under thick, stubbly pubic hair. The other fact that Fekki Ali considered concrete was that al-Safyah had done to both men what a man would usually do to a woman. That much was certain, and he had two pieces of evidence that I won't mention here. There was a third claim that Fekki Ali had a slight doubt about, though he wouldn't categorically deny it. Yet he swore by his grandfather Sulaiman al-Zaghrad al-Sinnari that he was prepared to die right away if he was proven wrong about it. That claim was that al-Safyah had a daughter and a son from a Bazawiyah lady who now lived at the Doum farm. Her name was Ni'ma Mashakel ("troubles"); Fekki Ali knew her and her parents, and had seen the daughter and son with his own eyes.

With regard to the issue of al-Safyah turning into a hyena, a lion, or any other animal, he believed it was possible. To him, the root of the matter was the milk, and he was certain that the ability to transform was inherited through breastfeeding. Before we take a look at the true story, however, we need to carefully examine what Fekki Ali regarded as indisputable facts, and those he considered probable or doubtful, and put them in the right context, i.e., read them in conjunction with the sum of gossip, testimonies, and whisperings in the mini-seminar at Adalia Daniyal's house on her *mareesa* day. We also need to weigh the testimonies of the two men who had had an actual experience with al-Safyah against those rumors, tales, and what the people and Fekki Ali considered indisputable facts, probable facts, or doubtful facts. We should remember to discard all parts that contradict those sources. In particular, we should discard al-Safyah's autobiographical accounts because she was naturally eager to spin the story in a positive light, one that would portray her as a helpless victim to supernatural powers. Besides, she was believed to have taken for granted some rumors that were in circulation and to have adopted them as concrete facts, so much so that she could no longer distinguish between fact and fiction; or, in Fekki Ali's words, "She's got everything mixed up."

But before I was able to give the final and authentic version of al-Safyah's story, Adalia Daniyal made a surprising confession about an incident that had taken place more than three years earlier.

Adalia said, "The rainy season was at its peak, and the workers were busy clearing the land for cultivation. Merchant X, the owner of one of the largest farms bordering Zahanah, visited us one Sunday. It wasn't my *mareesa* day, so al-Safyah asked me to bring them arrack and *asaliyah* from al-Hillah. I went to Addai's house and got everything they wanted. They had brought some meat from the souk, but I apologized and said that I could not cook it for them as I had to join my husband and children at the church. So I left them to drink and cook in the big *rakuba* near the *laloub* tree. After the prayers, I came back alone. My husband usually stayed until sunset to clean our

Lord's house and do the housekeeping. I left my 14-year-old daughter and her brother, who was two years younger, to play with their friends until sunset. We had access to our neighbors' place through a small door that we always left open. So I went into our neighbors' house, which was closer than ours to the church, and through that access door, I walked directly onto the *rakuba*. There I was stunned to see al-Safyah on top of the *jallabi*, who was submissively lying facedown. My scream alerted them; al-Safyah quickly pulled her thing out of the *jallabi*, who was so terrified that he wet himself. They started to apologize and implored me to keep it secret."

Adalia claimed that she had refused to accept a generous financial gift offered by the *jallabi* but that he had insisted and swore he'd divorce his wife if she didn't take it. He left the money for her and vanished.

"They went to the Mother's House. Al-Safyah didn't have a house of her own at the time. And from that day on, I knew that al-Safyah was both male and female. And I kept a safe distance."

Adalia didn't divulge this story to anyone except Fekki Ali al-Zaghrad, who, in all secrecy, passed it on to all. Adalia assured me that al-Safyah's thing wasn't long; rather, it was short, fat, black, and covered in thick hair. Fekki al-Zaghrad described it in one word: "Big!"

I was not inclined to circulate my friend's claim that he had made al-Safyah shave off her pubic hair and discovered that she was a virgin or that he was the first man in her life. But mentioning that claim might open a new window for all of us to get to the bottom of the matter, particularly if we added his assertion that he "was the one who showed her stars in broad daylight, not the other way around."

The "al-Safyah scheme" seemed to have put the feasibility study temporarily on hold. People's primary focus was now on finding out the truth about al-Safyah. The bank thing could wait—it was still January. However, there were always people who would go out on a limb, and al-Safyah was surely one of those. She came by with three men to ask about the study.

"I'm sorry but it's not ready yet. I've been too busy," I said.

"Busy with your friend's issue?" al-Safyah asked, staring at me defiantly.

"With many things," I said, trying to avert an impending confrontation. "But I'll have it ready tomorrow morning."

She said in a sharp tone that frightened me as she stared at me with aggressive red eyes: "You'd better do something useful and leave the gossip and chitchat to sluts, sodomites, and pimps." Her tone left no doubt that she placed me in all three of those categories, particularly the last one.

We went to the bank—Abrahait, al-Safyah, Mukhtar Ali, Lam Deng (Adalia Daniyal's husband), Fekki Ali Wad al-Zaghrad, and I—with the feasibility study, which had been written on clean white paper. We had to rewrite it three times before we finally had something neat enough to present to the bank.

The bank office was a magnificent building that stood out like a vain elephant. It was painted dark green and was the only two-story building in that area. My companions were wondering how to reach the manager's office upstairs—whether they were going to take the stairs or the elevator, and in the case of the latter, how to use it. It was Wad Ammoona who put an end to their speculation. Wad Ammoona, who had started work as an office boy at the bank only a few days earlier, took advantage of a brief halt in the calls for errands and came to chat with the Jungo outside the bank and to rave about the bank's tile mosaics, the Western-style staircases, the air fresheners, and the electric water coolers. He advised them to take utmost care so that they don't fall down and break an arm or a leg—or even worse, a neck. They listened attentively, with cautious smiles on their faces. He went back in for a while, then returned and invited us into the reception hall. Everything there was sparkling and clean—except the Jungo, even though they had done their best to make themselves presentable. They were now the dirtiest things in that place that Wad Ammoona had worked so hard to clean, since the early hours of the morning, with the help of two women the bank had brought in from Khartoum specifically for that purpose.

Because the instinct of bankers went on full alert whenever they sensed any danger, the cashier shouted at us: "Hey! What's up? What is it that they want, Wad Ammoona? Didn't I tell you not to let people in without permission?"

I took a few steps forward and said, "We want to see the bank manager."

"What do you want from him?"

"We have something to discuss with him."

"Do you have an appointment?"

"No."

"Can I know what is it that you wanted to see him about?"

My answer was firm: "No. We have to see the manager in person."

"The manager is in a meeting. Wait for him in the veranda or under the tree. Wad Ammoona will call you in when the meeting's over," he said, gazing at us and trying to read our reaction. I could feel him sigh in relief as we went outside, and before we were too far away, I overheard him rebuking Wad Ammoona. Before long, Wad Ammoona came back.

"If you have the proposal in writing, the manager said he will study it and respond to you," he said.

Fekki Ali said, "If he wants to see us, it's fine. If he doesn't want to see us, that's fine too. Does he think we're going to eat him? We're here on business. Go tell him that, Wad Ammoona."

Wad Ammoona twisted his lips as if to say "as you wish" and also "it's none of my business," but we also read between the lines of his gesture and knew that he meant to say we were not up to this task.

Fekki Wad al-Zaghrad loudly recited some incantations and a few short verses from the Holy Quran. His lips and tongue didn't stop until Wad Ammoona returned with a smile so big that his smooth cheeks glistened.

"Please come in," he said. "His Excellency the manager is waiting for you." He went ahead of us, swaying his hips in that feminine way of his, but we didn't pay much attention because we were all used to it. As we entered, we saw two policemen who hadn't been present when we first came in, and we wondered how they had made their way in. We knew both of them: their names and the names of their parents, brothers, and relatives. They were from al-Hillah. We exchanged brief greetings, and they looked a bit surprised. We went up into a spacious office that smelled of money, Wad Ammoona in the lead, cheerful and proud, intoning a famous woman's song.

The manager welcomed us and said he was happy to see us. But we could see clearly that he was trying to quickly find out what we wanted. "Welcome, welcome. Please be seated." I introduced him to the members of the delegation one by one. When it was Fekki Ali's turn, I made a particular stress on the fact that he was credited with numerous noble deeds, alluding to the fact that he could cause tremendous harm to *anyone* at *any time.*

I talked about the role of the bank as we all understood it and explained the purpose of our visit, making particular reference to the feasibility study. He smiled as he glanced furtively at al-Safyah in her new dress, of the "Mutual Advice" brand. His lungs were now probably full of the fragrance of her cheap "Bit al-Sudan" perfume. Trying to look alert and focused, he said, "Give me the feasibility study. I'll read it and share it with the investment manager, then I'll let you know what my decision is. I'm so glad you've come by, and I hope you'll become permanent customers." His tone suggested that he meant to say, "Now get out." Al-Safyah, who seemed to have understood nothing of what he had said—or perhaps she was the only one who had understood—said, "So are you going to give us a loan for the tractor and the plow or not?"

"First the matter has to be studied, and we have to conduct a risk analysis," he said, smiling.

Fekki Ali volunteered to explain what the manager meant to say. "He means we should go now and come back later for an answer."

Abrahait, who announced his presence by clearing his throat twice, said, "We'd better go now. We'll surely receive whatever we're destined to receive."

Without uttering a word, the manager took the feasibility study from me with a smile and flipped through it briefly before placing it on the paper tray. As we went out, Fekki Ali whispered in my ear, "If only I could find out his mother's name, I'd give him hard time. Son of a bitch—he sighs like a true sodomite. He asks for a feasibility study, and when we give it to him he tells us to go and come back later?"

Although we employed our proven skills in tracing rumors and facts, we failed to gather any personal information about the bank manager. Even Wad Ammoona couldn't find out his mother's name or his sign of the zodiac. We had almost given up our attempts in despair when Abrahait suddenly came to our rescue, "Alam Gishi," he said.

Employees who are not native to the locality tend to lead a monotonous life, banding together in one unit and keeping a good distance from the native population. While such a secluded pocket provides them with shelter against rumors and gossip, they can't resist the beauty, tender-heartedness, and humaneness of any self-confident girl. Expatriates are the most vulnerable, as they always long for home and family. To them, the female is a symbol of the continuity of life and a source of warmth. Women in al-Hillah don't really know this, but they nevertheless act—albeit unconsciously—according to that vision. Whether giving or taking, whether boasting or acting modestly, they do so with a significant measure of honor, dignity, and privacy. By their very nature, they are closer to the role of the sister, friend, wife, and lover, than to that of the opportunist or professional prostitute. They are descendants of good families, and they are likely to become good housewives in the future.

Alam Gishi knew those girls. She knew them well. Fekki Ali stretched out his limbs; the ball was in his court now. The man's name was Belal Hassan al-Turki; his mother was Nafiesa bit Abdallah. First, he added the number corresponding to each letter of the first name of the son and mother only, and then he identified the manager's birth sign. With the help of physical properties such as the color, length, and type of his hair, Fekki Ali managed to trace the man's weaknesses by using the book *The Sun of Greatest Knowledge*. He then referred to the science of letters, astronomy, the science of trees, and the so-called black magic. Then he dipped his cane pen in ink and started to write. He did not begin with "In the name of Allah, the most merciful, the most compassionate," but rather with "A (declaration) of immunity from Allah and His Messenger." He wrote it seventy-seven times. He wrapped the paper around a root known as the hoopoe root, inserted it in carefully cleaned shoots from a stem of the castor oil plant, and stirred the mixture with the claw of a male *sinber* bird. Then he asked that a man who had not performed the ritual ablutions take it, burn it, and scatter the ashes in the air on Friday before the call to dawn prayers. That same man was then to draw an image of Solomon's seal on the ground exactly one time.

Alam Gishi's period was now two weeks overdue, and there was no doubt she was pregnant. We rejoiced and started preparations for the newcomer. It didn't matter to me whether it was a boy or a girl; I just wanted a beautiful little baby to live with us and seal our relationship. However, there was no harm in picking a name for now. We agreed to name it Mohammed if it was a boy and Ganish if it was a girl. We had yet to reach an agreement on the names in case it turned out to be twins: she suggested two difficult names of Axumian origin, while I was in favor of two Arabic names. So discussion on the matter was put on hold until further notice. Alam Gishi clearly wanted a baby girl. It was that very desire that had prompted us to get married in the first place. And it was that desire that lent deep meaning and profound pleasure to our lovemaking. I couldn't resist her words, "By God, make me pregnant! I want you to make me pregnant!" My desire coursed over when I heard those words. I discovered that I viewed sex as something inseparably related to reproduction. Pleasure was not a target per se. Each time I had sex with Alam Gishi, I couldn't stop thinking about having a child. My friend viewed sex as a human duty, a necessity for one to become a perfect human being. To al-Safyah, sex was a purely psychological matter, evidence of one's fundamental identity.

"Without reproduction as its underlying objective, sex is reduced to a sort of mechanical pleasure exercise," I used to tell him.

"So you believe in 'a love story behind every single sex act?'" he asked.

"And a child. What's the value of love without children in mind?"

He laughed at me. "You're too romantic," he said, mimicking the jargon of Egyptian romance films.

My relationship with Alam Gishi had developed into a solid love affair. I sensed that from gossip and rumors in discussions at the *mareesa* houses. And I thought Alam Gishi had the same impression. I was told bluntly at the Khadoum house last Monday, "That woman loves you. And you know that when an Ethiopian woman loves a man, only death can separate them. Congratulations."

And they said the same to her. "They asked me, 'What have you done to that man?'" she once told me.

If what they were saying was true, then I must have fallen in love for the first time in my life. If not, our relationship was still in need of a definition. Yet it had the ability to last, despite the lack of a definition, so long as the baby—girl or boy—kept waving fingers from within our bodies, our desires, and our affectionate touches, so long as it kept giggling inside us.

Fekki Ali al-Zaghrad had once told me that I was going to have a long marital life with lots of children. Al-Zaghrad was a nickname that literally meant the one who ululated. Fekki Ali was a pious man, a grandson of a religious man named Sulaiman al-Zaghrad, whose name was cited in the book *Kitab al-Tabaqat* by Wad Daifallah. But Fekki Ali al-Zaghrad strongly believed that the al-Zaghrad mentioned in Wad Daifallah's book was a false one because Fekki Ali's grandfather, Sulaiman, had never worked as an assistant to *mareesa* makers, as the book mentioned. He had come from Dar Gimir in Western Sudan to study under Sheikh Mohammed al-Hameem. His grandfather was a truly pious sheikh who could perform miracles, such as turning water into curdled milk. And all he had to do was ululate, and the obstacles disappeared from his path, and those who had been absent returned, and those who had been distant came closer; difficulties dissolved themselves when he ululated, and grief was driven away. People there believed in Allah, His messengers, His angels, and His demons. They also believed in Fekki al-Zaghrad, and they accepted his predictions as faultless prophecies and divine revelations. That fact might have lent a great deal of stability to our marriage, particularly since Alam Gishi was an unequivocal believer in Fekki al-Zaghrad. For my part, I thought of him as a man who had certain proven skills and the power to influence others, which were driven purely by worldly and material faculties. He appreciated and respected my opinion, although he also believed he possessed spiritual powers, had djinn servants, and was knowledgeable in the secrets of plants, the science of letters, and palm and face reading. Furthermore, he claimed to be a descendant of the Prophet, and of *al-Ashraf*. I once asked him who *al-Ashraf* were. "They're the Quraish, the Prophet's tribe," he replied.

"I thought the Arabian tribes that migrated to Sudan were from Gohayna," I said.

"We're the descendants of al-Hassan and al-Hussain, sons of Fatima and Ali,[1] may God's peace be upon them," he said, smiling.

"I see," I said. I was preoccupied with memories of the two youngsters who had been martyred—one at the hands of Yazid ibn Moawiyah, and the other at the hands of Moawiyah ibn Abi Sofeyan himself—in ancient times in the Arabian Peninsula and al-Sham.[2]

---

[1] Fatima is the Prophet's daughter; Ali is her husband and the Prophet's cousin.

[2] The name for the Eastern Mediterranean region, roughly equivalent to modern-day Syria and Lebanon.

19 THE SHIT REVOLT

It was May, late May. It had been over a month now since I moved to the farm to prepare for the new agricultural season. The ten acres I had bought needed to be cleared of *kitir*, *laout*, and *taleh* trees. I had two workers to help me: Mukhtar Ali and Ibrahim Osman, nicknamed al-Shaygi. Although Ibrahim was originally from the Gaalieen tribe, his parents, on the advice of some relatives, marked him at birth with the Shaygiyah tribal facial scars so he could avoid the fate of his brothers who had all died before the age of five. The trick worked for him: he was almost fifty now.

Both were active and energetic Jungojorai with good farming experience, skillful in clearing the land and harvesting, and well versed in indigenous pest control tactics. No one was better than them in that domain except al-Danabari, who was very skillful in combating locusts.

Both were single. Mukhtar was older, in his late fifties. Al-Shaygi, in his late forties, was tall and well built, with a brown complexion and a thick mustache. Both were illiterate. We'd been living there almost permanently since March, in a hut and a *rakuba*. We used the hut to store our food and belongings, and as a shelter when it got too cold. The *rakuba* was for sleeping, napping, and chatting. Our kitchen was the open outdoor space; we used stones for an oven. And any place where people couldn't see you was a lavatory. We rode on donkeys to procure our water from the Setit River through the Zahanah inlet, the nearest one to us. We stored it in huge steel barrels. Water was the only thing that brought us into the village once a week. We had sufficient supplies of food: *kajaik*, dried meat, *om takasho, kambo, frendo, waikah,* salt, and dried chili. We also had plenty of sorghum flour, enough to last us for months. And add to this the fresh meat that the forest lavishly bestowed upon us in the form of rats, rabbits, birds, turtles, boar, pythons, etc., and we ought to have considered ourselves in a small paradise where everything that a Jungojorai dreams of was at our disposal. I must say, though, that food in general is not a big issue for a Jungojorai; he can eat anything that flies, anything that swims, and anything that moves on land—except people, that is.

Since I had decided to be one of the Jungojorai, I made up my mind to integrate myself fully into the fabric of this community. While I took a convenient shortcut—a woman—to achieve this, there were some rough lessons that I still had to learn, particularly the harsh nature of the work. With the help of my social insurance entitlement, which I had received the previous month, I paid the price of the land and left the balance with Alam Gishi to procure her personal needs. She had brought in another woman to lend her a hand at the telecom company's residential compound, and had agreed to share her salary with her. In fact, we were trying to protect our upcoming child.

Al-Shaygi and Mukhtar Ali did not cost much. Apart from the daily meals that we all shared, they needed only cigarettes, snuff, and *mareesa*. The *mareesa* was homemade: al-Shaygi used the porridge and *kisra* leftovers and some flour from the stock to produce a thin type of *mareesa* known as *baganiyah*, which is actually closer to *asaliyah*. They didn't drink it in al-Hillah, where it was not very popular, and where it was dubbed "the *mareesa* of the faithful." I was not particularly fond of *baganiyah*, being loyal to date arrack and imported alcohol. That was when I had surplus money. When I was broke, I quit drinking, unwilling to buy on credit.

We cut down all the big trees and used the big trunks to make twenty huge charcoal ovens. It was a backbreaking job, but it gave us a strong sense of achievement: we had managed to create value out of nothing. I had made it clear from the very beginning that I was going to share the charcoal sales revenue equally with Mukhtar Ali and al-Shaygi. The result was an incredible amount of work completed in record time. We sold three shipments to charcoal brokers in Qedaref, Khashm El Girba, and Showak. The terms of the sales were on-site pickup, which was less profitable but spared us the trouble of loading and transportation, as well as endless taxes, bribes, and levies that policemen invented as soon as they saw a truck loaded with coal.

The number of Jungo in al-Hillah began to increase. The agricultural season was about to begin across the entire East, and the lack of finances brought the bank issue to the fore again. The Jungo were aware that the bank had extended loans to large-scale farmers in Qedaref and Fashaga, all the way to Khashm El Girba and Kasala. It had supplied them with tractors and plows, as well as cash loans—or *salam*, as they were called. The Jungo were wondering why their request had not been considered. Why should they be discriminated against? They were the experts of that land. They were the ones who cleared, cultivated, and harvested it, and the ones who fought its pests. They were the ones who produced sorghum and sesame. Why wouldn't the bank trust them? That issue was the main topic of discussion among the Jungo. They were penniless in that miserable month of May: no jobs, no money, no *mareesa*-drinking festivals. As the price of sorghum skyrocketed, so did the price of *mareesa*. But thanks to the generosity of the *mareesa* sellers, the Jungo could still drink on credit: money borrowed was documented in the form of scratches on the walls. They could also provide their personal belongings as security or mortgage: cassette recorders, sunglasses, shirts, radio sets, anything of value, and things of no value too.

Thanks to those arrangements, the Jungo could still meet in the *mareesa* houses. There we had long debates about the bank and its role in the community. Many were in support of going back to the bank with a new proposal: that they should give us a small loan and a tractor with a plow. Twenty people who owned houses registered in their names volunteered to mortgage their houses as security for the loan. I too offered my small farm.

The Jungo who were gathering in front of the bank were a surprise to no one except the bank employees and security. All of al-Hillah's men, women, and children knew that the Jungo were going to go to the bank on Saturday and that they had only one request: "Try us with one farm, one tractor, and a loan of no more than five hundred thousand pounds."

We were approximately one hundred Jungo, Jungojoraya, and children. We were soon joined by small-scale merchants who had been denied loans. The frustrated merchants revealed many of the bank's secret deals with large-scale merchants and owners of large farms. They specifically told us that the bank wanted them to work under the large-scale farmers so that the latter could pay back the bank's loans.

The bank manager did not seek the help of police and security as there was no demonstration nor any threats of violence. It was a peaceful round of negotiations led by al-Safyah and myself. The rest listened and looked on—their contributions were keeping silent, remaining disciplined, and refraining from instigating a riot.

The bank manager had two reservations. First, he couldn't extend a loan to a group that had no official recognition. We were neither a union nor a registered company: we were just a group of people—an anonymous group, as he called us. The other reservation was also clear: he wanted a guarantee. He wanted some registered land as a guarantee, or some kind of financial guarantee. That was the bank's policy. We told him we had twenty residential plots in al-Hillah, and a small ten-acre farm—no property in city, no valuable assets, no real land. We said if we had any of those things, we wouldn't be so poor, and surely wouldn't be small-scale farmers. He said the bank's mission was to support the poor and small-scale farmers, but on terms that protected its capital. And of course, he couldn't go beyond his mandate and violate the bank's policies.

"I'll communicate all these points to the head office in Khartoum and we'll wait for their decision," he finally said. Al-Safyah, who had kept silent ever since we walked into the manager's office, suddenly said, "So are you going to give us the loan or not?"

"Right now, no."

Al-Safyah turned to me and said, "Let's go. What are you waiting for?"

Before we left, I thanked him for his hospitality; he had served us cold water and two Pepsi bottles brought by Wad Ammoona. Outside, the Jungo were waiting in small groups. They surrounded us at the entrance, but Abrahait, who was in charge of organizational affairs, said without consulting me, "Let's all meet tonight at Addai's house, in the backyard."

Under a full moon, some 300 people thronged the Mother's backyard, the usual place for parties. At the outset, Fekki Ali recited verses from the Holy Quran. His voice trembled when he reached the verse "*And we wanted to confer favor upon those who were oppressed in the land and make them leaders and make them inheritors.*"

He was followed by Father Peter, the Church pastor, who read a small prayer from the Bible: "But now, all you who light fires and provide yourselves with flaming torches, go, walk in the light of your fires and of the torches you have set ablaze. This is what you shall receive from my hand: You will lie down in torment."

The debate centered on one thing: what should we do? Boycott work in the fields? We'd be the first to starve. Continue to work as laborers? We wouldn't gain much: we'd continue, season after season, to spend all the money we earned, and the only people who would benefit would be the *jallabis*, the investors.

"Rob the bank," a Jungo suggested. The group's response was that they didn't want to be jailed or have to confront the police, which could result in losses and injuries. Suad Yohannes, mother of one of the two policemen, said, "If we kill our sons in the police, or if they kill us, what will any of us gain?"

Suddenly my friend chimed in, "Fight them with shit."

The entire place fell into utter silence. The word sounded strange, as if it had been uttered by mistake, or as if they had misheard him.

"Yes, with *shit*. Don't you know *shit*?" he said, his eyes shining with resolve, leaving no room for doubt. They laughed, taking it as a joke or something from one of his bizarre adventures.

"You've all heard of the Indians, haven't you?" he continued. "The Indians forced out the mighty British with a simple weapon: shit. The elderly among you—Mukhtar Ali, Fekki al-Zaghrad, Abrahait, al-Shaygi, Addai, and others—surely remember Mahatma Gandhi. He was the leader of the shit revolt."

Little by little, people began to grasp the idea. And they slowly appointed the first hundred people who would do the required job. And then they named the first fifty, then the first thirty. Everything was set. Early the next morning, when the employees woke up, they were unable to leave the residential compound for work. Piles of fetid shit stood defiantly at the door. So they tore down the cane fence, and had to turn the broken canes into a bridge, which they crossed to get to the street. When they reached the bank office, it was swamped in shit. No one could come near it, and an army of green flies took over and became the sole owners and general managers of the place.

The bank management sought the assistance of the public health workers, who argued that clearing shit was beyond the scope of their duties, as they were exclusively contracted to clean dry substances. The bank manager asked the police to arrest the perpetrators and force them to remove the shit, but the prosecutor's office turned down that request, saying that defecating in public spaces was not a crime punishable by law and that there was no local ordinance prohibiting it. "And how would we identify those who had defecated—by the shape of their shit, or by its color?" Deep down, they sided with the Jungo, as the bank was known to be associated with a particular political group that they were not part of.

The bank manager and a team of five officials took their Land Cruiser and left for Qedaref. The next day, a hundred Jungo laid shit inside the deserted compound: inside the rooms, on the beds, and inside the purified water containers. They put a good quantity of shit in the refrigerator, the electric appliances, and the utensils. They left another stock in large plastic shopping bags under the beds and in the kitchen, and also hung some bags from ceilings. On the third day, all the Jungo were so desperate to get out of al-Hillah at any cost that they accepted to work clearing shrubs for some merchants without bargaining on the price for their labor.

One week after the incident, the bank officials returned in the company of a truck full of riot police armed with machine guns, tear gas, rubber batons, shields, whips, and a firefighting truck. They tried to wash off the dirt with pressurized water from hoses connected to the fire truck, but to no avail, for the stuff was so thick and sticky that water only served to spread it around. The riot police stayed for a full month in a small camp near the bank. Although the compound was totally deserted, some neighbors continued to deliver shopping bags full of fresh and fetid shit by throwing them over the walls.

Al-Shaygi and Mukhtar Ali returned to the fields, and my friend went back to Qedaref and on to Khartoum, while I stayed in al-Hillah to entertain Alam Gishi. I didn't see Wad Ammoona, and when I asked Alam Gishi, she said he had been in Qedaref and had only reported to work at the bank that morning. He was to resume his work at Addai's house in the evening. I wondered why he was wearing himself out working so much when he had no one to look after—even his relations with his mother were severed.

"Wad Ammoona is working hard for the sake of Azza," she said.

Alam Gishi told me a widely known story, which was identical to Wad Ammoona's version. When Azza was released from prison, she took Wad Ammoona with her. She had promised both him and his mother that she would take good care of him, as if he were her own son, and that she would enroll him in school. But she was soon confronted with endless problems from her family. Her father and brothers gave her two options: either to quickly marry whoever was willing to marry her or to quit the work she had engaged herself in as soon as she was released. Selling tea and coffee at the al-Gooni souk was a mean job and a big embarrassment to the wealthy family. They wanted her to stay at home. But Azza rejected all the options and defiantly continued to work at the al-Gooni souk. The number of clients grew, and she opened a small restaurant beside her coffee shop—it offered traditional meals. She enrolled Wad Ammoona in a private school in Hai Karfis and rented a house in Hai al-Asra, which was near her work. She was decent and respectful, was not known to engage in any unlawful activities, and did nothing to annoy the neighbors.

Despite all this, her brothers were far from convinced. They plotted to scare her out of Qedaref—they didn't care where she went. She was aware of their plot and was ready to resist it. Two of her brothers broke into her house and beat her several times, and a group of paid thugs attacked her at work. In all these incidents, she fought back fiercely and boldly. They eventually changed their tactics and targeted Wad Ammoona instead. They commissioned some homeless boys and benzene addicts to beat him on his way to school or wherever they found him. Some perverts among them even tried to sodomize him, but he managed to ward them off, thanks to the fighting skills his mother had taught him. When he informed Azza, she set an ambush for them and beat them severely. In her rage, she stabbed two of them, killing one and incapacitating the other.

And so she found herself behind bars again, this time convicted of premeditated murder. Although the family of the boys, who had come out of the blue, agreed to take blood money, she couldn't afford it even after it had been reduced to only five hundred thousand pounds, following extensive negotiations that many kind-hearted people conducted with the family of the deceased. That reduced amount was still too much for the lonely woman. Her poor friends tried their best to help, but the little they eventually managed to collect didn't make any difference. Only Wad Ammoona continued to work with Addai and others to collect the blood money so that Azza could be set free. About a month earlier, he had told me that only one hundred pounds were now outstanding, so his trip to Qedaref might have been for that purpose.

When I met Wad Ammoona this time, I saw a great hero in him. When I asked him about Azza, he talked about how brave, generous, and humane she was and expounded the suffering her family had put her through. I asked if he had approached the Zakat office. He let out a sarcastic laugh. First, they had asked him to submit a certificate of poverty from the local council, then a copy of the verdict, then a biography of Azza. Finally, they said the funds allocated for defaulters this year had been exhausted, and he had to wait till next year. The following year, it was the same story: the funds allotted for defaulters had to be reallocated to the cause of propagating faith among *al-Moallafatu Gloobahom*, i.e., those who showed potential for embracing Islam. They said they would try to accommodate his request the following year. But Wad Ammoona was aware that the Zakat office had paid millions of pounds to prominent merchants from Khashm El Girba to settle their debts to the bank after they swore to God that they were bankrupt. At the same time, those allegedly bankrupt merchants were known to have huge assets: tractors, trucks, buses, properties, stores of building materials, and trading agencies.

I asked him about his mother. He said she had married a prison guard right after her release, and when her new husband was transferred to Shala Prison in al-Fashir, she went with him. Since Wad Ammoona refused to go with her, and since her husband was not enthusiastic about taking him along, Ammoona agreed to leave him with her trusty friend Addai. They had lived together in Om Hagar after Addai retired from service in the Popular Front for the Liberation of Eritrea. Wad Ammoona had no difficulty adapting himself to life with Addai; he had been born in al-Hillah and had lived there for a good part of his childhood.

At Addai's house, he met Alam Gishi, who took good care of him. He wasn't able to tell what brought the two women together. And when I later asked Alam Gishi, she simply said, "Business."

It was a challenging time for me: unemployment, preparations for the new agricultural season, preparations for the baby, and the now-unemployed Alam Gishi. Despite all this, I volunteered to pay half the outstanding amount of the blood money, but Wad Ammoona refused to take it, for what he considered objective considerations: first, it was the beginning of the season, and I needed every penny to prepare my land, and I had no experience in farming and might underestimate how much money was needed; second, he wouldn't be able to afford the other half of the amount until the end of October, as he had just paid a big installment last week, from his share in a savings plan with friends. He wouldn't be able to fully pay back the remaining amount until June. So Azza would have to remain in prison past October anyway. He suggested that I invest my money in my land and make my contribution at the end of the season, if all went well. I was embarrassed by how warmly he thanked me, and before I left for the fields, he came to our hut in the evening and gave me a piece of advice: "Don't take a large amount of money with you. You don't know what will turn up on the road. And don't trust just anyone." He wasn't willing to provide any further explanation. He promised to stay with Alam Gishi in her hut to serve her until I returned. "Don't worry. Alam Gishi is my sister," he said.

Rainfall became an almost regular occurrence after the mid-June storm. It was quite heavy rainfall, although some experienced Jungo believed it was not an exceptionally bountiful season. "It's not an extraordinarily good start, but it's a promising one. If the initial rains are heavy enough, then the entire season will be successful," they said.

I was advised to start early. Before long, the fields teemed with Jungo chanting away their weariness as they patiently plowed and spread sesame seeds, exerting no end of sweat to produce food to feed millions, while they themselves were left deprived of their dreams. They didn't have the patience to think things over. The shit revolt didn't inspire any other ideas, projects, or positive actions in them. It disappeared like a silly joke that briefly amused them before dying down. So they went back to work, which was where their real value lay, and forgot everything else. The Jungo wanted money, and the only way to get money was to work long and hard, which would in most cases land them under the death tree in Fariek Girish in al-Homra, or under some other tree somewhere.

We woke up one morning to some strange news about bandits—*falloul* or *shifta*—at the Khor Anater creek, which ran through the center of the western farms, between al-Shagarab and al-Hillah. That place had remained secure even during the Eritrean-Ethiopian war, and during the war between the government army and the armed opposition in the 1980s and 1990s. That was why people were astonished to learn that the bandits were not Ethiopians or Eritreans. They were Sudanese, and more precisely, they were Jungo, and some had been identified by name. They carried axes, spears, daggers, and swords. About ten black men had looted a pickup truck that was carrying passengers to the al-Shagarab camp. They took all the valuables in the passengers' possession: watches, money, and new shoes. They also took away a pistol the driver had hidden under his seat, along with a case of imported spirits. Later the same day, they attacked the checkpoint at the Showak and Shagarab junction, seized a Kalashnikov machine gun and a GM3 rifle, and fled into the Zahanah forest on a pickup that they had taken from the checkpoint, which was later found near the village of al-Jairah.

When news of such stunning incidents reached al-Hillah, it gave birth to equally stunning rumors. Rumors went the rounds that the Jungo had begun to revolt and were now attacking the government army at Zahanah and Hamdayeit with the help of weapons obtained from Eritrea. Taking the rumors for granted, the military and security authorities called in the garrisons of Khashm El Girba and Qedaref to crush the Jungo revolt. Instead of sending an army, the government, an expert in local strife and armed revolts, sent a fact-finding committee headed by a senior security officer. The committee, which was guarded by an armored vehicle, visited the operation theaters and interviewed the victims. It then set up a local committee that interrogated the residents before filing its report:

> Five seasonal project workers are committing subversive acts for unknown reasons, most likely driven by want of money. They are armed with a pistol, a GM3 rifle, a Kalashnikov machine gun, and knives. Some of them were army ex-soldiers. They are not inclined to shed blood. The residents were able to identify them as Taha Koko Nimir (retired soldier), Abdallah Khair al-Seed al-Tayeb, Burhan Takhali Waldo, Deng Mayom Ajang (former soldier), and Ibrahim Osman al-Shaygi. They are now somewhere in the Zahanah forest, and may have crossed the Setit River to al-Homra, or they may be roving somewhere between those places and Ethiopia.

The report recommended that the roads linking al-Hillah to al-Shagarab—the Hamdayeit-al-Jaira road and the *al-Hafeera-Zahanah* road—be guarded and that a military patrol search for the gang in the Zahanah forest. The report stressed that no citizen should be arrested or harmed in any way and that the army should abstain from involvement in any armed clashes except if the enemy opened fire first or set an ambush. They left behind a full contingent of highly trained riot police—roughly built youngsters with robust muscles and athletic bodies, their heads shaven in the style of the army commandos. The residents nicknamed them the owls, which reflected a mean opinion of them.

I should have been the first to guess that al-Shaygi had joined the bandits. Although he had left without making the slightest hint of his intentions, I remembered he harbored deep grudges against the bank because he believed that the bank and the government were biased toward rich merchants, and against the Jungo. In fact, we all shared this belief, but did that justify intimidating and attacking citizens, and stealing their money and property? And who knows? Such acts could well lead to human lives being lost. There must be a missing link somewhere, and Mukhtar Ali and I tried to identify it. We finally concluded that al-Shaygi and his companions might have wanted an easy life and easy money. Work in the fields was hard, and one could barely make ends meet with income from that work, and only for a limited period of time. The workers had no access to social insurance, health insurance, end-of-service benefits, or pensions—it was a futile life, a "vain life," as Mukhtar Ali put it. But now they were risking their lives. Easy money leads to easy death. We made up our minds to go find them, at the very least to learn the facts of the matter.

20 ALAM GISHI'S REVOLT

I understood from Wad Ammoona's message, delivered verbally by a Jungo, that Alam Gishi was sick and that I had to come see her as fast as I could. I made the necessary arrangements for the farm with Mukhtar Ali and took Hamdayeit's morning truck to al-Hillah. I found her at home, drinking coffee with Wad Ammoona. She was beautiful and smiling as usual, though she looked somewhat pale. I also read some disappointment in her face, as if she had not been expecting me to come. Wad Ammoona went outside to give us some privacy, pretending he had some chores to do.

She said she had not been willing to tell me about her illness and that Wad Ammoona had acted on his own. She started speaking in an unusually aggressive tone. "I had a miscarriage two days ago," she said. "The baby was in its fifth month." It was a big shock to me. It had never occurred to me that such a thing could happen. I felt a severe pain in my stomach, and a feeling of failure came over me. I tried to avoid looking at her belly, tried to convince myself that it was one of those rough Ethiopian pranks and that the baby was still there, alive and kicking. The more seconds passed without Alam Gishi backing off from her painful prank, the more vividly I saw the world falling apart and dying before my very eyes.

"Everything is finished between us," she snapped. I hoped all this was nothing but a bad dream. The woman who was standing in front of me bore little resemblance to my wife and darling Alam Gishi. "Each of us has to take a different route," she added in the same sharp tone. When I asked what she meant by that, she kept saying she just didn't want me anymore. I began to think that she might have gone mad. I said I loved her and would never leave her; I was her sweetheart and her legal husband. I told her she'd give birth to another child and said that if miscarriage was painful to her, it was even more so to me. I embraced her. She was ice cold, as inanimate as a rock, and kept repeating in a painful mechanical tone, "It's over. It's all over now."

"Leave her alone for now," I advised myself. "Let her get over the shock. A day or two and everything will be normal again." But I was too perplexed to settle on any particular course of action. In my bewilderment, I began to look out for Wad Ammoona. It didn't take me long to find him; he was always exactly where you wanted him to be. We discussed Alam Gishi's condition. He said she had been in this condition since the day of her miscarriage. He advised me to consult Addai, saying she was the only person who could convince her to reverse her decision. We explained everything to Addai, who sympathized with us. She had been by her side during previous miscarriages and was well aware of the inner turmoil they caused her. She asked us to walk around for an hour or so until she had had a word with Alam Gishi in private.

After her meeting with Addai, Alam Gishi was a bit better; she showed a bit more leniency and tolerance toward me. However, our relationship became increasingly tense. Neither of us was to blame for the abortion. I didn't blame her, and she didn't hold me responsible either. But she was acting unusually aggressively toward me. I'm not referring only to the biting and kicking and deliberate soiling of my clothes but also to a campaign of demonization, as she went around accusing me of exploiting her and stealing her jewelry and money. Fekki Ali al-Zaghrad diagnosed her condition as "lunacy."

Addai kept urging me to be patient. She was worried that Alam Gishi might have been bewitched; indeed, people here had done far worse things. Could it be that Alam Gishi was suffering from simple frustration as a result of exhaustion? I thought of taking her to the

Tigani al-Mahi Psychiatric Hospital in Omdurman. In my bewilderment and grief, I missed my friend; he could have come to my rescue with some quixotic solution. I did everything in my power to improve the situation, but to no avail. My last hope was for Alam Gishi to become pregnant again and give birth to a healthy baby. I adored her and was not prepared to let her take any other course of action in that rough territory. Women here worked as Jungojoraya, makers of local liquor, or prostitutes, or a combination of those things. But none of that suited Alam Gishi. Before we got married, I had thought of her as someone who could work in any of those domains, including prostitution. Indeed, as a prostitute, she had entertained me as a client, and I had admired her ability to provide pleasure. I was also aware that at one time, she had worked as an arrack maker and as a Jungojoraya for several seasons. But now, I saw her as an innocent, fragile person, shy and helpless; a good-for-nothing child; a mother at a loss. Leaving her alone at this juncture would mean leaving her to meet her doom.

I stayed with her at home in al-Hillah for fifty straight days, during which time she occasionally behaved normally, but mostly acted insane. She frequently had a compelling desire to get pregnant, though at other times she showed no desire at all. The time I spent with her was truly insane, rife with tumult and pain, though not entirely devoid of pleasure.

I took leave of her and returned to the farm, leaving her in the company of Wad Ammoona and Addai. Hardly a month had passed when Wad Ammoona sent me another message with a Jungo informing me that Alam Gishi was pregnant again: she had missed her period that month. There was something else too: she was determined to go back to her ex-husband, and I might miss her entirely unless I rushed back. The first thing that sprang to my mind was that Alam Gishi must surely have gone mad this time. The only sensible option I had was to take her to Khartoum as quickly as possible. I made the necessary arrangements for Mukhtar Ali to take over responsibility for the work and provided him with sufficient food and money, enough to sustain him and the workers to the end of the season. Once again, I found myself on a Hamdayeit bus to al-Hillah. Wad Ammoona met me at the bus terminal and told me the story in detail. Had it not been for Addai and him, Alam Gishi would have already left for Hamdayeit. He was confident that she was not insane and advised me to act wisely. She was adamant that she would go to Hamdayeit and that I had to divorce her because she wanted to reunite with the father of her two daughters. She said she had already consulted him on this, and he had agreed, and that he was now waiting for her.

"If you refuse to divorce me, I'll go to Hamdayeit against your will," she said bluntly.

"But you're pregnant!"

"I'll send you the baby after I give birth," she said indifferently.

Everyone was convinced that demonic forces had a hand in this and that envious people had stirred up an evil plot with some sorcerers. Fingers were pointed at many, including Fekki Ali al-Zaghrad himself, although he categorically denied any involvement, swearing by the Prophet and by Sheikh Mohammed al-Hameem and his grandfather Sheikh Sulaiman al-Zaghrad. He even offered to cure her, but she refused, insisting there was nothing wrong with her; it was the others who were insane. I asked her why she had to leave, and she said she just wanted to be reunited with her ex-husband and live with her daughters. That was all.

"And what about me?"

"It's up to you. There are plenty of women. Pick who you like."

A conciliation team composed up of respectful and influential men and women from al-Hillah was quickly set up. They talked about the sacredness of matrimony and social ties, about the devil, about evil men and evil women, and about envy, and fate.

"I want to go back to the father of my daughters," she told them.

"But you're married."

"I want him to divorce me."

"I won't divorce you. You're pregnant. Deliver the baby first."

"I'll send you the baby right after delivery, unless there's a miscarriage like the last time!"

Her last comment alarmed me—it could only come from a lunatic. I would divorce her if she could convince me that that was what she really wanted, and that her desire was not prompted by some psychological disorder. Suddenly, a new idea came to me. "I'll let her go to Hamdayeit and stay with her daughters," I told them.

The conciliators were taken aback. "The father of her daughters is there," they said.

"He knows she's not divorced. I'll leave it up to both of them," I said.

"But she's still your wedded wife."

"That's a different issue. It will be resolved by the law."

People had a whole range of opinions on what came to be known as "the Alam Gishi story." At the intervention of the manager of the telecom company, the resident judge, the local council director, and some conciliators, an agreement was finally reached. Alam Gishi agreed to call off the plan to go to Hamdayeit on one condition: that I don't stay with her. I could stay with Mukhtar Ali until the situation was resolved. We both accepted the deal, although she agreed only reluctantly.

I left her at the house that Addai had left for us, hoping to be able to cure her during this transitional period. I decided to begin the course of treatment from Hamdayeit: to visit her ex-husband and consult him. I truly hoped he could help. I took Wad Ammoona along because he had shown great interest in accompanying me and also because I needed him. Although he was younger than me, I confess that he was also more socially mature. We took the Hamdayeit bus, a truck somehow reconfigured to carry people. It had narrow steel seats and steel windows that were left wide open in all seasons. People rode inside it, on top of it, and to the right and left of the driver: it would go at full speed, hopping over pits and creeks like an old fox trying to outrun its hunters. Its roar was overheard from long distances across the nutrient-poor trees of the savannah, attracting the attention of rabbits, rats, monkeys, and of the Jungojora deployed in fields deep within the farms. The driver kept reminding us that whoever wanted to take the bus to al-Jairah, al-Hafeera, Hamdayeit, or the adjacent villages had to wait for the bus along its route, which meandered through the Zahanah forest, between *taleh* and kitir *trees*. In this rainy season, the bus let out thick smoke as it struggled with the wet, muddy soil.

Passengers were chatting about rain, the advantages of early seed sowing, and other hot topics. For some reason that was beyond me, I found myself thinking about al-Safyah. I had always drawn comparisons between Alam Gishi and al-Safyah. In fact, there were no big differences between them. Alam Gishi would find herself, unconsciously or intentionally, committing acts or saying things that hardly reflected her true self. Al-Safyah, on the other hand, was adjudged (during mini-seminars at Adalia Daniyal's house last summer) to have two characters: a visible, more dominant character, which we dealt with daily, and another one that would become visible only when she was sexually aroused. So both women had two characters, assuming we could call al-Safyah a woman, based on the testimony of the two men and that of al-Safyah herself.

Wad Ammoona, who rarely lacked talking points, confided to me something he said he had never shared with anyone else. It involved my friend. After his incident with al-Safyah, my friend spoke with Wad Ammoona in private and told him he wanted to ask him a few questions that he wanted clear and candid answers to. Wad Ammoona agreed.

"Are you homosexual?" was the first question.

"No," was the answer.

"You need to identify yourself," he said nervously. "No one knows if you're a woman or a man!"

"I am neither a woman nor a man. I perform the functions of both men and women. So I am both a man and a woman," Wad Ammoona said, trying to tease him. "I am a *wixi*, midway between a boy and a *chicksy*," he added, echoing how a friend in Qedaref used to describe him.

Perplexed, my friend said, "Speak more clearly. What do you mean by women's functions and men's functions? What do you mean by *wixi* and *chicksy*?"

Wad Ammoona replied, "Tell me which one you'd like to hear about—men's functions or women's—and I'll give you a practical explanation."

Suddenly Wad Ammoona went silent because the bus had come to an abrupt halt that violently jolted all the passengers. Before we could hurl abuses at the driver and curse his mother and father, we saw masked men circling the bus. A familiar voice shouted,

"Come down, one by one, silently. Women and children, stay where you are. Men, bring your bags down with you."

We dismounted. The trunk of a large tree had been laid across the road, at a spot where the road naturally narrowed. Although they were masked, we recognized all of them, except for a few who stood a bit farther away carrying machine guns. We knew we had to pretend not to recognize the looters. We needed to obey and pay, keep our mouths shut, lower our heads, and avoid eye contact with them. One of them, known as Taha Kooko, said to us men, "We want half the money that each of you is carrying. And driver, we want *all* the money you've got, plus the money sent from Qedaref for the merchant Adam Idris al-Bilalawi. *Hurry up*!"

We swiftly carried out their orders. Taha, who was apparently the spokesperson for the group, added, "We are not *shifta*. We are victims of injustice who want to reclaim our rights. We won't work like slaves anymore. We'll take our rights by force. Tell this to the fat merchants who are sucking your blood."

After taking the money, they pushed the trunk away and let us go. In a flash, they vanished into the forest. Wad Ammoona said to me after they had gone, "Didn't I advise you not to trust just anyone, and not to carry a large amount of money with you? Did you see your friend al-Shaygi?"

A noteworthy addition: the Jungo were all armed with Kalashnikovs. There were around twenty of them, and some wore government army uniforms. More importantly, they acted quite calmly and seemed neither in a hurry nor confused. When we arrived at Hamdayeit, people were talking about a government patrol that disappeared yesterday and about a Jungo revolt.

The fate of the Jungo wasn't exactly my biggest concern at that particular moment. Wad Ammoona expertly led me to a house where Alam Gishi's daughters lived with their grandfather, a rich, talkative old man. The elder daughter looked like her mother, except that she was a bit taller. The younger daughter also looked like her mother. Both were attractive and slender. They gave us a warm welcome when they understood I was their stepfather. They asked about their mother's health, noting that they hadn't seen her for over two years. After a while, their father came in. The grandfather withdrew.

We were astonished to find out that she had separated from her ex-husband in the same way she had from me. "She said she hated me," he said nervously. "I left my daughters with my parents and divorced her—and she married you. That woman's very strange. Something's wrong with her."

"People in al-Hillah think that it was you who deserted her and took away your daughters," Wad Ammoona said.

"That's not true, I swear to God," he said nervously. "You can ask all the people in Zahanah. I asked scores of people to mediate, but she refused. She left the girls with me and ran away. People advised me to divorce her so that she couldn't disgrace me. And I divorced her on their advice."

"So what should I do?" I asked helplessly.

"Divorce her. Divorce her as soon as possible," he said confidently. "That's the only solution."

"I've never known another woman my whole life. There was no one before her, and there will be no one after her."

"Divorce her, man," he said, as if he hadn't heard me.

"And will you take her back? Will you remarry her?"

"Yes, I will. She's the mother of my daughters. And if she decides to leave me again, I'll divorce her so you can take her back."

I thought he couldn't possibly be serious, or perhaps he wasn't aware of what he was saying. But he sounded dead serious. It was just the two of us; Wad Ammoona had sneaked out, as usual, when he felt the subject needed to be discussed between the two of us. The two daughters had left earlier with their grandfather.

He went on, showing no sign of changing his position: "One turn for you and one turn for me; all according to the Sunnah of Allah and His Apostle. If you don't like this arrangement, look for another woman." Then he added, "I wonder what it is about her that makes you cling so strongly? Women are like the tail of a lizard. If you cut it off, it grows back. And if you cut it off again, it grows back again—twenty times."

"I really don't know if . . . "

"Divorce her, man," he interrupted me. "If you don't, she'll kill you and flee to Ethiopia. Even the devil won't be able to find her again. I know those Ethiopian women. They're either faithful to you to the very end or they desert you once and for all—there's nothing in between. They don't know what compromise is."

"But Alam Gishi's sick."

"You're the one who's sick. That woman wants her daughters and the father of her daughters. Why are you standing in her way?"

"But she's pregnant with my child."

"I know," he said matter-of-factly. "When she delivers and your baby is strong enough, we'll send it to you. When she deserted me, I left my daughters with my mother. You also can give your baby to your mother, or your aunt, or any of your relatives. And when Alam Gishi comes to hate me, you can remarry her. It's so simple. Don't get upset about it."

Insane as it sounded, his logic managed to win me over, and when I left I was determined to divorce Alam Gishi. At least, I told myself, she would be in safe hands and would lead a happy life with her husband and daughters.

He thanked me and assured me that the moment she came to hate him again, he would send her back to me, with a divorce note in her hand.

I told Alam Gishi as we walked to the bus, "Please take care of that guy in there."

"I will," she said, letting out her first smile since the beginning of the crisis.

The bus left under the guard of the army and riot police, as had become the custom recently. Alam Gishi was the epitome of beauty, her eyes shining with overwhelming joy, although a streak of madness marked the blue rings around them. Alam Gishi was the only woman in my life, the only woman that I truly loved. By "the only woman" I mean to say she was the one who helped me discover my inner self and was the first woman to conceive from me. That was a truly unique human quality: to have someone who was willing to have a baby with you. Another advantage that I don't think any other woman shared with Alam Gishi was that she communicated in a language I understood, always using the right words and the right music. I had never thought our relationship would end so painfully. Up to the last moment, and even after the bus took off, I thought she would change her mind, but when she waved goodbye through the bus window, our separation became a reality. The people around me looked at me pathetically, and some of them consoled me with words they thought would make me feel better. "She'll come back to you. She certainly won't find a better husband," they naively reassured me.

Yet the best consolation I received was from the Mother and Wad Ammoona, who arranged what might have been the best night of my life, had it not been for my low spirits. To my surprise, they brought in al-Ajouz, accompanied by his *om kiki*, and Boushy, a pet name for Boushai, the Shuluk singer, a very pretty girl whose mother was from al-Homran, one of the Arabian tribes in the region. Addai was aware that I liked Boushy's company. So there we all were in the big hut. All the furniture had been removed, the floor was covered with a straw mat over which some plastic mats—cheap, but soft and beautiful—had been laid. The Mother herself took care of sponging my back with soap and massaging my body with scented *dilka* dough. She then left me in the hands of al-Ajouz, Boushy, and three young girls who sang to me in a space filled with the scent of sandalwood and other incense.

"Sing 'Mutual Advice' for me," I asked them.

Boushai and I shared glasses of my favorite drink: Ethiopian red gin. Al-Ajouz helped himself to some, and we offered the girls Pepsi and Stim. We all danced to songs by the Ethiopian singer Tamrat, played on the Mother's recorder. We sang in Amharic, Tigrinya, Arabic, and in many ancient Blue Nile languages whose origins weren't clear to us—were they from the Angassana, the Wataweet, the Broon, the Gumur, or from other tribes? Boushai sang a popular Shuluk lyric, one of the hits by the pretty singer Viviana.

At 10 p.m., the Mother whispered in my ear, "What's your wish for tonight?"

"For tonight only?"

"Yes, for tonight only. Supper is not a wish because it's ready and will be served soon. And the song 'Awadeyah Cries for Seven Days on End' is outside the wish list too. And I don't think you need to hear 'Mutual Advice.'"

"Let al-Ajouz make a wish on my behalf—he can choose 'Mutual Advice' if he likes," I said.

"I wish you happy dreams," al-Ajouz said, laughing.

The Mother said, "Ok. Let's see what kind of wish Boushai has for you."

"I wish he'd drink the rest of the gin on his own," she said as she searched for her headscarf.

Amid the laughter, the Mother said to the girls, "Do any of you want to make a wish for him?"

They laughed and started to sing "Awadeyah Cries for Seven Days on End."

I wasn't sure if I was drunk or sober when I said, "I wish al-Safyah would tell me a story about the Jungo; or I wish Wad Ammoona would tell me a story about the prison."

The Mother's laughter caused her large breasts to shake. She said, "Al-Safyah is busy treating sesame with pesticides at the al-Zubaidi farm. Wad Ammoona left—he said he was tired. But I'll tell you my life story. I'm sure you'll find it more interesting than al-Safyah's life story."

We all had supper together. And when I was completely drunk, they left me alone. I fell asleep almost immediately. In my dream, al-Safyah returned from the al-Zubaidi farm on a huge black camel. She said to me, "I've shown your friend stars in broad daylight. Now it's *your* turn."

21

ADALIA DANIYAL'S ORDEAL

In Adalia Daniyal's house, there were ten recorders fitted with big speakers. She kept them in a large steel box that she bought from Keren and that was originally used for storing ammunition during World War Two. In the box, there were also plenty of sunglasses, large Adidas shoes, twenty NATIONAL three-wave radio sets, and other smaller items. Adalia Daniyal called the box "the trust safe," although the items stored in it couldn't be classified as trusts. Actually, they originally entered the box as trusts or security, only to be gradually exchanged for food or drink, or, in very rare cases, sold for cash. This would happen in the summer months, toward the end of the sorghum-harvesting season. At that time, the Jungojora would have run out of cash and started to sell off their collection of outfits that they had built up during the sesame-harvesting and sorghum-cutting months—the period from October to early December, or the "fat months," as the Jungojora called them.

Like all arrack and *mareesa* makers, Adalia Daniyal was very disciplined and professional. Whenever a *faddadi* asked her to "keep this recorder," she immediately assigned a value to it and scratched the transaction onto one of the walls of her room, which served as a sort of debit account for all transactions: all orders of arrack and *mareesa*, as well as all cash borrowings. A true Jungojorai would claim back his trust only when he had enough money to buy it back. However, they always preferred to buy a new collection of outfits during the fat months—outfits that reflected the latest styles.

Smarter and more calculating Jungojora would develop intimate relationships with arrack sellers. The age difference was never an issue, nor was the beauty of the female partner, for all women are pretty in the eyes of smart, mature males. People here believe that every woman—regardless of her age, beauty, color, or tribe—has something to give a man and that all women are pretty enough to enable a man to reach his climax. The *faddada* sum it up by saying, "A truly virile man is never selective."

But the most important condition in the unwritten contract was that a Jungojorai must have only one woman at a time and that a *faddadiyah* must have only one Jungojorai at a time. This was clearly a difficult condition to fulfill, and the Jungojorai would in most cases fail to abide by it. Idleness and good food often awakened the demons of lust in him. And the women were particularly attractive from December to April, because they didn't take part in clearing shrubs or cutting sugarcane then, but instead confined themselves to the lazy life of the household, making their livelihood by selling liquor and homemade perfumes, and by selling tea and coffee at the souks during the day and outside their households in the evening. Only a few resorted to prostitution, which hardly yielded any income, as all men were penniless during those months and bartering took over. Besides, men were in short supply during those months, as most of them would leave to work in sugarcane farms. So a fierce competition would emerge among the many beautiful, idle women for the few men who opted to stay in al-Hillah and make their living by mortgaging their belongings or entering into intimate relationships or marriage until the hard months had passed. The Jungo dismiss those who depend on their female partners for their living as being "mean." Then the harvesting season would come, the period when those intimate relationships would break down, and spouses separate.

Adalia Daniyal was married to a devout Catholic. She too was devout, observing prayers and serving at the church along with other women. Her young boys Abab and Tony were already training themselves to become devout by imitation. Adalia was aware of the risks of bringing up her kids in a house frequented by drunkards who used obscene language and knew little about courtesy and decent behavior. They would speak freely about what happened inside huts and *rakubas* under the cloak of darkness and didn't hesitate to describe their most intimate encounters with women, and their unrestrained laughter might have suggested to children that their way of life was the proven recipe for true pleasure. That was why Adalia never allowed her kids to get close enough to hear such unchaste conversations, and that explained her commitment to the church and her keenness to take the kids along, so as to spend the longest time possible away from home, particularly on Saturdays, her *mareesa* day. If they happened to come home earlier than usual, she immediately sent them to the house of her uncle Abdallah Majok, an accountant at the produce market. They would have lunch there and return home just before sunset. The *faddada* would have left by then, and the kids would find their share of *mareesa*, perform their prayers, and go to bed.

Lam Deng had his reservations about this pious program for the kids, and indeed about Adalia's philosophy of raising children. But he gave in to her will. Perhaps he was trying to avoid a confrontation with his domineering wife. Perhaps he was trying to spare the kids the specter of family feuds. Perhaps he was adhering to his Christian values of forgiveness and tolerance.

Adalia Daniyal appreciated all this, but she adamantly believed that upbringing was exclusively the mother's jurisdiction and that the father's sole role—earning money—was outside the perimeter of the household. His failure to carry out his share of the responsibility should in no way bestow upon him other responsibilities that were not originally his, particularly raising Abab and Tony.

But was Adalia Daniyal really so firm and strict? Others always know more about you than you know about yourself. An outside view is always more objective and thorough. There are many others, while you yourself are merely one person. So which view is the more credible? The others have a thousand eyes, 500 hearts, a thousand ears, 500 mouths, a thousand legs, and a thousand hands. You are merely one single person. Which party should we believe? Which party is more capable of uncovering the truth and identifying lies and fabrications?

In a mini-seminar on Khamiesa al-Nubawiyah's *mareesa* day, the audience verified the authenticity of the following incident: On the day Kaltouma, daughter of Khamiesa al-Nubawiyah, was married to the Jungojorai Abdaraman, a dialogue about "pleasure" started up right after the wedding. It was a fresh, simple, and heated discussion. Alam Gishi did not start it, and indeed the comments she made were neither the most astute nor the most controversial, although no one could deny she spoke with authority. But yesterday, at a group discussion held on the sidelines of Khamiesa al-Nubawiyah's *mareesa* day, the ladies present talked about the "first time," as they called it, that Adalia Daniyal realized there were important things in her life as a woman that she had not experienced. They dismissed her claim as an unsuccessful attempt to portray herself as an innocent person. Such a claim, they asserted, hardly befitted a woman who had been married for twenty years and had given birth twice. However, Adalia Daniyal asserted, "I swear to God, I've never experienced this thing you're talking about. Not once."

They probed her with questions, "Is your husband *okay*?"

". . ."

"Does he *come* too early? Does he growl like a dog?"

"How many minutes does he last?"

"Does he play with you first or not?"

Then they talked about their individual experiences with their men, indirectly pointing fingers at Lam Deng. The problem lay not only in the fact that he was uncircumcised but also in the fact that he was hasty and dealt with the matter as if it were a tedious duty. They took pity on her, as someone who had never had the chance to feel like a woman.

For one full year after that, the Jungojoraic hive-mind kept a close watch on Adalia Daniyal. She decided to be more like her friends, who knew how to enjoy themselves as women. She wanted to experience what they had spoken about with such conviction:

"I don't know if I'm on earth or in the heavens."

"It feels a bit like numbness, a bit like drowsiness, a bit like a dream. It's something you never want to end, but it goes away suddenly."

"A type of pain, a sweet pain."

"It's beyond description, sister. You have to experience it to know it. It's something from our Lord."

"No, no, sisters. I don't like to talk about these things!"

She tried with her husband Lam Deng, but the game always ended early: ejaculation, followed by a coarse sound, brief prayers to thank the Lord, and then he'd fall asleep. In the past, she didn't bother because she was content with the pleasure of repeated penetration and the warm arms of her husband, which made her feel as if she were the center of the universe. Now, however, she wanted to go beyond all that to the point that her friends had described to her and convinced her to pursue. Adalia couldn't stand Lam Deng anymore, although they had sex only once a week. Lam Deng attributed this change to the tumults and vagaries of women. There were numerous references to this in the Bible, and also in the Holy Quran, as he understood from some Muslims. Lam Deng was petit and plump, and had piercing clever eyes. He wasn't the talkative type. In the summer, he worked on red brick ovens by the riverbank. He was third in rank at the church, after Father Peter and Mother Mariam Kudi, a beautiful pious virgin whose ancestors were from the city of Deleng in the Nuba Mountains. According to testimonies in the group discussion, she had scored high marks in beauty contests in Kenya before fully devoting herself to the church and ending up in this remote spot.

Lam Deng made a confession to Father Peter: his wife Adalia Daniyal was acting strangely and had asked him to be circumcised.

"Doesn't she know that circumcision is only observed by Jews and Muslims? We were created in the image of God, and we don't distort that image."

"She's well aware of that."

"So why's she doing this? Does she want to become a Muslim?"

"No, she's still a devout Christian. I don't know what's happened. It's really strange. I asked Mother Mariam Kudi to take it up with her on Sunday. They're both women so communication should be easier."

At a group discussion held on Khamiesa al-Nubawiyah's *mareesa* day one Saturday, the following was confirmed: my friend heard about what later came to be known as "Adalia Daniyal's ordeal." As usual, he imposed himself like some new messiah. "I'll be the first to make Adalia Daniyal feel like a true woman," he promised me. "I'll take her to climax."

"Just make sure your experience with al-Safyah doesn't repeat itself," I said, teasing him.

"Those are two different things," he replied seriously.

After many successive flirtatious maneuvers, he managed to meet her privately in one of Addai's huts. "From the very first moment," he bragged, "I discovered that all the allegations made by drunken males and vain women are false. She had an orgasm as soon as I kissed her. She meowed like a cat, recoiled, and then stretched her limbs. Then she gazed at me frightfully for a while before running away."

So on Sunday Adalia Daniyal had nothing to tell Mother Mariam Kudi, other than saying that the circumcision issue was a foolish idea.

But who's stupid enough to believe that story?

22 THE COMPASSIONATE ROBBERS

Work at the fields was in full swing. The most distinctive feature about that agricultural season was that the bank was actively involved in financing large-scale farms. It also extended loans to its own employees, who cultivated large swathes of land with sesame and sorghum. The bank manager, for one, sowed a thousand *feddans*[1] with sorghum in the fertile land located between Khor Maghareef and the Zahanah forest, an area that came to be known as "the bankers' farm."

The Jungo were hard at work; they needed cash, and they were being paid promptly. We had to admit that the bank had invigorated the local economy. New activities were introduced by the bank employees, who, with the help of bank loans, imported milking cows of the famous Friesian breed and established poultry farms. Those two activities alone created jobs for at least thirty youngsters. Another advantage was a marked drop in the price of eggs, which now joined the list of consumable items, thanks to intensive advertising and some imitations. Another advantage was that the price of milk dropped to just fifty piasters per pound. And the quality of the milk was better now too—it had less water content. The milk was more hygienic as well, as it was stored in large receptacles that were washed twice a day.

The bank staff invented a new loan system—*katafalli*, as people called it. A rich bank employee would lend money to someone, who

[1] One *feddan* is 4,200 square meters.

must have a guarantor and must sign an unconditional undertaking to pay back on demand the cash equivalent of a specific number of sorghum sacks, valuated at the current market price. On the maturity date, the borrower would have to pay back the loan in kind, i.e., the same number of sorghum sacks, multiplied by two. The difference, though, was that the price of sorghum would always more than triple by the maturity date, usually the period between May and August. As a result, the borrower would end up paying four times the original loan.

They also improved the transportation system, having introduced, for the first time in that region, comfortable passenger buses that operated between Showak, Abboudah, and al-Hillah during the summer season. The three minibuses were owned by two bank employees. That made sense. Instead of keeping funds within its locked coffers, the bank decided it was only natural that it should extend loans exclusively to its own staff and large merchants at that initial stage, until the bank developed sufficient confidence in the creditworthiness of ordinary citizens. Many appreciated the bank's policy and credited it with bringing life to the village again. Now, they argued, every productive resident could sell their products to the bank staff—even charcoal, firewood, and the aromatic *taleh* wood. The backyards of the bank employees' houses were packed with piles of those commodities. "We used to transport charcoal all the way to Khartoum," one person said, "and had to pay countless bribes on the way. Now Siddig al-Awad, or even the manager himself, spares us the trouble. They're prepared to buy any item of value."

Yet despite those countless advantages, there were still nitpicky people who were oblivious to the benefits and who were critical of the bank's interference in their private lives in many direct and indirect ways. They kept a full record of the bank's malpractices, and a series of seminars was held to discuss them. At a mini-seminar in Abrahait's house that marked an obscure festive day called "Solomon Day" or "King Solomon Day," the topic of discussion was the amount that Siddig al-Awad, the bank official, had promised to pay Amol Jang if the latter embraced Islam. Although Amol Jang was present in person, his testimony was largely ignored, and the audience seemed to endorse the version of our friend Mukhtar Ali, who asserted, beyond doubt, that Siddig al-Awad had received a huge amount of money from a man with a long beard.

"I almost took him for Osama bin Laden. If Osama bin Laden hadn't been in his Tora Bora hideout at the time, I would have thought it was him in flesh and blood: tall, fat well-built, light-skinned, with a long beard, thick hair, plenty of money, and bodyguards too. He came to Qedaref, and Siddig met him there." Mukhtar Ali swore by God and by the Prophet that he had seen him and heard their conversation.

The Mother briefed the audience on a futile attempt to make her provide information about the identities of the Jungo who took up arms and found shelter in the Zahanah forest and to identify those who sympathized with them and who opposed them. Wad Ammoona disclosed a proposal by the bank manager to marry Boushai secretly. The audience seemed to think that the marriage might have taken place, despite Boushai's categorical denial, "I would rather throw my sex to the dogs than give it up to that arrogant thief."

Adalia Daniyal said, "I refused to sell them my recorders. They offered a very low price, below cost." After a fit of hysterical laughter, which sounded more like sobbing, she said, "They were the ones who advised me to have my husband circumcised."

But the most surprising testimony came from Abrahait, who had always been reserved, suspicious, and reticent. He said to me, "They're the ones who ruined your marriage. They lured Alam Gishi with gold and money. You're not wanted here. They'd love to see you leave, or even die. Take care. You've been accused of instigating the Jungo revolt and inciting your friend al-Shaygi to become an outlaw."

It was the first time that one of the seminars had concluded with less than solid results. Its findings can be summarized as follows: "Unless Fekki Ali has a say about this, there's nothing that can be taken as an undisputable fact." On the sidelines of the seminar, however, there were whispers that it was Fekki Ali and no one else who had mobilized his demons, his yellow books, and his green and black magic in favor of the bank staff because they paid him more. Fekki Ali could have destroyed them all, particularly after Alam Gishi had provided him with the names of their mothers, employing a combination of feminine guile, masculine resourcefulness, and Wad Ammoona's foxiness. It was common knowledge that Fekki Ali had traveled to the town of Basonda and stayed there for two full weeks. Basonda, as was well known, was the seat of all the custodians of the secrets of the tree science, the so-called "green magic." As the adage goes here in the East, if the people of Basonda reject you, the people of the cemetery must have summoned you.

23

ALL STRANDS OF GOSSIP END UP IN WAD AMMOONA'S HANDS

Wad Ammoona, the bank office boy, was the only one in the town who held all the strands of gossip and facts, and he was probably behind many of the major events in al-Hillah. The bank employees gave him special treatment, even pampered him, on account of his rare wealth of information, which some referred to as "bed knowledge."

When his mother Ammoona first came to Qedaref from the remote western part of Sudan, she worked with the Jungo in the fields. She would put her little boy under a narrow shade of canes and *adar* plants, on an old bed sheet spread out on the ground, with some dates or candy for him to share with the flies and ants. Wad Ammoona learned his first lesson from his early companions: patience from the ants and meanness from flies. In a place where children grew up fast, if they were fortunate to escape death before the age of five or even in their mothers' wombs, he was brought up by his mother and three aunts, who had joined their eldest sister a few months after her arrival in al-Hillah. The aunts eventually ended up in Saudi Arabia. Al-Tayah, a woman based in the Kirinteena district of Jeddah who was an expert at investing in attractive young girls, convinced Ammoona that it was in the best interest of her younger sisters to be brought up in her custody, and she promised to make beauty queens of them: they'd live in prosperity, and she'd find them decent jobs that suited their age. So off they went, and no one heard from them for years. Wad Ammoona was finally able to touch base with them years later, after the inauguration of the telecom company's branch office in al-Hillah.

So you could safely say that the only person Wad Ammoona had lived with continuously was his mother. Ammoona was a pretty woman from Kordofan, which people always referred to as the remote west. We can't take as truth all the rumors about her personality and her origins, nor can we say for sure what jobs she had worked or which men she had been with. However, it was commonly known that she had been put in jail many times and that she was continuously hounded by certain jailors. She was a belligerent and brave woman. And did I mention that she was attractive too?

Certainly, the only thing that Wad Ammoona inherited from his mother was her skin color, assuming of course that his father was not the Yemeni man he claimed. People said Wad Ammoona should have looked far manlier, on account of the harsh conditions he had endured with his mother at the prison and in the fields. But this was Allah's wish. And if you believed in the old maxim "Living fire begets cold, impotent ash," you could not totally rule out that Ammoona was indeed the mother of Wad Ammoona. Before joining the bank as an office boy, he worked at Mother Addai's house, where his role was twofold. He fetched and carried things for the Mother and her female staff (which involved bringing flour from the mill, buying sugar and coffee from the local grocery, serving clients and guests, warming up water, and fetching firewood). His other function was baking *kisra*, which was his favorite hobby. Both roles were relatively respectable. But he also did other unusual jobs that were regarded by many as indecent: cleaning the private parts of senior employees, merchants, and wealthy women, for example.

He was handsome and elegant in his simple dress, thick black mustache, and clean-shaven face. You would see him in every house in the town, on special occasions and at all other times as well. He was the only person who had a permanent right to enter any house in al-Hillah at any time he chose. He was lively and cheerful, kind-hearted and peaceful, and he was a good singer, particularly of women's songs. Since the age of sixteen, he had been known to be an expert in painting henna for women and in giving dance lessons to brides-to-be. He knew every detail about everyone, big or small. He couldn't keep a secret, and no secret was beyond his reach.

The bankers liked him and employed him as an office boy on the recommendation of Alam Gishi. He was a slightly different person now, perhaps because of his new work environment, where he spent eight hours every day running up and down the stairs. He quickly developed additional interests, such as peeking into client accounts and getting to know who owned how much, how much *X* withdrew, and how much *Y* deposited. Those tasks would have been too difficult for anyone except Wad Ammoona. This semi-illiterate man, who had received only a few months of education during Azza's intermittent stints outside of prison, had a wealth of techniques that he drew on in order to gain access to vital information he needed for his nighttime chats at the Mother's house, with women in their houses, or during his individual "private parts" grooming sessions. As a way of fending off boredom in his tedious work, he would entertain his clients with the likes of "Do you know how much Hussain the *jallabi* deposited into his bank account today?"

A cunning person like Wad Ammoona naturally knew when information about client balances was needed most and who would pay fortunes to gain access to it, such as debtors and relatives. But the type of information that he was very willing to offer free of charge, and would even pay from his own pocket in return for attentive listening and words of praise, was bedroom information. On countless occasions, he bought *mareesa* and *asaliyah* for the *faddada*, and packs of Bringi cigarettes for the women, and treated his guests to savory grilled meats just to show off his precious bedroom information.

But Wad Ammoona's most unenviable habit was indeed "selling" private information. Foretellers and false *fekkis* would pay fortunes for information about their patients: their concerns, who they suspected was behind their ailments, and how they felt about the person providing a cure.

Despite his incredibly busy schedule, Wad Ammoona was utterly faithful to Addai, offering her a free private grooming service once per month. He loved to proclaim that Addai had the loveliest smell, particularly between her thighs. He always classified people according to the odor of their private parts, and one of his favorite sayings was "A naturally pleasant smell is a blessing from Allah."

The private-parts-grooming profession had come into being in tandem with the opening of the bank branch and the telecom company, and with the arrival of gas station workers and of a bunch of fresh university graduates who took up jobs as administrative officers in al-Hillah, as well as the arrival of senior military officers assigned to the now-expanded local military post. All those developments took place over the past ten years. The new profession was invented by a spoiled administrative officer from Omdurman, who once saw Wad Ammoona at his house busily preparing a hair-removal wax for his wife: a mixture of sugar, lime, and carnation extract. At the very first sight of him, the experienced officer was able to read Wad Ammoona inside and out—he wasn't deceived by the thick mustache that lent him a false masculine air. So he boldly asked Wad Ammoona to wait for him in the sitting room after he had finished his wax job. There he told him about Abdo Zahra, who used to provide an invaluable service to him and to senior officials, ministers, and proprietors of now-famous companies, and even to former heads of states. He said he sorely missed Abdo Zahra "in this desolate village where even a donkey would break its bonds and bolt off due to boredom."

At first, Wad Ammoona suspected the intentions of the officer and thought he might want a dubious bedroom service. But thanks to God, he came to understand what the officer really wanted.

"But I've never done such work," Wad Ammoona complained.

"I'll teach you. You can make a fortune from the job. Besides, it's a decent profession, just like a barber's. And it's not too complicated."

So the officer worked hard vouching for Wad Ammoona to potential clients in an attempt to put the business on solid ground.

24 HUNTING WILD BOAR

The grass had reached towering heights, thanks to a bountiful rainy season. Heavy rain had paralyzed transportation between the towns and villages, including the trucks that supplied us with flour sent by friends or merchants down in al-Hillah. To avoid starving to death, the Jungojora who were working with me decided to go hunting for wild boar, which was abundantly available in those areas. Its meat was delicious, and the Jungo believed eating its liver improved one's eyesight. Although boar hunting was extremely dangerous, every Jungojorai claimed that he was by far the best hunter, with a proven track record. There were five of us at the farm: myself; Mukhtar Ali; Abdaraman al-Bilalawi, who had, only a couple months ago, married Kaltouma, daughter of Khamiesa al-Nubawiyah (we still called him "the bridegroom"); a retired soldier whom we nicknamed *al-Himreeti* on account of his reddish complexion; and a young woman called Hawayyah Bit al-Malayka (daughter of the angels).

I was the only Jungojorai who admitted to never having had the privilege of hunting or eating that creature, so I didn't take part in the heated debate over whether a boar went into and out of its hole head-first or bottom-first. The discussion became so heated that people began calling each other names: "mean," "miserable," and "son of a bitch."

After drinking our remaining stock of *mareesa*, we hoisted our axes and knives and went into the forest. The wild boar was a large animal that could grow up to the size of a calf. It had strong, short legs, solid hoofs, and two tusks, as sharp as the horns of a bull, that protruded from its mouth, which it used in self-defense. A single thrust of one tusk could tear a hyena into two. All animals steered clear of that aggressive creature. The only threat came to it from the Jungojorai, who employed a host of techniques to catch it.

On that day, the Jungo were so entangled in their debate that they paid little attention to the task of catching the boar. I was more concerned with getting sufficient meat to feed my team for over a week, until the land was dry and the roads were accessible again. I kept urging them to focus on hunting, but they were determined to first establish how it got into its hole. It was a matter of personal dignity now.

We found the boar's hole. The experienced Jungo said the boar was not in it, although its footsteps and the strong smell meant it must be nearby. Some wool found hanging in nearby thorny shrubs belonged to a female boar, so her male partner could well be inside the hole: there was a consensus among them about this finding. They asked me to climb a nearby *laloub* tree to keep out of the reach of this stupid but extremely dangerous animal.

The three men took perfectly calculated positions around the hole and asked Bit al-Malayka to go find the animal with the help of its smell and its tracks. "When you find it, position yourself so that it's between you and the hole, and when you're far away enough, throw a stone in its direction, and it will run back to its hole." The Jungo would be waiting there to see for themselves how it would go in: head-first or bottom-first. They would hunt it only after it had entered. But that was not how the boar ought to be hunted. The proper way, Mukhtar Ali later told me, was by blocking the entrance with stones, thorny plants, and large blocks of wood. When the boar encountered this, it would hesitate for a moment, and before it could decide what alternative route to take, the Jungo could attack it with axes.

As we stood there in suspense, silently waiting for the boar, an idea crossed Abdaraman al-Bilalawi's mind. Without telling the others, he moved from his position behind a big *tundub* tree just behind the hole and headed toward the entrance of the hole as if he wanted to check on something. Some guessed he might have heard something inside, particularly since he was the closest to the hole. To our astonishment, the moment he reached the entrance, the male boar dashed out, pierced Abdaraman with its huge tusks, and drove him along with incredible speed into the forest. Without hesitation, we all ran after it to rescue poor Abdaraman, who had been taken by surprise and didn't even have time to scream.

We were expecting him to fall off the animal's head at any moment. We chased it for almost an hour, following its tracks, which were clearly visible on the wet soil. Braving exhaustion, we continued our chase through to sunset. We must have gone too far west, for we found ourselves at the outskirts of Mount Esayr. There we met an old Jungojorai who advised us to go back and forget about poor Abdaraman. "For your own safety, go back. The boar must have taken him up to the mountaintop, where his masters are," he said. When I naively asked who those masters were, my knowledgeable companions winked at me, tacitly telling me to shut up—the masters were masters of the underworld.

I later came to realize that I was the only one who didn't know that the old Jungojorai who had appeared out of the blue and advised us to turn back was himself one of the underworld people in disguise. On our way back to the farm, we talked about Abdaraman's fate, which resembled the fate of all the previous husbands of Kaltouma, daughter of Khamiesa al-Nubawiyah. We felt deeply sorry for the tragic loss and prayed for him. The weird thing, though, was that this tragic accident didn't distract the Jungo from their debate over the position the boar had taken in entering into and leaving its hole. Mukhtar Ali swore that the boar had come out bottom-first and then very quickly changed position, snatched up Abdaraman, and drove him to God knows where. The other Jungo had a completely different version of events. Bit al-Malayka and I didn't catch sight of the boar, neither when it came out of its hole nor when it got hold of Abdaraman. Bit al-Malayka had been tracking the male boar among the *kitir* shrubs. I was lost in my own grief and daydreaming atop the huge *laloub* tree I had been advised to take shelter on.

Ultimately, we settled on a small turtle, an old monitor lizard, some locusts, and two fat wildcats.

25 BOUSHAI

After fierce battles between the Jungo and an army battalion based at the Zahanah military post, the central government was alarmed by the mounting security threat posed by what it called the *shifta*, or armed gangs. In public, it blamed foreign forces that were working hard to topple the national government and undermine its "renaissance model." It made specific reference to the opposition, the Eastern Front, the Free Lions, the Bija Congress, the Justice and Equality Movement, and many others. It even mentioned the name of Eritrea, and as a cosmetic touch or for the sake of unifying the internal front, it added Israel to the list. Yet from the accumulated experience of the central government that had been at war with its own citizens since independence, the decision makers were aware that the revolt was driven solely by the Jungo, and the proper way to deal with it did not involve excessive force—that would be like using a nuclear bomb to kill a mosquito.

We were well into the second half of the rainy season now. The grass had grown tall, as high as the *kitir* and *taleh* trees, and some *adar* plants had grown taller than the farm huts. The rainfall was so heavy this year that it killed all the pests that posed a threat to the crops at their early stages of growth. Those pests, including rats and some species of locusts, were trapped in their underground hideouts by the torrents.

As the rainfall intensified, moving around on the black, fertile, muddy soil became all the more difficult. The Jungo knew every inch of the terrain. The army didn't. The Jungo could infiltrate into Eritrean or Ethiopian territories to retrieve their weapons hidden in the bush. The government army didn't have that privilege. The Jungo were fighting because they felt they were not being treated fairly and because they wanted money. The government soldiers weren't sure what cause they were fighting for. So it was an uneven battle, and the confrontations often ended in favor of the Jungojora and with heavy losses on the part of the government forces. The government's victory parades only served to demoralize citizens and to fill children's minds with nightmares and difficult questions about the value of life and death. Those parades never managed to conceal the humiliating defeats. One day, we woke early in the morning to the sound of military marches. We took to the streets, or more accurately, to alleys formed by thorny *kitir* bushes that kept goats and donkeys away from the cane fences. As if some invisible force was guiding our steps, we all headed to the main square near the Sudanese Red Crescent office. There, two bodies were on display, hanging from two large wooden crosses. They were the corpses of two men known to everyone in al-Hillah, including the children. The one in a government military uniform, whose large fetid body was swollen and covered with flies, was Ab Bakar Habeela, Haloum al-Zaghawiyah's ex-husband. The other one, wearing a filthy galabia and long underwear, was the once-skinny but now-swollen body of Abdallah al-Hardallo, who was once so full of jokes, but was now so silent and sad. Adam Lahsat, nicknamed "the martyr's mother," chanted "Allah is the greatest" into the microphone seven times before announcing the following: "Every day we will bring in two of these Jungo dogs and hang them here."

The square was immediately renamed Victory Square. Intoxicated and overly excited soldiers opened fire on the inanimate bodies. The morale of all of us sank into a deep, dark well as we returned home, our minds filled with one question: what's next? At a mini-seminar on Om Jabir's *asaliyah* day, we quickly concluded that the whole demonstration was a show of vengeance and intimidation. We agreed that the rich employees must have been overwhelmingly terrified. One or two people in the audience mentioned that Fekki Ali was considering leaving al-Hillah for good: he had built a house in the al-Haj Yousef neighborhood of Khartoum. He had been quoted as saying that business was better there. "The Khartoum residents are fed up with doctors and private hospitals. The *fekkis* are working like heavy-duty machines, making fortunes and building great connections, while we're all sitting here watching while *X* is killed, *Y* is crucified, and *Z* is expelled to Ethiopia."

Siddig al-Awad loaned me enough money for four sacks of sorghum, valued against the current market price. He hinted that, despite many question marks about me and my friend who had escaped to Khartoum, he wanted to do me a favor, for God's sake, so that I could pay the labor charges and so that I shouldn't lose the capital I had invested. I played dumb as I signed a debit note for three times the quantity of sorghum I had received from him. I had no other alternative.

Despite all the long months I had spent away from Alam Gishi, she never left my thoughts. Mukhtar Ali devoted all of his time to me. Only after a great effort on my part did I finally convince him that we should be partners in the small enterprise we had been working on since the beginning of the season, before al-Shaygi left us to join what the government sometimes called the *shifta* and sometimes "the mutineers." Al-Shaygi had caused me difficulties, and I was now under police surveillance. I was summoned for interrogation at the security offices in *Hai Fellatah* on five separate occasions. And Wad Ammoona confided to me that I had been put on the blacklist.

My relationship with Boushai was unique in three ways. First, she admired my knowledge, or as she put it, my ability to "know everything." She often told me that she had hoped to be an intellectual, or at least a university graduate, but she had to leave school at the age of fourteen because her family couldn't afford the fees and the expensive uniform. So she saw in me an unfulfilled dream of hers.

Second, she admired how faithful I was to my former wife and darling Alam Gishi. That was rare, she said, in these times when men hardly showed any loyalty at all. Although she didn't say it directly, it was clear to me that she was eager to replace Alam Gishi.

Third, I was helplessly attracted both to very dark women and very pale women, particularly ones with tall figures and long, voluptuous legs. I loved them even more if they were good singers or dancers, or gifted in any other way, even the way they spoke or walked. Boushai was indeed a perfect example of such a woman, even more so than Alam Gishi. But what set Alam Gishi apart was that she was the first woman on earth who had asked me to help her conceive and give birth to a baby girl. I couldn't fulfill her desire, which later became mine too. More importantly, she was honest and candid. And the way she talked was charming, as if her entire body were talking. Alam Gishi was incomparable; there was something special about her. Boushai was unaware how unique Alam Gishi was and that her attempts to replace her were in vain. Perhaps she might be more successful if she lowered her sights and tried to attain a stature close to Alam Gishi's rather than to literally replace her. I did like Boushai, although I dealt with her with extreme caution because I didn't want to commit myself—for once I commit, I do whatever it takes to fulfill that commitment, whatever the cost.

In fact, at least so far, I hadn't felt the need for a partner in bed. I was still obsessed with Alam Gishi. I still loved her and saw her in my dreams each night—and I lived with memories of her every second of my life. I had an intuition that I would fail with Boushai. That was certain. I didn't believe Abrahait's claims that Alam Gishi had conspired against me with the bankers or with others. I simply convinced myself that there was no plausible explanation for what she had done. The Mother once told me that my condition was deteriorating by the day. In fact, my relationship with women was governed by intricate psychological conditions, even though it remained smooth and hurdle-free.

Just as Alam Gishi used to entertain me at midnight, Boushai now visited me and sang for me before I fell asleep. She sang in the Shuluk and Baria languages, and she memorized two songs in Amharic, which I loved. She was twenty-seven years old, although she looked twenty or thirty years older: the type of life she led was so full of work that it seemed impossible that her days contained only twenty-four hours.

Many would be astonished, as I indeed was, to know that Boushai's family consisted of a single person: herself. Her father, a Shuluk who had joined the Sudan People's Liberation Movement under Commander Abdel Aziz al-Hilou, was martyred in a battle on the outskirts of Hamashkoraib. Her mother died shortly afterward. Her brother Alala migrated to Australia, and no one knew the whereabouts of Ali, her other brother. The last time she saw Ali was two years earlier. Her mother's family didn't like them, due to ethnic considerations, despite the fact that their father was a Muslim. Her younger sister Abook joined al-Tayah, Ammoona's sister, in Saudi Arabia.

So Boushai ended up alone. And she was up to the challenge. She worked making local liquor, just like all the poor women here. But she was not known to have had any affairs with men; at least Wad Ammoona was not able to get any information on that regard, and no seminar could ever establish a link between Boushai and any man, Jungo or otherwise. But that didn't mean Boushai had no admirers or boyfriends. Everyone liked her, and many women valued her friendship and enjoyed keeping her company, sometimes spending the night with her. She had turned down two marriage proposals and one offer of an extra-marital affair. People were now talking about a clandestine marriage between her and Turkawi, the bank manager, citing the mobile phone he had given her, the first mobile phone to enter the eastern district of al-Hillah. They reckoned that our relationship was driven by my need for someone to entertain me and by a futile attempt on her part to marry a self-made man. We both found solace in one another, and as I said, I admired Boushai's perseverance and how hard she worked to earn a living. There was more to it, though: Boushai was the first person in the entire eastern district to buy a digital TV receiver. She didn't use funds sent in by Abook from Saudi Arabia, for Abook had yet to send any and was still working to reimburse al-Tayah for her travel and residence expenses. And Boushai still hadn't heard from Alala in Australia: she had no contact with him.

So she worked selling *mareesa* and *asaliyah*. That was by no means an easy job, for dealing with drunkards called for great amounts of patience and diplomacy. At first glance, drunkards seemed serene and kind—they talked about stuff like boars and argued over whether they entered their holes with head-first or bottom-first. They talked about adventures with hyenas: they loved its meat, which was credited with curing some ailments, and even its excrement was an effective means of treating asthma and bronchitis. And they held long sessions full of gossip and chitchat. All this would happen in the first few hours, unless there was someone among them who got drunk right away and started the quarreling prematurely, disturbing the peace and putting the house master's nerves on end—those quarrels could eventually lead to police intervention in which case the hostess wouldn't be able to sell her stock of *mareesa*.

In the absence of such a drunkard, the next few hours were the time when clients would enjoy songs. They would sing to themselves, using empty *mareesa* utensils as drums in the absence of a proper *dalluka* or a smaller drum *(shatam)*. Others would entertain themselves by flirting with the house master or her daughters, or chatting with them about marriage, love, and family. But the most dangerous thing about those intermediate hours was that clients would feel a compelling desire for sex, which would usually lead to fights with other men: a husband, a brother, or a boyfriend. The fight often involved local weapons, which were used skillfully and wrathfully.

Only a clever and well-trained house master could keep control of those unruly drunkards. She needed extraordinary crisis management skills, because she worked in a minefield. Some of the risks included being stabbed, fracturing an arm, someone jumping into a neighbor's home, police intervention, confiscation of work tools, and a long term in prison. Boushai developed her crisis management skills from the drunkards themselves. Through her long association with them, she could now classify her clients into distinct categories: a drunkard who was prone to starting fights, a drunkard who would fall asleep on his stool immediately after the first glass, a beginner who would wet his clothes like a baby or burst into tears, and a well-balanced *faddadi* who could control himself and would quietly listen to the songs or pick up his walking stick and leave or who might simply spread his turban out on the ground and fall asleep in a corner of the room. Using this in-depth knowledge, she was adept at managing her clients.

Boushai refrained from sleeping with the Jungo. "They're filthy: they rarely wash their clothes or their bodies. Their smell is strong enough to knock a falcon out of the air!" she would say.

Boushai needed her diplomatic skills on another front too: the bank, also known as the monster that intervened in every tiny detail of her daily life. Turkawi narrated to her numerous times, through Wad Ammoona, the story of his less-than-attractive wife who hardly showed any interest in him as a man and husband, her sole passion in life being money. It could hardly be said that they were in love before they got married—he only married her because she was his cousin.

"Why is he telling me this?" Boushai asked herself.

Making local liquor was a crime punishable by the law, and surely the police and intelligence agents could devote a small part of their time to uprooting that illicit business. And just as surely, Turkawi could keep them away. But he could bring them in too, for all the investments that police officers and senior officials made were either financed by Turkawi personally or by the bank. But Turkawi, as he personally explained to her, was too God-fearing to involve himself in an illicit relationship with her, and she surely wouldn't want to disgrace herself. So he proposed a secret marriage—*orfi*, as it was called—and cited texts from the Shiite traditions to convince her. But she despised his arrogance and could never forget the strong odor of his armpits the first time they met.

"I don't want to get married—neither publicly nor secretly. Neither *halal* nor *haram*."[1]

But those who knew, Turkawi could tell you with all certainty that the battle was far from over at this point. She met him only once. He came to her place disguised as a Jungojorai, and only when he was well inside did he expose his true identity. Yet their indirect daily encounters continued through Wad Ammoona, who communicated messages between them as meticulously and perfectly as an electronic recorder, according to Turkawi's instructions.

It was Wad Ammoona who recommended Boushai to the bank manager. The latter had confided to Wad Ammoona that he was in desperate need of a woman to sleep with. This had to be arranged in strict secrecy. She had to be clean and pretty, with no relatives or jealous lovers who could cause trouble. After thinking it over, Wad Ammoona came up with Boushai. But when the huge telecom company began its operations, Wad Ammoona's services were no longer needed as Turkawi could speak with Boushai directly at any time he chose. In fact, Turkawi had used Wad Ammoona's services only reluctantly, for he was aware that Wad Ammoona communicated his messages not only to Boushai but also to the entire village. But he had no other choice.

When Turkawi failed to convince Boushai with regard to either a secret marriage or paid sex, he made what he called a 'humanitarian request': for phone sex. He explained the process. She refused at first, but on his insistence she eventually gave in.

That would explain the scene that took Wad Ammoona by surprise one day. Walking into Boushai's room, he was astonished to see her on her stool, moaning and groaning and making sounds that could only come out of a woman during hot sex. She was

---

[1] *Halal* means religiously permissible. *Haram* is the opposite.

holding her mobile phone close to her mouth. Surprised at seeing him, she screamed, turned off the phone, and burst into laughter. He asked her what she had been doing.

"Nothing. Nothing. What did you hear?"

"Nothing," Wad Ammoona said, laughing.

Talk of war was the hottest topic. Talk about the execution of Halloum's ex-husband and Abdallah Mahdi, their crucifixion, and how the soldiers had shot at their dead bodies prevailed over speculations about rainfall and the bank intrigues—many had interpreted those events as the bank's retaliation for the shit revolt. In fact, no one remembered that revolt anymore. It was alien to the norms of the community and was gradually dropped from the daily roster of gossip and the agenda of the mini-seminars.

After the killing of the two Jungojorai by government soldiers, the news of war subsided. The Jungo were said to have retreated to the outskirts of the town of Tesseney, where they would probably stay throughout the rainy season, living off money they made when they sold the weapons they had captured from government forces to the Zubaidiyah in the East Front. That was their largest source of income, apart from trading alcohol. They were actively engaged in smuggling alcohol imported from Eritrea and Ethiopia into the town of Khashm El Girba, and on to Khartoum and Atbara through the Botana plains. Thanks to them, pleasure seekers could savor the Ethiopian *anisha* in Abu Hamad, Dongola, and Wadi Halfa in the extreme north, and in Nyala in the extreme west.

Al-Shaygi visited me late one night, in the company of some friends. It was midnight, dark and rainy, and the howling of wolves shattered the imposing silence and sent shivers down our spines. In celebration of the reunion, I slaughtered a male goat from the stock that I kept as a strategic reserve. We drank tea and coffee, and they told me about their adventures, their triumphs, and some of their debacles. They laughed when we remembered the Hamdayeit bus incident and how they pretended they had never met me. "Here's your money. We kept it for you," they said.

I took back my money. They asked me many questions that I answered honestly.

"We're determined to give those bank people a lesson," they declared. "We'll show them stars in broad daylight. But not now—you'll know when the time comes. Until then, we'll be in Eritrea."

That reminded me of what Adalia Daniyal had once told me. "The Jungo have developed an Ethiopian habit: they never give up their rights."

They tried to comfort me about the loss of Alam Gishi, but I was enraged when one of them called her a slut. I defended her passionately, telling them things that men in that community normally never mentioned. I told them I loved her, adored her, and had forgiven her for anything she had done. I told them that honor and chastity were attributes of the soul, not the body. I told them a man who couldn't live with his woman's few vices was depriving himself of her numerous virtues. I told them a profligate woman was far more honorable than a devout man. That was part of what I told them.

26

MY FRIEND THE REBEL

My friend returned to al-Hillah after a long absence, during which time he had been in Khartoum, or perhaps other places he found interesting. It was obvious now that al-Hillah had become his favorite spot. He mentioned this to many.

"This is the most beautiful place I know."

He was of the opinion that robbery, taking up arms, and waging guerrilla warfare against the government army were futile exercises that would get the Jungo nowhere unless such actions were guided by some political theory and social analysis and unless they had a meticulously defined objective that was attainable under the current circumstances. He volunteered to lead the theorization effort. To do that, he had to intermingle with the Jungo, to live with them in *kitir* bushes and gloomy creeks, within firing range of the government army, sharing moments of fear, assault and retreat, hunger, deprivation, defeat, and victory. One of his favorite sayings was "Theory detached from reality is like cooking a meal on a bare flame: it ruins both the meal and the flame." To him, the underlying factor behind the failure of the rebel movements in Darfur was the lack of theorization. Arms alone wouldn't help. And a rifle whose gunpowder was not made up of both dreams *and* thought would only serve to kill its owner.

He asked me to take him to the hideout of the armed Jungo. I warned him that he might not be able to stand their way of living. Although he could eat virtually anything, just like the Jungo, he was a city man in the end, and he risked falling into the hands of the enemy, which would lead to one of three results: a slow and painful death, injury, or a swift end.

He shrugged off my advice, as he usually did when someone warned him about the risks involved in one of his undertakings. "I'm not going to die anytime soon. I know that. If you're not prepared to die, nothing can kill you!"

I knew no one could win an argument with him. But I was also aware of the odds he was up against or more accurately, the odds that were destined to defeat him. I reminded him of his adventure with al-Safyah, which ended in disgrace, and of the tragic end of his adventure with Abrahait Waldo Is'haq, when a twenty-year-old woman gloatingly stuck her caramel tongue out at us. I also reminded him of his futile dialogue with Mother Mariam Kudi, the church pastor, when the faithful nearly killed us, and of his dispute with Wad Ammoona, which the latter won. I also jogged his memory about some other unnecessary adventures that he had stupidly plunged into. "Even putting all these aside, this new adventure could actually kill you," I warned him.

"I believe in one thing: the successful man knows how to capitalize on his failures. As for the al-Safyah affair, it's the pure fabrication of the Jungo and Jungojoraya. How can a woman rape a man?" He accused me of adopting the Jungo's manner of thinking, of being obsessed with what he called "an urge toward an organic interpretation of phenomena," a term that he must have made up on the spot because I had never heard of it before, from him or anyone else; there was a touch of Freud about it.

"How come? It's impossible!" he said, laughing.

"Even if she had a thing that was *big*, in the words of Fekki Ali al-Zaghrad?" I said, mocking him.

"When did Fekki al-Zaghrad see it? And how?" he fired back. He went on a spree of refutations, turning all the failures I had just cited into victories, into marvelous triumphs.

I took him to my plot of land. He stayed with us for five days before al-Shaygi escorted him to the Eritrean border. Since then, we only heard about him through occasional reports that were fenced with thorny *kitir* and *haskaneet* plants, and tainted with September's sticky clay, and laden with fear, with caution, and the howling of the humid southerly wind. But reports kept coming to us in Tigrinya, in Amharic, in Bijawite, in Jungo Arabic, in the jargon of the Randok, and in the dialect of the Rashayda nomads.

He frequently sent me messages, through visitors or mutual friends, and I always wrote back, albeit cautiously. He once asked me to send him what he called a daily schedule of the bank employees' movements. The first report was to cover their movements over a full week. And then I was to make a second report two weeks later. The schedule was to be reviewed every three weeks to calculate the deviation ratio accurately. I did the job perfectly, with the help of Wad Ammoona—indirectly though, because I too didn't trust the latter and suspected that he might be a double agent. I also cultivated my relationship with Boushai, who was still continuing her phone sex sessions with the bank manager. Although she knew very little about his daily life, we benefited immensely from her relationship with him because she could ask him to come to her house at any time, and he would definitely obey, coming stealthily and in disguise, making sure that no one knew of his movements. Those encounters represented an ideal opportunity for the Jungo warriors to deal with him. I wasn't sure what the Jungo's intentions toward the bank and its staff were exactly, but there was one thing I knew for certain: those intentions were malicious.

27

A GIRL FROM ASMARA

She was believed to have been the first to have tried with him. Zeinab Idriseit was a young, proud woman who had led a free and prosperous life in Asmara for nearly seven years. When she was called up for conscription, she crossed the border and stayed in al-Gargaf for a week before some kind people led her to al-Hillah and on to the Mother's House. At the door, she met Wad Ammoona. She didn't try to conceal her admiration.

"I didn't expect to find such smart and elegant men here!"

"You sure will," the house ladies said. They didn't elaborate. A question passed through their silence: how come we never thought of Wad Ammoona as a man before? They had always treated him as a friend, a brother, an obedient servant, and sometimes as their godfather. Addai explained to her what Wad Ammoona's role was and urged her to seek his assistance on any matter and to treat him kindly.

She was classified as a first-class bedroom girl and was briefed on the job description and ethics. She had two conditions. First, no sex without an "insulator," i.e., a condom. Second, she reserved the right to accept or reject the client at her discretion. No coercion. Then she added a statement that instantly placed her in the professionals' category and cast heavy doubts on her claim that she had come here only to evade conscription. Twisting her mouth coquettishly, she said, "Because of Addai's good reputation, I didn't want to talk about money earlier: what's my share, and what's hers?"

Addai was forced to accept all her conditions because she was in desperate need of new blood, a new face. She sent Wad Ammoona to the al-Kitra Souk to buy a large box of condoms, according to the specifications that Zeinab Idriseit had set, including the manufacturer's name and the year of production. She also provided him with a sample for comparison and reminded him to check the expiration date. She kept a large supply of the best-quality condoms in her suitcase.

"Treat Wad Ammoona like your brother," Addai told Zeinab, in an attempt to protect her boy from any dubious sex-related intentions the newcomer might have. The house girls had told her about the comments Zeinab had made when she first met Wad Ammoona at the door and added their own interpretations and embellishments to them. The girl from Asmara smiled and didn't utter a word. Later on, she said to Wad Ammoona, "You're the most handsome man in the whole village."

"Is that so?" he asked shyly. It was the first time he had received such a candid compliment.

"All the men here are filthy. Their body odor would knock a falcon out of the air—unlike the men in Asmara, who are as beautiful as angels." Talking more openly now, she added, "You ought to live in Asmara. Take a job in a bar or a hotel—you could earn a fortune."

She told him how she had been a rising star, an icon in Asmara. "If it hadn't been for the conscription! I hate war, and death, and the sight of blood."

He told her about the more refined people who had come from Khartoum, Madani, Qedaref, Kasala, Port Sudan, and Obayyid to work at the bank or elsewhere: at the telecom company or the gas station, with the police and security forces, at the crop market, and in the local council. There were also army officers and the owners of large farms, and their sons too. He explained how al-Hillah in the daytime was totally different from al-Hillah at night. Most of the people he mentioned came to Addai's house to enjoy an excellent dinner. Many others, including high school teachers, came for breakfast. He assured her that he and Addai would make sure she saw the VIPs, not the Jungo.

She told him she felt that there was something between him and Addai. He swore to God that her suspicions were unfounded. To him, Addai was no more than the master of the house—an employer—and professionalism dictated that he not transgress certain bounds. Convinced by his reply, she made advances on him. Okay, he said, but he had to attend to some of Addai's requests first.

Only the next morning did she realize beyond a shadow of a doubt that he wouldn't come. She fell asleep.

28

THE BEDOUIN SHEIKH'S VOW

The plots of land cultivated by the bank and its staff were estimated at three thousand *feddans*. They were part of a large swathe of fallow land covered with *kitir*, *taleh*, and *seyal* trees, as well as seasonal shrubs such as *boos*, *nal*, and *adar*, which would turn green during the rainy season. That swathe had been designated by the British colonial authorities as grazing land for the cattle of the al-Homran and Lahawieen Bedouins who roamed the area.

The bank's acquisition of that land would not normally have been an issue, but it was the last of a large expanse of fertile land that had been persistently swallowed up by greedy merchants over the past twenty years, forcing nomads to the outskirts of cities and towns. Many traded their cattle for small pickup trucks and houses, opened grocery stores or restaurants, and became town dwellers. But many others held on to their cattle and nomadic life.

It was the latter group who brought up the land issue. They presented an old document that dated back to the colonial rule, signed and sealed by General Gordon Pasha, the British ruler at the time, specifying the boundaries of the pasture zone. The document had been held in the safe custody of one sheikh Abbas al-Lahawi of the Lahawieen tribe, who had kept it in a goat-leather bag hidden in a steel box whose original purpose was to store unused ammunition from the Italian-British war. It reeked of sheep hair, dozens of rainy seasons, and the frailty of languid times. And there was a fetid odor about it—the smell of the betrayals of successive national governments and rulers. It had been waiting patiently like a decaying old landmine. The Bedouin sheikh spread the document right on the ground, despite desperate attempts by the committee members to convince him to place it on a large iron table. It was read hastily, as if it were a school text that had been learned by heart.

The Bedouin sheikh threatened the bank employees with dire consequences if they didn't waive the titles to the land, including planting rights. He vowed to divorce his wife if he failed to carry out that threat. He said he didn't fear a government that was too weak to stand up to a gang of thugs who were looting and plundering in broad daylight. He concluded his tirade with an ominous threat: "Actions speak louder than words."

Without paying attention to what was said next, he folded his document carefully and went out silently, followed by his seven companions. Two days later, they heard the bank manager's comment, "Let him soak his document in water and drink the liquid. Does he think the English are still here? Apparently he's still living in a cave."[1]

Judging by their intimate knowledge of the Bedouins, the members of the conciliation committee suggested that some money and words of apology would probably diffuse the Bedouin sheikh's rebellion and tame it to the level of mere words and chanting. So a high-level delegation took off, loaded with a large sum of money and a promise of one hundred sacks of sorghum for the sheikh. The sheikh gave them a warm welcome. At first, he showed some reluctance to accept the amount and the pledged sorghum, but before long he accepted because he didn't want to disappoint his guests. Later, a member of the delegation said the ease with which the sheikh had accepted the money suggested that he regarded it as a right, not a bribe, which meant that he was still sticking to his position. No one believed him,

[1] A reference to a story related in the Holy Quran about young men who had been persecuted because they converted to a faith that was not the state's religion. They fled to a cave for protection, where God kept them asleep for over 300 years.

and his opinion was quickly dismissed. The sheikh himself asserted that accepting the mediation of guests was the minimum gesture of hospitality expected from a host. And when a Bedouin sheikh says something, he means it.

"But he swore to divorce his wife," the mistrustful member said.

"A Bedouin who doesn't take that oath three times a day would be considered ill," they replied, mocking him.

The mistrustful member wasn't entirely convinced; he had other arguments that supported his position, but he decided to keep them to himself for fear that they might classify him as a traitor. Besides, he was keen to maintain a secure and lasting relationship with the bank. "So let's forget about the Bedouin sheikh," he said to himself.

It was said that when the bank listed the enemies of progress and civilization in al-Hillah—the troublemakers and instigators of tribal strife—my friend and I were at the top of the list. No wonder, then, that I was summoned to the security office for interrogation in its grand building behind the souk. There was one main question they wanted me to answer: "Why did you come to al-Hillah?" They began with that question, and after a long round of interrogation, they ended with it too. Why *had* I come to al-Hillah? Well, I had never really asked myself that question. I should have. My friend and I had visited numerous places—villages, towns, and the wilderness. Since we were laid off in the public interest five years ago, we had never stayed in any one place longer than we had in al-Hillah. It was here that I married the first woman I had ever known and loved, Alam Gishi. And it was here too that I first took up farming and had land and a house of my own. Perhaps that was part of the wisdom behind our being created: cultivating the earth.

I can't remember what my specific answers were. But I do remember having mentioned Alam Gishi's name at least twenty times, although they never asked me about her. They said they knew everything about me and about her, and there was nothing more that they needed to know in that respect. They wanted to know one thing: why had I come to al-Hillah? Deep inside, I was aware that

that question was the magic key to some hellish circle. If I turned that key, I would lose myself in that vicious circle, fall into a maze with no exit. My instinct kept me on the circle's surface, and I was eager not to go any deeper. In the jargon of the security forces, this was called maneuvering, or being convoluted—a serious condition that was generally handled with direct blows to the head. But they didn't resort to that method then, as they believed it was outdated and could be counterproductive at that time.

29

"IT'S HELL. THAT'S WHAT IT IS."

It was mid-October, which meant that the farmers were done harvesting sesame. And the sorghum, too, was ripe: its canes and ears were dry, waiting for the harvester. There were rumors circulating that the bank had imported a large number of modern harvesters. Each machine could reap as much as a hundred *feddans* in a single day, using only three skilled workers who came with the machines, plus one unskilled worker to do some heavy lifting work.

The harvesters were procured during the last month of the labor season: the time that the Jungo had long been waiting for, when labor charges reached their peak. Here they were, staring helplessly as the devilish machine went about doing the job they used to do—mercilessly throwing them into idleness and laughing at them with its disgusting metallic vibrations. Those machines, which were also owned by the bank staff, effectively cut the cost of labor to almost a quarter of its original rate.

As a final blow to the demoralized Jungo, the bank intended to import, for the next agricultural season, a chemical that would prevent all weeds and parasites from growing. The bank was also planning to bring in a machine that could uproot all trees, large and small, in just fifteen minutes, thus eliminating the need to remove trees manually—the manual process required a full day to remove one small tree, and there was no guarantee that the tree wouldn't grow back again. Such machines and equipment had never crossed the minds of the Jungo and still seemed like fairy tales to them, although they had seen the huge sesame harvester with their very own eyes, had seen its terrifying arms that writhed on the ground like wounded snakes—the grating of its belts and the bellowing of its exhaust pipe could be heard hundreds of meters away.

The Jungo had gathered spontaneously from nearby farms and neighboring camps and villages to take a closer look at this creature that galloped through the sesame stalks and just moments later spewed the grain into jute sacks, throwing the dizzy canes onto the dry black soil. They had once seen sorghum harvesters, but those were unsuccessful in these rough terrains, which had too many creeks and forests—to say nothing of their high cost. But this creature here had been manufactured by the Chinese specifically for the topography of the East, and it provided an effective solution to the problem of fuel shortages and high labor costs. The more advantages the Jungo heard about, the more frustrated they grew.

"Have they made a machine to impregnate women too, so that we can seek other work in this world?" one Jungo commented.

Those machines had a profound impact on every aspect of life in al-Hillah and beyond: in al-Jairah, al-Hafeera, Khor Maghareef, Fashaga, Hashaba, Zahanah, Hamdayeit, Mount Esayr, al-Homra, Tesseney, the outskirts of Qedaref, around Samsam, al-Jannah Barra, al-Layah, Hajar al-Asal, al-Hoori, Om Sagata, al-Aradaibat, al-Magran, al-Mafazah, al-Hawattah, Doka, the upper Dinder River, Awlad Shaigoug, the Ghanam farm, Aradaibah Korsi, and Aradaibah Tigani.

The Jungo felt coldness and bitterness in their souls. In al-Hillah, their undisputed stronghold, the impact was most evident. A striking example was the Mother's House: the number of its clients, Jungo and small farmers, declined sharply; girls and other workers lost their jobs, and many moved to neighboring towns, particularly Khashm El Girba, Kasala, and Qedaref; some went all the way to Khartoum. Some women resigned themselves to selling tea, coffee, *sheesha*, and food for truck drivers along the highway. Even Wad Ammoona was believed to be preparing to move to Khartoum for good, and there were rumors that he was poised to make a big leap after an influential person seemed to have expressed an interest in him.

All this happened in just one month. But it was the most critical month of the year, during which a Jungojorai would complete his outfit and might manage to place large cash deposits with his friends, the local liquor makers, or with Addai's girls, who had always served as small banks for the Jungo: compassionate, honest, and interest-free. In the same month, women would normally build up stocks of sorghum that they bought from small-scale farmers at cheap rates. They always kept a sack of sesame to sell later after the prices went up, when the crop market opened to receive the new season's production, or when the sesame company entered the market as a buyer, or when a some disaster or other raised the price.

As the days went by, a privileged few gained fortunes while the Jungo, the small-scale farmers, and the women stood by and watched. Many fled the town, including Fekki Ali al-Zaghrad. The bank manager left too, after unidentified men made an attempt on his life. Scores of Jungo moved to places near Hawattah or to the outskirts of Qedaref. The message they carried to the Jungo in those places was, "the bank is bound to come to you, so you'd better be on the lookout for other means of livelihood."

The military presence intensified in al-Hillah: police, central reserve forces, popular defense forces, community police, public security officers, and economic security officers. Aggressive drafting campaigns were unleashed to conscript young men and women—and even some older people—for the popular defense forces. It was obvious to all that there was something wrong, something they couldn't quite pinpoint, though they could understand or at least guess the underlying motive: money. Al-Hillah was in the throes of a cruel rebirth, as crucial as the moment when gold was discovered in the New World, diamonds in Pretoria and Cape Town, and cotton in Sudan. It was the moment when easy money was discovered. And it was a strange type of fever: the fever of money.

With the *googo* on her back, al-Safyah descended on our farm, escorted by her team of five Jungo. In the morning, they worked with us on harvesting and cane cutting. They were happy, chanting beautiful old harvest songs that had almost dried on their lips. For several weeks, they had been driven out of work by faster and more precise machines. Now they had a great enthusiasm for work. Another team—Towr Morah Morsal and three Jungo—joined us, and they were followed by Worl Ajang's team, then Mohammed Wad al-Nawaymah's; and then came al-Sadek Abbas' team, accompanied by al-Tayeb Kabsoon and Hassan Obaid—or "the wolf," as he was nicknamed; and others still. It was as if the Jungo had been invited over the radio, which they listened to at all times. Songs filled our blue skies, and we had wonderful celebratory nights.

The crop was harvested in just five days; the canes were chopped up and made into one large pile that was fenced with thorns to fend off animals. Mukhtar Ali and I agreed that we should put al-Shaygi's share aside and divide the remainder with the Jungo on equal terms, but the Jungo firmly opposed that arrangement. However, they did agree that five sacks of sorghum should be allocated for *mareesa*. We dispatched the sorghum on a truck to al-Hillah. It was the first shipment of sorghum to enter al-Hillah in that eventful season. As it turned out, it was also the last.

Regardless of my personal opinion of what happened and whether it was good or bad, I want to put on record that I was not involved in the events that ensued—I was away doing the harvesting work and was busy preoccupied with news of Alam Gishi. In fact, the latter task occupied most of my attention, and I couldn't keep track of the developments involving the armed Jungo and the frustrated nomads who joined forces with them. So I missed a series of seminars that the Jungo organized in nearby farms and camps, as well as the most recent ones in al-Hillah. I also lost touch with Wad Ammoona, who was now preoccupied with the bankers and shuttling back and forth to Khartoum. As a result, I was cut off from the world, with no one to provide me with information and alert me to developments.

But I'll never forgive myself for being taken by surprise—just like a pest or an animal—by the event that rocked the entire place. During an unplanned seminar, or, more accurately, over a hundred emergency seminars organized in the streets and houses of al-Hillah, the audience suddenly found themselves talking about one thing: fire. Let us listen to some of the descriptions of the scene as voiced by eyewitnesses. They were actually making these comments to themselves, as everyone was too perplexed to listen to others for a description or an explanation.

"It's Hell. That's what it is!"

"Truly, son, this has never happened before, not since the people of Thamud,"[1] one old lady said, trying hard to make herself heard.

"May Lord Jesus be with them," Mother Mariam Kudi prayed in front of the horrified kids who had taken refuge in the Church. They imitated her as she drew the icon of the Holy Trinity. They prayed to the Lord to compensate the owners of small-scale farms for their massive losses.

"Amen."

It happened at 1 a.m. People woke up to a massive fire in the middle of the fields. Giant flames were reaching up to the clear blue sky, like a dragon trying to lick the stars with its flaming tongue. It had started as a sporadic flame. Moments later, the entire place was ablaze, the flames reaching into the sky and turning the whole place into an open fireworks display. It was an infernal festival beyond words. The screams of terrified children, the wailing of women, and the mumblings of the drunkards added to the miserable drama. Then barrages of bullets sprayed out from Zahanah forest. A contingent of central reserve forces and police marched aimlessly around the village. They couldn't go beyond al-Hillah, which was the only safe zone. So they busied themselves with building meaningless military formations.

At sunrise, the fire called off its festivities, leaving dark spots on the ground, like henna on the feet of some legendary bride, offering thousands of *feddans* of her body as a sacrifice to the wind.

---

[1] Referring to the people of Thamud, an ancient nation that Allah punished for their failure to heed His commands.

30 THE BODY LYRICS

People really didn't know anything about Mother Addai because they presumed they already knew everything they needed to know about her. And that was why no thrilling events or stories involving her were ever related; I never heard anyone talk about her life, her past, her family, her origins, or even her real name. They took her for granted: like the water, the sky, the day, and the night.

Wad Ammoona and I sat invoking memories of Qedaref Prison. Our conversation drifted to Addai.

"If Addai died now, who would inherit her place?" he asked.

He was not expecting an answer. His question was rather a continuation of his account about Addai. She was hardly seventeen when she joined the Eritrean People's Liberation Front. Wad Ammoona and all the others considered this an undisputable fact. They also firmly believed she was a fierce, belligerent, and beautiful fighter—a shrewd, battle-scarred commander who had experienced triumphs and defeats, had seen comrades and friends die, and who had been wounded and arrested, and who had then escaped from detention. Prior to the revolution, she was a friend of Mengistu Haile Mariam when he was just a *falloul* roaming the borders between Sudan, Eritrean, and Ethiopia. It was believed that one of her parents was Eritrean and the other Ethiopian, or that both were Ethiopians, or that both were Eritreans. Those clear contradictions were the only details that people in al-Hillah believed about her. My encounters with her were too brief to allow me to verify that information. She was always busy attending to some household matter or to a client's request, or issuing directives to the girls or to Wad Ammoona. She was entirely devoted to her work.

Wiping his pretty face with his palm, Wad Ammoona asked, "You don't know me very well, do you?"

I was taken by surprise. We were at Addai's house, and it was the morning following my darling Alam Gishi's escape to her husband and daughters. Wad Ammoona had devoted himself to entertaining me. We shared some refreshing glasses of *asaliyah*. After a moment of hesitation, I said, "Well . . . I know you to some extent."

"But all you really know about me is from gossip and conversations at the *mareesa* houses, right?" he asked, laughing.

"You could say that," I admitted. "We never had time to sit together like we are now. I hardly even know the Mother. And there are some stories you've related to me and to Alam Gishi—about the prison, the cook, your mother, and Azza. And I'm sure there are other things I can't remember now."

He said in a heavy voice, "I can't find anyone to talk to about my own life, my personal life. There are a lot of things weighing on me. I need a friend I can confide in, someone to give me advice, to help me tell right from wrong."

What an absurd situation I found myself in. He wanted me to be his counselor when I couldn't tell right from wrong in my own life. I said, "Of course I'd love to listen, but I can't give you advice. No one on this earth truly knows right from wrong. But you can talk to me as a friend and as a brother."

He fanned the *sheesha* coal with some palm leaves. Ashes scattered in all directions, exposing the live red coal.

"My life is like this coal. I haven't had a moment's rest," he said.

Suddenly he fixed his eyes on me, "Am I a man or a woman?" he asked. He didn't wait for an answer. He started explaining to me in a very low tone how he had discovered himself at the age of eighteen. He was swimming with some friends in the Basalam River, where they often played popular games such as "the crocodile and the diver," "the wooden rod," and others. During these games, it was inevitable that they came in bodily contact with each other. One day, however, he felt a strong quivering when he bumped against another boy while they were playing "the crocodile and the diver." He had always admired his playmate's agility and his skill in hunting birds and wild rabbits, which were abundant on the uninhabited eastern bank of the river. The quivering was so violent that he nearly drowned. He thought he must have been hit by a *barada*, a small fish that gave off an electric shock as a defense mechanism. That was the only explanation that Wad Ammoona could think of at the time. That incident didn't linger long in his memory, though.

The real turning point in his life was what happened with a stranger who visited the Mother's House one summer night. He was a markedly delicate man in his late fifties, slender and handsome, and soft-spoken. Women spoke to him freely about every matter as if he were one of them. When he saw Wad Ammoona, he called him, held his hands, and pulled him close to his face. He smelled of perfume—a perfume that, from that day on, became Wad Ammoona's go-to scent. He pulled him closer still, until Wad Ammoona could feel his breath on his face. He kissed him twice on his cheeks and ran his fingers across his lips. Rubbing Wad Ammoona's hair with his other hand, he whispered softly in his ear, "Take care of yourself. You're a prince." It reached Wad Ammoona's ears as "You're a princess." He was quivering in ecstasy as the man's words and kisses pervaded every part of his body.

I had heard a different version of that story before. Apparently Wad Ammoona's purpose behind relating it to me was to refute that very version, which he must have heard many times. It could well be that the other version was the authentic one and that Wad Ammoona was trying to mislead me. According to the other version, when the man saw Wad Ammoona, he rose to his feet as if he had been stung. He gave him a warm embrace and kissed him on the lips, just like men kissed women. It was also said—may Allah protect us all against the perils of gossip—that he kissed him somewhere else too, in the presence of several women, including Alam Gishi. Thank God Addai was not at home: she would have taught him a lesson. It was said that he had a long conversation with Wad Ammoona that no one else could hear because the man was literally whispering into Wad Ammoona's ear. But those inclined to speculation interpreted the whispers as "seductions and obscenities." A reference to that incident appeared in Wad Ammoona's memoirs, which were published years after he left his ministerial job and public service at large. In those memoirs, described by some as "indecent," his Excellency revealed that the stranger had handed him the keys to the future.

The stranger left the next day. Wad Ammoona never saw him again, but from that day on, he began to give paramount importance to his body and his appearance and to the way he walked—the way he moved his hands and hips. He clearly modeled his movements on those of women. He even confided to me that he wished he were a woman. He hated those masculine parts dangling between his thighs and longed instead for real breasts and a woman's face and for the feeling of menstrual blood flowing from him. His mother had noticed those inclinations early on, and she always admonished him: "Be a man, Wad Ammoona. Leave the women's stuff to women." Such comments offended him because at that time he never felt he was imitating women, but rather that it was his innate nature. He often had heated arguments with his mother.

"There's a woman inside me, deep inside me," he said suddenly, raising his hands in the air. I felt as if he had rid himself of a huge burden that'd been weighing heavily on him. He said he felt guilty and full of remorse for what he had done to the prison cook, and if he could go back in time, he would surely submit to that man's will. "I shouldn't have reacted so violently," he said in a sad tone.

When he calmed down, I shared something with him, though I wasn't sure how true it was: "Every man has a woman inside him, and every woman has a man inside her."

"No," he said, an anxious smile hovering on his face. "I have a real woman inside me, a crazy woman. She wants to come out by any means."

I felt he was being completely honest. I truly admired him and felt inadequate—I was unable to offer even the smallest help to him, not even some bit of advice. Although he looked confident and composed, he wanted me to answer his main question: what was wrong with him? He took the discussion one step further and asked me whether it was true that in America one could painlessly remove one's male organs and lead a normal life as a woman and get married. I said it was true.

"Is it easy to go to America?" he asked.

"Through the lottery," I answered him. That was the easiest question I had received.

"What's the lottery?"

I explained the lottery to him. He followed up with over twenty other questions. And when he sensed that he was overburdening me, he apologized: "Sorry to bother you with my personal problems, and to trouble you with such silly questions. You have your own problems, as big as mountains."

He was certainly alluding to the problem of Alam Gishi. I said I couldn't express how happy I was that he had opened up to me, and I encouraged him to speak even more freely. I wanted to ask him if he had ever had an intimate encounter with a man, but I didn't have my friend's courage—the courage to ask such questions and endure the consequences. I felt sure he had had such an experience, although he wouldn't admit it. As if he had read my thoughts, he changed the subject: "You know what? I always feel the Mother is the happiest person in the world, even though she has no children or family and never got married."

"True," I said. "Happiness is when you have a mission in life. Some people's goals in life are their family and children. Others find satisfaction in the respect, love, and friendship of those around them. Others go around trying to buy everything. Everyone knows how to make themselves happy."

"I find happiness in serving people and making them happy," he said.

We had a long and wonderful chat. I told him about my family and my friend's family and about Qedaref and the prison—from the perspective of a jailor's son. I told him about my life, although my experiences were few and poor compared with his eventful ones. He told me about his intention to settle and work in Khartoum. A bank official had promised to introduce him to a very important person there, someone very high up, very rich, very influential, and very full of lust. If he could get in good with that person, all doors would open for him. "You're worth your weight in gold, Wad Ammoona," the bank official assured him. "But here you are as worthless as goat dung."

I felt that statement was a bit of an exaggeration, although not entirely so. Years later, when my friend emailed me a copy of his non-fiction book *The Revolt of the Jungojoraya*, I was not surprised to learn that Wad Ammoona had risen to a very senior post—a political position he couldn't have dreamt of back then even if he'd been endowed with all the imagination in the world.

Before leaving, he said something I didn't understand: "Your friend's amazing!"

"What do you mean?"

Standing by the door, he looked me straight in the eyes, a coquettish smile on his face, and said, "I mean he's simply amazing!"

"You remember the other day, on the bus to Hamdayeit, when al-Shaygi and his group stole our money? Remember? You were saying something about my friend, but you didn't get around to finishing it."

"And you didn't ask me again. It's too late now!" he said, teasing me.

Leaving his fragrance behind, he went out, walking confidently and proudly. I ran after him and grabbed him. For the first time, I realized how delicate his hands were—as soft as a baby's. He laughed and said he would tell me only at the right time. I insisted. It wasn't my habit, but I felt an irresistible urge to know what had happened between Wad Ammoona and my friend, the patriot and theorist. Throughout our lifelong friendship, from early childhood to the present day, I had never noticed any homosexual leanings in my friend. We had no moral reservations against such things, but we classified ourselves as being attracted to the opposite sex—my friend liked to use the English term, "heterosexual." Yet I couldn't rule out that Wad Ammoona might have seduced him or that my friend might have wanted to see for himself if Wad Ammoona was truly homosexual. I knew that my friend, for the sake of proving certain ideas, wouldn't hesitate to go that far, and even farther. I knew that from experience. But I wanted to know what exactly had happened here. Wad Ammoona noticed my sense of urgency. It was a weak point that I was sure Wad Ammoona wouldn't fail to exploit.

"You want to know?" he asked coquettishly.

"Yes, I do. Now!" I said, mimicking the way he talked and trying to hide my anger.

He came back and sat beside me on the big bed, crossed his legs and lit a Bringi cigarette. As soon as he started to talk, I could tell from his expression that he was making up the whole story. I could smell its freshness as it dripped off his tongue. When he was being honest, just a moment ago, his face had looked different. I abruptly asked him to stop and go get me a bottle of cognac. He smiled, stood up, and went out quietly.

31

PROPHET SOLOMON'S SEAL

A rational man like me could not have stayed on at al-Hillah a single minute longer. Those who had stayed awake all night watching the festival of fire that consumed all the sorghum fields were now too drowsy to take notice of us as we sneaked toward al-Homra in Ethiopia. We were a small caravan full of fear: my friend Mukhtar, al-Safyah, and myself, along with many other Jungo. Addai was our leader. She carried a small but heavy bundle that contained all her wealth, in the form of gold. She looked exhausted, perhaps because she was so fat. It had been more than thirty years since she had retired from the battlefield and chosen an easier and far more convenient lifestyle. Although we were all terrified, we couldn't leave without her. We were all indebted to her. On the way, every one of us was eager to lend a hand and help her carry her wealth. We all swam to the other bank. The Mother swam far better than most of us. We marched onto rocky terrain that was nevertheless so genial and compassionate that it sympathetically contracted under our feet to shorten the distance to the Ethiopian border, our initial destination and first line of safety.

Many of the Jungo were carrying mobile phones. They called their friends and relatives back in al-Hillah, who informed them that troops from the army were chasing us on foot—their vehicles and machinery couldn't cross the river. But we were also warned that they might seek the assistance of fighter planes from Qedaref or Kasala. So we had to hurry to the Ethiopian border. The moment we crossed al-Homra Creek, we heard a roar behind us. We reckoned the fighter would not bomb us, now that we were well inside the Ethiopian territories. However, the Mother directed us to take shelter under the many trees that were scattered along the creek. The plane hovered over the trees, stirring up a thick dust storm that blinded and distracted us, causing many of the hungry and weak among us to fall down. It was apparently trying to keep us near the creek until the soldiers arrived. When it went away for brief intervals, the Mother would redeploy us. During one of the intervals when the plane was gone, she ordered us to run down the creek deep into the Ethiopian border. When the plane returned, we were no longer there. It flew back. When we were sure that the plane wasn't going to chase us inside the Ethiopian territories, we reassembled by calling out each other's names. Only 24 reported to the meeting point. There was one person missing. I had counted 25 people in the group after we crossed the river. It did not take long to realize that the missing person was Addai. We went off in different directions in the bush and along the creek to search for her. We called out as loudly as we could. Following the same route we had taken, we went back to the site where we had been besieged by the plane and to the place where she had last been seen. No trace of her. Some Jungo suggested she might have taken a different route into Ethiopia. She was no stranger to that place: thirty years ago, she had been a *falloul* roaming those territories and looking for passersby on the outskirts of al-Homra and Tesseney. Others said she might have been afraid that the Ethiopian soldiers would take her money. Everyone had a theory. But the fate of Addai remained unknown until a welfare officer in the refugee camp told us, two weeks later, that they had found a decomposed body five miles to the east of al-Homra creek, under a *seyal* tree. She had most probably been killed. No money or personal belongings were found with the body.

Half an hour into the Ethiopian territories, we were met by Ethiopian officials and civil leaders, as well as military and medical teams, UN officials, and representatives from the International

Organization for Migration. We were interviewed and searched for weapons. They only found a few axes and daggers. That was followed by medical checkups. Then we filed applications for political asylum, a term many of the Jungo had never heard of. The officials specified the camp that was to accommodate us. We traded our names for ID numbers. An anonymous Ethiopian organization provided us with some food and water. We spent the night in cramped tents. The UN later began building more comfortable accommodations with lavatories, washrooms, and a small clinic. We were exhausted, hungry, filthy, and broke. I, for one, was literally penniless; the only things I had left were sorghum sacks, but I had left them with Addai, who had left them behind in al-Hillah and then disappeared into the Ethiopian wilderness. All the Jungo were as penniless as I was because they hadn't worked enough that season to earn any money. Had it not been for the food and accommodation offered by the UN organizations, we would have starved to death. We were soon joined by other families and other Jungo who had come from Hamdayeit, al-Gargaf, and Zahanah.

Exactly three months later, in early January, Alam Gishi sent me a message informing me that she expected to deliver in a week's time—she invited me to the baby-naming ceremony, if I could make it safely to Hamdayeit. I was alone in the tent when the messenger, who was later identified as Is'haq al-Muslati, came in. I had spent most of my time alone recently. My friend Mukhtar Ali, after only one week in the camp, had become bored and decided to go to Fariek Girish to join some old friends. He invited me to go with him, suggesting that we could work with the Ethiopian farmers as day laborers, i.e., as Jungo. To him, that was far more decent than staying in the camp like beggars waiting for charity from the Europeans. I didn't like the idea and tried to convince him to wait until things had calmed down a bit, but he left for Fariek Girish along with al-Safyah and some other Jungo.

The messenger told me that Alam Gishi was in good health and very happy and was living with the family of her husband's father, who loved her and her children. He sat on the only chair in my tent and had set an old black Samsonite briefcase down beside him. While I was of course happy that she was going to give birth to our child very shortly, I was both sad and disappointed to learn that she was happy and that her husband's family loved her. Didn't that mean the chances of her divorcing him had become very slim, almost zero? When he read the grief in my face, the Jungojorai said there were plenty of women in Fariek Girish—beautiful, slender women. He described them as "sugar," which was the sweetest thing in that part of the world. He suggested that I should go there and look for one to marry. He promised to facilitate the matter for me through his network of acquaintances and relatives. He said I could choose from many different ethnic origins: Bilala, Fellata, Talsa, Zhubarana, Baza, Jaalieen, Dinka, Takroon, etc. It was evident that that freak attached special importance to the tribal origins of women. From the way he pronounced the names of the tribes and from his facial expressions, which were abundantly clear even in the faint light of the lantern, I could sense that he classified those women on purely aesthetic grounds: a knowledgeable person could tell the difference between one woman and another by her tribe; each tribe had its own flavor.

He added in a confident tone that suggested a scholarly knowledge of people, particularly women: "As for Ethiopian women, this is of course their homeland. The country is full of women; each one is prettier than the other."

"None can compare to Alam Gishi," I said.

"Many are more beautiful than her," he said defiantly.

"It's not about beauty," I said, trying to explain what really mattered to me.

"What's it about, then?" he asked. "Are there women in this world who are better at sex than other women? Are there women made of clay and others made of fire? I'm trying to understand."

In an attempt to help him understand, I said, "It's not about sex."

"So what's it about? Do you mean love?" he asked sarcastically. "You mean there's no other woman you can love? Sorry, I'm just trying to understand."

In an attempt to help him understand, I said, "Of course there are many women, but . . . "

"So," he interrupted, intensifying his siege, "what is it that Alam Gishi has that no other woman has?"

"I don't know. I really don't know."

"I do," he said coolly, confidently.

"Tell me," I said quickly. "I don't know."

Looking into the distance, and as if he were talking to empty space, he said, "Alam Gishi is a demon, a female djinn."

"A demon?"

"Yes." He put his hand on my shoulder in a strange way. "That's what she is. She came straight from the river. This country is full of djinn. They're living with people, but no one can see them."

"And how do *you* know about them?" I asked the tall, brown-skinned man standing there with glistening skin and a clean-shaven face.

He took in a short breath and swallowed nervously, "I just do."

As I hadn't seen this Jungojorai before, I got a strange feeling he himself might be a djinn. I found myself scanning him, particularly his legs and toes, searching for the signs that were said to be associated with the djinn. The djinn were widely known to have the feet of donkeys, or sometimes of dogs. But the man's feet seemed perfectly human, and there was nothing strange about his appearance, except that he was perhaps too clean-cut, too eloquent, and too confident.

He said he was the first man in the entire East to meet Alam Gishi, and he took that as a great honor, implying that he was distinguished in some way. He had been working at Osman Eisa Haroun's farm near the al-Hashaba Bridge. Alam Gishi told him she had escaped from al-Homra prison and was afraid the Ethiopian police might capture her and return her to custody. He hid her in his hut for a full week, provided her with good food and drink, and bought her new clothes to replace her "lice-infested" garments. He had no reason to dispute her story about the prison and the Ethiopian police until early one morning, when he felt an urge to go to bed with her. When he undressed her, he was astonished to see the djinn seal stamped on her back.

"On her lower back, near her bottom. It looked like Prophet Solomon's seal," he said. He drew an image on the ground.

"Did you see this seal or not?" he asked me.

It looked like the star of the Prophet David, with its strange triangles. I had seen this figure numerous times since I was a teenager. *Fekkis* would draw it on paper and give it to women to burn and inhale as a way of exorcizing evil spirits and bringing good luck to them and their children.

"There *was* something," I admitted. "But I swear to God I never asked myself whether it was a seal, a tattoo, or a mole. But it did carry some resemblance to the image you drew on the ground."

In fact, the thing that I had seen on the back of Alam Gishi looked exactly like the image this Jungojorai, Is'haq al-Muslati, had drawn on the ground. It was a prominent marking and was exactly where he said it was. But I was giving myself some space to maneuver.

"That was the seal of Prophet Solomon," he added matter-of-factly. When he asked her about it, she ran away. He never saw her again until he saw her with me in al-Hillah.

"She wept and said to me, 'Please don't reveal my secret, Is'haq, son of Dreng. Please don't tell anyone.' But I'm telling you, for the sake of God."

"But how did you know that it was the seal of the djinn?" I asked.

He said he had spent all his life on the banks of the Setit River, from Hashaba, al-Jairah, al-Hafeera, Hamdayeit, al-Homra, Zahanah, and all the way to Khashm El Girba. That region was the seat of the biggest djinn kingdom in the world, the djinn of Prophet Solomon, who all dispersed after his death. And Khashm El Girba in particular was mentioned seven times in the *Book of Mysteries*. The King of Kings of the djinn, known as al-Anwar, lived in the Om Osood area, behind the shrine of Sheikh Absharah. Many of the residents of Khashm El Girba had seen him. He appeared once every year, on the anniversary of the day when a fish gave Solomon back the seal that the djinn had stolen from his wife.

So on that day each year, the river would flood over and the ancestors of the fish that had swallowed the seal and given it back to Prophet Solomon would come onto the shore, and people would pick them up with their bare hands and grill or boil them. That was an annual punishment inflicted upon them by the King of Kings of the djinn, on a special day they dubbed "the fish-hitting day," though they should have called it "the fish day" because if that one ancient fish ("the grandmother") hadn't returned the seal to Prophet Solomon, Solomon wouldn't have gained control over the djinn and that fish's descendants would not have fallen victim to vengeance. So the king would appear on that day, but the people wouldn't recognize him because they were ignorant of the secret science. He would appear in the shape of a crocodile, a strange bird, a fish that no one could catch, or any other beast he chose.

As if he wanted to sum up his statement with some sort of theory or revelation, al-Muslati said that whoever happened to sleep with a female djinn could never again enjoy sex with any human female. He assured me that he had not touched another woman ever since he slept with Alam Gishi fifteen years ago.

"Have you touched another woman since Alam Gishi?" he suddenly asked. Before I could reply, he added theatrically, as if he were in playing a role in a black comedy, "She's got to come back to me. I won't be able to die until that happens."

"So you're in line with me," I said cynically.

"It's not just me and you. There are thousands and thousands of men waiting all over the world," he said in an oddly serious tone.

I decided to keep silent. I wished he would vanish for good. I didn't want to see him again. I wished the whole thing was a dream. He stayed on till midday, talking about the djinn's kingdoms, their homelands, their names, and their sweet women. They're everywhere, he said, in every form you can imagine. Half of the trees around us could well be djinn. They can transform into insects, birds, animals, or people. Their ranks include Muslims, Christians, Jews, and nonbelievers. There are smart djinn and stupid djinn, honest djinn and deceitful ones. He assured me once again that all the djinn in the entire East were the servants of Prophet Solomon—they had dispersed all over the universe following the death of Queen Balqees, Prophet Solomon's beloved.

I unfortunately asked him about the old Samsonite briefcase that lay by his leg. My intention was to move the discussion away from the djinn and Alam Gishi. He squatted on the ground and silently put his hands on the briefcase, trying to look calm and composed and to lend himself a mystical aura. He brought the small oil lantern closer and turned the old rusty numbers on the combination lock. It opened, and inside I saw a big book whose pages had turned yellow. The book was so big it almost filled the entire briefcase; the remaining space was filled with dried plants that I had never seen before—or perhaps the lantern was too faint to allow me to identify them. Opening up the first page of the book, he said: "Come on, read."

I said I preferred for him to do the reading.

"No. I want you to see for yourself."

"See what?"

"The book."

I came nearer but still kept a good distance. I didn't want to implicate myself in what I thought of as senseless magic and sorcery, which could only serve to deceive ignorant people. As if he had heard my thoughts, he said, "This is just an ordinary book, authored by Imam Galaluddin al-Anbar, may God bestow his blessings on us as he has endowed us with his knowledge. I found it with an old sheikh who wouldn't lend it to me, so I had to copy the whole book out by hand."

I said I preferred that he do the reading. And so as not to sound rude, I said the lighting was too poor for me to read, and so was my eyesight. He started, "In the name of Allah, the most gracious, the most merciful" and then read two pages. What little I could make of them was that whoever disputed the content of that book would put himself in danger and sustain grave losses, while those who believed in it would reap many advantages, of which he provided some examples. I thought he made some references to a sacred oath and Allah's greatest name. He said whoever knew Allah's greatest name would own a quarter of the universe. He claimed that the secret key to Allah's greatest name lay within the book he was carrying. I didn't want to ask any further questions, afraid that that would drag me to even darker areas and tempt him to stay on with me for the whole week. He volunteered to read the full title of the book for me—*Galgaloteyat al-Asrar* or *The Trove of Secrets*—and then told me of another book titled *The Letters of Fire*—both were by Imam Galaluddin al-Anbar.

He said he could tell me about my future and fortunes both in this world and the hereafter, if I wished. He added that it was from this very book that Mukhtar Ali knew that his end would be below the death tree.

"Where's the Mother's jewelry?" he suddenly asked me.

"Some thieves killed her and took it," I said innocently.

He smiled, as if to say, what a fool. He said he himself had almost fallen under the same misconception when he heard that she had been found dead and her treasure, estimated at nearly a hundred million Ethiopian Birrs, was missing. The only proven fact in the story was that the Mother had been murdered. But who killed her? And where was her treasure? Those were questions that only he (in al-Homra) and Allah (in the universe at large) knew the answer to. He, for one, would never divulge the secret, but Allah might one day, at His discretion.

Deciphering the mystery behind the Mother's death was not a particular priority for me. What I needed more was a good sleep and some peace—I needed to get rid of that evil man and also his book. But he suddenly asked me, "Do you want to know when you're going to die?"

Taken aback by the abrupt question, I asked him whether he knew the time of his own death. He said he didn't, but that was only because he didn't want to bother himself with such things. Yet he was aware that the matter was of paramount importance to some people, particularly city dwellers who usually planned ahead for their future, and he thought I was that type of a person.

"No. I don't want to know," I said, which was not exactly the truth. He paused for a long while, then shut his book and put it carefully back into his old cracked Samsonite briefcase. He rose to his feet, dusted off his clean galabia, and bid me farewell. I could still see him in the austere light of the lantern when he called out in a coarse voice, which sounded as if it came from some forgotten grave: "You're going to die at the age of seventy-five years, two months, and three days, early in the morning, in a foreign land far away." I heard his laughter pierce through the darkness of the camp as he gradually vanished, leaving behind a host of questions, some grief, and the heavy darkness.

A few minutes later, a young Jungojorai named Abul Naja Saeed, from Khashm El Girba, came in.

"That man talked to you about the djinn, didn't he?"

"How did you know?"

"He's in an intimate relationship with a demon. Everybody knows that. He lives in al-Hafeera, by the river. He told you his name was Is'haq al-Muslati, didn't he?"

"Yes he did," I said nonchalantly.

Looking me straight in the eye, he said, "What's wrong with you? Are you afraid? What the hell did he tell you? He's the biggest liar in this whole region. Don't tell me you believed him. What did he tell you?"

"Nothing. Nothing," I said, trying to sound normal.

I decided to go to Hamdayeit early in the morning, no matter what. It was only ten minutes away from al-Homra by local transport, or half an hour on foot. The problem was how to sneak out of the camp and back into it without the social welfare officers noticing. Besides,

I was now the camp sheikh and leader, the spokesperson of the refugees, and my absence even for a single hour would be felt instantly. More seriously, I would be risking my life because if I got caught in Hamdayeit, I would definitely be executed in a matter of seconds, just as dozens of Jungo had been executed.

The fierce fighting between the Jungo and the government still showed no sign of abating. There were rumors that young men from the Lahawyieen and Homran tribes had joined the armed Jungo. Their numbers were estimated to be in the hundreds, and they were believed to be honing their shooting skills on the outskirts of Tesseney in Eritrea. And to lend the situation even more excitement, Israel was added to the list; some swore that they had seen Zionist elements conducting the training. Others denied that the Lahawyieen and other nomads had joined the Jungojora army. It was certain, though, that the government was negotiating with the armed rebels through a regional mediator. People were saying that another peace agreement was in the making, this time for Eastern Sudan.

The news of war was not exactly the focus of my attention. I was preoccupied with one thing: the deceitful words of a man named Is'haq al-Muslati, particularly one statement that I couldn't forget: "You're under the spell of a demon."

I couldn't wait to see my baby, even if for just a few moments. I wouldn't take the baby from her until he had been weaned. I just wanted to see it; that was all. I discussed my plans with Tesfai, the social welfare officer, who warned me of the high risks involved and briefed me on the escalating tensions between the government, on one hand, and the Arabic nomads and Jungo, on the other. The latter were now speaking for the entire east of the country, demanding its legitimate share in the country's power and wealth. He warned me that even if I managed to escape from one side, I might not be as successful with the other. He suggested instead that Alam Gishi bring the baby to al-Homra: our meeting place could be the customs zone by the bar that overlooks the river separating the two countries. That spot was only ten minutes away on foot from the house where Alam

Gishi lived with her girls and their father. He assured me that the meeting could be arranged under the patronage of the International Red Cross. He would alert them in good time to bring Alam Gishi and her baby. There was no point risking my life, he said: I should be rational and show some patience. I accepted his suggestion and waited, albeit impatiently.

One day, the social welfare officer came and asked me to prepare to meet my child the next day. He was now two months old and in good health. I could see his mother too. They were aware that Alam Gishi and I had separated on her wishes. Tesfai knew the whole story, having heard it from those who had escaped from al-Hillah with me, though everyone had their own version of it.

I was lonely, as had been my habit in recent days, and felt a deep grief and utter alienation. I became ill-tempered. A few days earlier, I got into a quarrel with a Jungo woman who had stolen some snuff from a man. They brought her to me to resolve the dispute. She was angry and blamed me for all the homelessness and misery. I had never been so ill-tempered before, and my position as the camp sheikh dictated that I show prudence and self-restraint, not anger and rashness. Yet I found myself reciprocating her obscenities and anger. Later I felt deeply sorry about the incident.

Al-Safyah came in all of a sudden. She was now fully integrated into the Jungo army and had aspirations beyond farm work, food, and drinks. She confided to me that she intended to go to university to study to be a lawyer. With the help of God, nothing was impossible. Wad Ammoona, for instance, finally found someone in the capital to look after him. Even my friend's prophecy—about an imminent victory and about them gaining a privileged position in Khartoum once the peace agreement had been signed—might come true.

She then told me that Mukhtar Ali had gone to the death tree of his own free will, after his health had seriously deteriorated. She, his friends, and even al-Shaygi (during his occasional visits to Fariek Girish) failed to dissuade him. So she left him there and came here to seek my help. The message she carried from him was, "Go back right now to your family in Qedaref. Don't stay a single second in the East. Otherwise you'll meet the same fate as me and all the Jungo: the death tree. I really hope you escape this miserable fate."

My relationship with Mukhtar Ali was one of a father and son, to say the least. Mukhtar Ali had taken good care of me and my friend, and had been our mentor and guide during our early days in al-Hillah. It was Mukhtar who had deciphered the mysteries of al-Hillah to us through his captivating tales. The least I could do now for Mukhtar Ali in his present ordeal was to visit him in Fariek Girish at his death tree and dissuade him from submitting to death. I didn't think twice. I went with al-Safyah to the camp management and obtained a permit to visit the city. It was valid for only one day—more than enough time. I could go and come back before the 6 p.m. curfew. If Mukhtar Ali agreed, I would bring him along and have him registered as a refugee. He would have access to free food and accommodation: just the bare essentials, but something is better than nothing. And I could host him in my own tent.

Suddenly she came closer and whispered to me that my friend, not al-Shaygi, was the actual commander of the Jungo and Bedouin army. He was the one who had sent her to me. He wanted to meet me at Fariek Girish to discuss something she considered important: my joining them. I tried hard to compose myself as I articulated my message to him: I had always been a civilian, and I would remain a civilian. I hated guns, the word "war" terrified me, and I wouldn't kill a human being whatever the differences between us or however offensive he had been to me. I explained my opinion to her with regard to killing helpless soldiers as a way of solving problems. I knew she couldn't fully understand my point of view; maybe she thought I was a coward, because her commentary on my tirade was, "Death is solely in Allah's hands." Fortunately, though, she did understand that the sole purpose of my visit was to see Mukhtar Ali and that I had no intentions of seeing anyone else in Fariek Girish.

"Not even your friend?"

"Not even my friend."

Al-Safyah kept talking all the way there. That was not her habit; apparently she had now adopted talking as a profession, a way of staving off idleness. She who had always hated war now had no option but to live with it. She related detailed accounts of the Jungo's encounters with the government. And even though we were alone on the road, she sometimes lowered her voice to a whisper when she wanted to communicate what she regarded as secrets that others shouldn't hear.

Fariek Girish was not far from the camp, especially as we were going to take the public bus from the souk. The al-Homra souk was in the same condition I had seen it years ago: more of a dingy set of accommodations than a souk, with shabby restaurants and small pubs that sold cheap spirits, beer, and *oozu*, an alcoholic drink popular with poor Jungo. The only change in al-Homra was that the presence of the Ethiopian army was now more evident; more personnel had been deployed to contain the military activities on the border and protect refugees. An interested visitor could enjoy a brief sexual encounter for just four Ethiopian pounds (birr). Beautiful girls in tight, revealing garments and fake gold braids woven in with their hair sat on their doorsteps inviting passersby to their lairs. Al-Safyah sped up whenever she came across one. Suddenly she stopped at a small bar, ordered a beer, and invited me to a glass or two of *oozu* if I wished, before we continued our journey. She said she was going to buy Dashin beer for Mukhtar Ali. I told her openly that I had no money, and she said she had enough. Only then did she confide to me that my friend had sent me some money but that she wouldn't give it to me until I got back to the camp so that I wouldn't waste it on women.

I said I wanted to buy something for Mukhtar Ali. Taking a sip from her beer, she said, "Mukhtar Ali doesn't need anything. He just wants to see you."

The beautiful barmaids paraded in front of me, unchastely showing off their sexy bodies. One of them shamelessly sat on my thighs. I dismissed her politely and told her in Amharic that I was not particularly helpful when it came to what women normally wanted from men. I deliberately used that lengthy expression because any shorter version might have sounded indecent, or even aggressive. And she had done nothing wrong; she was just doing her job. She stared at me in surprise, as if to say, "Oh, I understand." Then she vanished, calling off the marvelous demonstration of her body. I had enjoyed the show, and it was fulfilling to feel that these beautiful women found me attractive, even though money was involved.

Al-Safyah had been watching me from the corner of her eye. I thanked God for two things: first, I had no money, and hence no authority to make decisions; al-Safyah was in command, and it was entirely up to her to decide what I could and couldn't have, including women. The other thing was that I had long been in a state similar to an insect's hibernation. I mean to say that I didn't feel the desire for sex any more. And all the women who came to me in my dreams—the so-called "devil's women"—looked just like Alam Gishi. But my beloved Alam Gishi was not one of those women. I had never had sex with any other woman. She was the only woman in my life, and she always would be.

"Let's go," al-Safyah said when we had finished our drinks. She clapped; the waitress came instantly and stood by my side. "Santi Nu?" al-Safyah asked her in Amharic. The waitress quickly scanned our table, then said in a soft voice: "Five birr." Al-Safyah gave her the money. The waitress looked at me as she picked up the empty bottles and the two glasses, as if to say, "A woman's paying for him! Isn't that proof of what he told me earlier—that he's castrated? Poor man!"

We headed toward the death tree. At first I didn't recognize Mukhtar Ali. He looked many years older: emaciated, the bones of his face protruding, and perhaps a bit shorter than when I had last seen him months ago (I noticed that when he rose to his feet to greet me).

"I was sure you'd visit me before I died," Mukhtar Ali said as we embraced affectionately. He was clean, and his clothes smelled of incense.

I said I was determined to take him with me. That was why I had come, and I would never leave him in the shade of that tree. The huge death tree was listening to our conversation, dangling its long branches like the arms of some giant mythological creature. It gave off shade all year round, and its intense green color never faded. No one knew who planted it. That was hardly a surprise, as the *neem* trees were usually sowed by birds that would swallow ripe fruit and excrete their seeds hundreds of miles away. It must be over a hundred years old, since even the oldest people in al-Homra remembered it being the same shape and size even when they were just small children playing in its shade. Curlews and large parrots sang on its branches during the rainy season, and it played host to white cranes during their summer migration. Seven people lay under it now: five Jungo and two Ethiopians.

People told terrifying stories about it, for example, that it would tell its guests when they were going to die, whispering it in their ears in the early morning in what resembled the voice of an old woman. They also believed that it kept the souls of the dead on a branch where they would remain till Judgment Day. There were widespread stories that it cried and shed tears when any of its guests died under its shade, i.e., when they "gave back the trust," as was commonly said in those parts. Yet the strangest story involving it was about a Jungo who had been driven by poverty, illness, and hunger to decide to end his life under the tree. One day, he suddenly remembered that he had some sacks of sesame that he had entrusted to a merchant at the Hamdayeit souk. Those sacks, he thought, could meet his expenses for almost a year and pay for his medical treatment. So he decided to leave the death tree and go to Hamdayeit. He picked up his *googo*, bid his friends farewell, and started to walk off. But before he could leave the tree's shade, a branch dipped close to his ear and whispered in the voice of an old woman: "Where are you going, taking the trust with you?" He pushed the branch aside and tried to run away, but the branch held onto him and dragged him back into the shade. The poor Jungojorai was paralyzed and couldn't leave the tree's shade again—not until he died the next morning and his body was taken away.

Mukhtar Ali said he wouldn't leave that place except for his grave. "The tree has spoken. Tomorrow morning, God willing, I will give back the trust." He spoke with confidence, and it was obvious that he truly believed what he was saying. I almost burst into tears, but I remembered al-Safyah's warning that whoever cried under that tree would also die under it. I didn't want to die there, at least not then.

I gave him a Bringi cigarette. He smiled at me. I helped him back to his hard bed. Beside him was his googo: his faithful companion for over twenty years. "I knew it would kill me one day, would walk me to the grave, and would stand there laughing at me."

Al-Safyah reminded me that it was almost five o'clock, and she had to return me to the camp and then come back. I promised to come back tomorrow for Mukhtar Ali's funeral. She handed me the money that my friend had sent me. I had already received some canned food and clothes earlier in the morning when she came to me at the camp. I was in dire need of money, even though Tesfai, the social welfare officer, had presented me with a gift and some money for my baby and ex-wife, Alam Gishi. Tesfai was aware that I was penniless and that it would be extremely embarrassing for me to meet my baby for the first time and leave without presenting him with something.

The next morning, I woke up early, washed thoroughly, put on the new clothes that my friend had sent me, and took the money, the canned food, and Tesfai's gift, which I was hoping to present to the mother of my baby. We took a Land Rover 110 to the Sudanese border. On the way, my mind was preoccupied with many things. To my surprise, it wasn't just Alam Gishi and the baby that occupied my thoughts—as the international officials accompanying me no doubt expected. There were many people in my mind that day, and Wad Ammoona was prominent among them. I had understood from some Jungo who had recently joined the refugee camp in al-Homra that Azza had been released after nearly five years in prison, after Wad

Ammoona had found his way to a senior official in Khartoum and provided him a very special service.

But the most striking news about Wad Ammoona reached me ten years later, while I was in the United States: Wad Ammoona had become a federal minister under the name of Kamaluddin al-Yamani. How had that happened? That's a story that anyone from al-Hillah can relate to you in a mini-seminar on the *mareesa* day of any beautiful woman. Or you can read about it in my friend's book, which I referred to earlier, and which is titled *The Revolt of the Jungojoraya*. You can also read about it in Wad Ammoona's memoirs, which were published in Beirut. In those memoirs, his Excellency touches on many events in his life. He's very open and candid about some, but deliberately ambiguous and reticent about other more private matters. In those precious memoirs, his Excellency relates the story of his struggle for survival and how he became a notable person. The names of Azza and Alam Gishi appear repeatedly in several parts, and he refers to the Mother by her real name "Stefanis," which meant nothing to the admirers of the Mother simply because no one knew her by that name. That was not a particularly grateful gesture, in my opinion, as he owed a lot to the Mother. She had supported and nurtured him and had always been proud of him, even when he was a nobody.

Similarly, I didn't like his claim that he had been one of the leaders of the great shit revolt against the bank officials: he credited himself with playing a major role in that revolt. He claimed all of my friend's achievements in that revolt as his own. Not only that, he described me and my friend as "the arrogant ones." I don't know what he meant by those words. In another part, he called us "the dreamers." That was when he commented on the armed revolt of the Jungojorai. However, he did mention my name as one of those who had helped him understand himself. He said he was not ashamed of the sad chapters of his life because they were not of his own making. He had done his best under what he called "particularly challenging circumstances." The history that he should be held accountable for was the history of his own making: his achievements and his ability to pull himself out of what he called "the mire of poverty."

Yet the most beautiful and most sincere part of the memoirs was the section about the prison. That section was a great help to me in writing the second chapter of this novel, titled "the Prisoner, the Prison, and the Jailor." I must say, however, that I didn't copy the entire section, but rather used it as the backbone around which I constructed my chapter. I must also admit, in all honesty and in keeping with intellectual property rights, that I built the characters of the prison cook and Azza around those described by his Excellency in his memoirs. Most of the criticism those memoirs received from so-called guardians of morality and from conservatives centered on the parts about the prison. One critic said his Excellency the minister should have written about the glorious history of the city of Qedaref, and the role of al-Noor Ankara, one of the city's heroes, instead of getting stuck in the prison's mire. He also denounced the sexual insinuations, particularly when his Excellency talked about a childhood friend whom the prison cook used to sodomize.

I should also say that the thing the memoirs failed to depict properly was the character of the child who had been a friend of the boy who would later become his Excellency the minister. The memoirs portrayed that child as a victim of everyone, of every place and every time. That child, I think—in fact I'm pretty sure of it—was actually Wad Ammoona himself, and I have depicted him accordingly in this book. Anyway, those memoirs are available outside of Sudan, and you can get a copy quite easily.

I also thought of Fekki Ali, Abrahait, Addai, the beautiful Boushai—an endless list of people—until the Land Rover stopped by the bar on the eastern bank of the Setit River, the border between Ethiopia and Sudan. I was familiar with that bar, having visited it several times, and still held vivid memories of it in my heart, both pleasant and bitter. I was greeted by some barmaids who apparently recognized me, and by Ganish, the owner of the bar: how often had she and I had drunk together, quarreled, and swam in the river, completely drunk and stark naked? I read all that in her wide smile.

I looked for my son and Alam Gishi in all the faces I came across. Tesfai and a representative of the International Red Cross finally led me to a small room at the back. There were Alam Gishi and my baby, whom I immediately named Mohammed, after my father. Alam Gishi was at her best: the softest, sweetest, and most beautiful a woman could be. She was wearing "Justice," our favorite perfume. Her kohl was painted perfectly, as usual, adding to the beauty of her wide eyes. I made a request that I didn't expect her to respond to, but I just wanted to let her know that I still loved her. And that was certainly true. My affection for her had remained perfectly intact, untarnished by our alienation, or how she deserted me, or her insanity. My request was this: why didn't she come live with me at the camp, where we could bring up our child until we found another solution?

With a shy smile on her face and her hand ruffling the baby's hair affectionately, she said in Tigrigna, "Ani Naggamo Mafi."

I couldn't believe she had said yes. I couldn't believe she'd come to stay with me. How amazing the world of women is! How perplexing and crazy! Fifteen years have passed, but I still can't express my feelings, now, as I write my first novel, *The Jungo: Stakes of the Earth*, here in the state of Florida in the United States, with Alam Gishi and our three sons.

As we headed back to the camp in the Land Rover, I held my beautiful baby Mohammed on my lap, and Alam Gishi sat by my side, occasionally looking at me and smiling. I was the happiest man on earth. As I inspected the features of my baby to look for traces of our family, I saw on his lower back a small blue mole that looked like the image drawn on the ground by the suspicious al-Muslati: the seal of Prophet Solomon.

GLOSSARY

A

Abanghazi The sheep's bile—used to flavor the chili mixture; also added to *om fitfit.*

Abu A prefix that literally means "father of" and—by extension—"the one with." For example, *abu lamba* (see below) is the one with the lamb.

Abu Humar A nickname for arrack. (Humar is the Arabic for donkey!)

Abu lamba Translates into the one with (carrying) a lamp. It refers to a snake that glitters at night as if it were carrying a lamp.

Al sham The old name of the Eastern Mediterranean region, which included present day Syria and parts of Lebanon.

Angaraib A wooden frame bed, with strings made of dried local plants forming a net to sleep on.

Antat An insect that ruins the sesame harvest.

Asaliyah A date wine.

B

Baati A dead person who comes back to life.

Barbara A pickup truck with a tractor engine; a local means of transport.

Barta barta A mythical creature that has eight legs.

Bit A prefix meaning "daughter of."

C

Companions of the Cave Referring to a story related in the Holy Quran about young men who were prosecuted for having converted to a faith contrary to the state's religion. They fled for their refuge to a cave, where God kept them asleep for over 300 years.

D

Dalluka A local drum played mainly by girls, particularly at weddings.

Dilka An aromatic dough used in massage, believed to be highly effective in relieving muscle strain.

Dokhan A steam bath that married women in Sudan regularly take. A combination of aromatic wood (*taleh*) and locally produced perfumes, it lends the body a gleaming bronze color and a pleasant scent.

Dokhla Refers to the first night a groom sleeps with his bride. It is preceded by detailed rituals, including the so called "*rahat* cutting" (see below).

Doubait A form of Bedouin chanting.

E

Endaya A local bar that serves locally produced drinks.

F

Faddadi Another name for the Jungo (plural: faddada)

Faddadiyah A female *mareesa* seller (plural: faddadiyat)

Falloul The local name for bandits in Ethiopia.

Fateha The Fateha, meaning prelude, is the first *sura* (chapter) of the Holy Quran. It is recited during daily prayers and also as part of the marriage contract ceremonies.

Fatima The Prophet's daughter; married to Ali ibn Abi Talib, the Prophet's cousin, and the fourth Caliph.

Feddan A feddan is 4,200 m^2.

Fekki Fekki is a devout or religiously knowledgeable person who people call upon for treatment of all ailments, particularly serious diseases and psychological disorders.

Ferro The *ferro* is a torture device made of iron that is fixed tightly on the head. It was introduced by the Italians during their occupation of Ethiopia. It was believed that no one could tolerate the *ferro* for more than a few hours.

G

Gabour An insect that ruins the sesame harvest.

Garmasais A type of sari; a shiny colorful robe that covers the bride's entire body as part of the wedding ceremony. It's an essential part of the bride's dance.

Gishi A district chief of police in Ethiopia.

H

Hafeer A rainwater reservoir.

Halal Religiously permissible.

Haram Religiously forbidden.

J

Jallabi Literally means a toddler. It refers to a merchant or investor who is not a native of the locality; usually those hailing from central and northern parts of Sudan who roam other parts of the country on business.

Jungo A nickname for seasonal farm workers.

K

Kajaik Dried fish.

Kalash A popular rhythm in the Blue Nile Province of Sudan, particularly among the Barta tribes.

Ka'ouk An insect that poses a serious threat to the sesame harvest. *It*'s believed to have the ability to suck out the juice of the plants from a distance by simply flying over the field.

Karad A dry fruit of *taleh* (acacia) tree.

Kawal A wild plant used to make a popular dish.

kayta A rhythm dominant in the Nuba Mountains and other parts of Southern Kordofan Province.

Kisra A type of bread baked in thin sheets from sorghum dough.

Khor A creek; seasonal stream.

Kulaiga A sesame bale.

M

Madeeda Millet or date pie.

Mardum A rhythm dominant in many parts of Kordofan Province.

Mareesa A local drink made from fermented sorghum.

Mareesa day The day when a *mareesa* producer invites friends to her house and serves them freshly produced mareesa. They follow a rotational system, with each woman having a specific day so that each one should have an equal share of the market.

Masaweek Sticks of *araak* tree used for tooth brushing.

Mawlana A title for a religiously knowledgeable or devout person.

Mehayah A juice made of a piece of paper containing writings by a sorcerer or a religious man, dissolved in water—used as medicine.

Mouleeta A plant juice used to flavor chili.

Mushuk Mareesa residue, used to feed livestock.

O

Om baba The Ethiopian name for popcorn.

Om owaidat A local name of a bird.

Omda A local mayor.

Om fitfit A local name for the sheep bowel, a popular dish in Sudan, served raw, with chili and spices. *Om* is a prefix that stands for "mother of" and—by extension—"the one with." Fitfit means remnants or tiny pieces (maybe derived from the fact that the bowel is cut into tiny pieces, and embroidered with a special spicy mixture and served raw).

Om kiki A local musical instrument, like a violin, except that it has a single chord.

R

Rahat cutting An important part of the traditional wedding ceremony. A *rahat* is a strap made of straw or dried goat skin (recently the skin goat was replaced with silk or thread). As part of the bridal dance, the groom has to insert his hand under his bride's gown and cut the rahat (a symbolic gesture that he is the first man in her life and that she now became a married woman). He then tears it down to pieces and throws the remnants at the marriage aspirants to bring them good luck (in this case marriage).

Rakuba A thatch and wood structure, which usually serves as the living area of homes.

S

Sheesha A hookah, or water pipe.

Shifta The local name for bandits in eastern Sudan.

Sunnah Islamic traditions and teachings (based on the sayings, deeds, and directives of Prophet Mohammed).

T

Taya A type of site camp: a room built of straw close to the field where workers rest, cook, and spend the night.

Thamud Referring to the people of Thamud, an ancient nation that Allah punished for their failure to heed His commands.

Tum tum A popular rhythm in Central Sudan.

W

Wad Translates into "son of"—hence, Wad Ammoona is "the son of Ammoona."

Wad abrag A local name of a tiny, bright-colored bird.